STARGAZING ON THE
ORIENT EXPRESS

JENNIFER SKULLY

Redwood
Valley
Publishing

STARGAZING ON THE ORIENT EXPRESS
A ONCE AGAIN NOVEL

Book 5

Can a deluxe trip aboard the most romantic train in the world save their failing marriage?

As Marnie and Guy Slade head off for the vacation of a lifetime, traveling first class from Paris to Venice, on the surface, everything seems perfect. Until Marnie sees a strange text on her husband's phone and all the fears she's pushed aside about their marriage make her suspect he's having an affair. So when she meets a famous actor—and realizes he's flirting with her!—she can't help but be flattered by the attention.

But Guy has his own suspicions about Marnie's long work hours and her need to rush to the phone every time work calls. And now she seems to be enjoying the attentions of this actor far too much. With jealousy suddenly flaring between them, their passions are unexpectedly rekindled thirty years after their "I do's."

As they tour the magnificent Louvre and dine on gourmet cuisine in the Eiffel Tower, travel through the stunning French countryside, passing from the exquisite Austrian landscape and into the dazzling city of Venice, can the beauty and magic surrounding them entice Marnie and Guy to pledge themselves to each other all over again?

Join our newsletter and receive free books, plus learn about new releases, contests, and other freebies: http://bit.ly/SkullyNews

Author Note:

I hope you enjoy this ride aboard a European luxury train. A quick disclaimer to say that I have made modifications to train schedules and layouts to suit the story. Thank you for indulging me.

ACKNOWLEDGMENTS

A special thanks to Bella Andre for this fabulous idea and to both Bella and Nancy Warren for all the brainstorming on our 10-mile walks. Thank you also to my special network of friends who support and encourage me: Shelley Adina, Jenny Andersen, Linda McGinnis, Jackie Yau, Kathy Coatney, and Laurel Jacobson. As always, a huge hug of appreciation for my husband who helps my writing career flourish. And thank you to Wrigley who likes to snuggle on a blanket right next to me as the weather gets colder... well, at least for five minutes!

"I'm not saying he's cheating on you. But I am telling you to be very careful and watch every move he makes."

Marnie Slade tried to take her best friend's words with a grain of salt. After all, Linda had been divorced only a few months, after discovering her husband of twenty-five years had been cheating on her with his secretary.

She and Linda met for drinks in their favorite Palo Alto bar. Marnie had been late, another work crisis that couldn't be handled without her input. Linda was used to it, but Marnie hated her tardiness. People started arriving late because they expected you to be late.

"I honestly don't think Guy is cheating," Marnie said, a habit that had formed over the months of listening to Linda's increasingly bitter rants.

Linda was just looking out for her, but her experience had colored her entire outlook on life. As well as her outlook on Marnie's marriage.

"I didn't think Paul was cheating either." Linda's eyebrows rose as if she was still completely surprised. "Until I showed up at his office, bringing him dinner because he was working late. Only to find him doing *that*—" She spat out the word as if she couldn't even say what Paul had been doing. "—on his desk with *her*." She spat that word too.

Marnie had heard the story. Over and over. She felt her friend's pain. But the divorce had been final for six months. Linda had taken Paul to the cleaners, as the saying went, hiring the best divorce attorney in the San Francisco Bay Area. She got the five-million-dollar house in Saratoga, a hefty alimony payment, and their three kids' undying devotion. Paul got a two-bedroom apartment, car payments, mortgages, and his kids' revulsion. But he also had a girlfriend twenty years younger who seemed to adore him, and at fifty-five, Paul Honeycutt had never looked happier, despite the alimony he had to pay Linda monthly for the rest of her life. Unless she remarried, which she would never do just to spite him.

His happiness was the lump in Linda's throat, the ache in her heart, and the bitterness in her belly. With a trim figure and shoulder-length blond hair styled like Farrah Fawcett in the late seventies, she would have been a beautiful woman if it weren't for the bitter frown lines.

Marnie listened to her friend, the woman she'd known her entire working life.

"I mean, you have to wonder why Guy suddenly started losing weight," Linda said as if she hadn't made the point before.

"It was because of his brother." Guy's brother Chris had died of a heart attack nine months ago. He was two years younger than Guy, only fifty-three. "That put the fear of God into him, like he was a heart attack waiting to happen too."

Linda put her hand over Marnie's on the table. "I know." She squeezed. "It was awful for him. And for you. But Guy only started losing weight four months ago. If his brother's death was the reason, why didn't he start before?"

"That's only when I first noticed it," Marnie said, knowing she sounded defensive.

"I know that's what you think," Linda said gently, her voice laced with a note Marnie couldn't identify. It certainly couldn't be jealousy.

Marnie felt forced to go on justifying. "He started a couple of months before that. I just didn't see the change." As a physical education director, Guy had always worked out, but he'd still put on a few pounds over the years. And now he'd started to lose it, fast.

"But wasn't four months right after *she*—" Another word spat out. "—started as the new principal?"

She. Sharon Bennett, the elegant new principal at Guy's school, who was accomplished, efficient, and only forty.

Marnie wasn't worried. But she should never have told Linda that the new principal was an attractive woman fifteen years Guy's junior. Her best friend latched onto that image as if it was the history of her own divorce replaying itself in Marnie's marriage.

"And that *woman*—" Linda had a way of lacing the word with venom. "—was young enough to be Paul's daughter. That's what they want when they're in a midlife crisis, to feel like they can keep up with somebody years younger than they are. Even if it's only fifteen years," she finally got around to adding, bringing the discussion back to Marnie and Guy.

They, they, they. Why did Linda always have to lump Guy together with Paul? Obviously, it was because Linda no longer trusted any man. And she knew how to push Marnie's button of insecurity, despite how many times Marnie said she wasn't worried about elegant and classically beautiful Sharon Bennett.

Marnie considered herself a good-looking woman, but she

knew people thought she looked good "for her age." At fifty-five, she'd kept her figure, weighing exactly the same as she had on her wedding day thirty years ago. But she had to dye the gray out of her brunette hair, her eyelids were a little droopy, and she had those irritating lines fanning out from her lips and wrinkles at the corners of her eyes. Being CEO of a San Francisco-based, multimillion-dollar company with multinational contacts and five hundred employees, she was a woman in her prime, at the pinnacle of her career. She was the main bread-winner in the family, making more than double Guy's salary as head of the physical education department at a private school.

Of course, he could have been principal instead of Sharon Bennett. But he'd turned that job down even while Marnie was working her butt off to keep the board of directors happy, maintaining their respect and support, and earning the money that paid for their sons' Ivy League educations. But Guy never wanted to hear about her work issues. In fact, there was an unspoken moratorium on work talk once she got home.

She wouldn't think about that now, about how much it had pissed her off that Guy hadn't even told her about the job opening until he'd already turned it down. She had to get past that. What's done was done. She was determined to move forward.

"I really don't want to talk about Sharon."

"Sweetie," Linda said in a soft, cajoling tone, as if she felt terribly sorry for her. "That's my point. If you don't want to talk about her, your gut is telling you there's something wrong." She leaned in close, squeezing Marnie's hand sympathetically. "How long has it been," she asked quietly, "since Guy made love to you?"

That was the problem with best friends. You told them something one time, and they never forgot. They failed to get the hint that you didn't want to talk about it again. And Marnie did *not* want to talk about her sex life. Or Sharon. But saying that to Linda would only add fuel to the fire, and her friend would never let it go. Never. Ever.

So she gave Linda her stock answer. "That's just as much about me as it is him. Work has been a killer lately." She held up her hands. "I was late meeting you tonight. Again. It's never-ending. By the time I get home, I'm exhausted. Sex is the last thing on my mind."

Not exactly true. She'd always believed a good orgasm was a major stress reliever. But the few times she'd approached Guy in the last several months, he was too tired or had a headache or just plain wasn't in the mood, all those excuses usually attributed to women.

But she really, really, really didn't think Guy was having an affair. He wouldn't do that.

Would he?

Linda was sympathetic, as if she could read the question like a thought bubble over Marnie's head. "Sweetie, I understand. I just think it's better if you're forewarned. Don't be like me where you just walk in and it's this enormous shock. Probably nothing has happened yet, so you can nip it in the bud before it ever gets started. Just keep your eye on him."

Marnie hated to admit that meeting Linda once a week for drinks was weighing on her, actually making her question both Guy and her marriage. She wouldn't have all these doubts if not for Linda's persistence.

"If he was having an affair, why would he arrange such a fabulous thirtieth anniversary trip for us?"

Linda said exactly what Marnie feared she would. "First, he arranged the trip before that *woman*—" She once more spat the word as if Sharon were the girl Paul had cheated with. "—came on the scene."

"But if he was having an affair, he'd have canceled the trip." Her tone was defensive again. She tried to curb herself.

"Right." Linda snapped her fingers. "Like he'd give you a heads up that something was going on."

Marnie and Guy had watched a repeat PBS show with David Suchet, the actor who played Agatha Christie's Poirot. He'd taken a trip on the famous Orient Express, and it was so luxurious, so exciting that Marnie had said how amazing it would be to take a train from Paris to Venice, spending a week in Europe.

It had been a pipe dream.

But the next thing she knew, Guy had booked the trip as an anniversary present. When she said there was no way she could take off for ten days, he'd told her, as if he knew a damn thing about it, that she could take a vacation if she arranged it months in advance.

She'd made the mistake of telling Linda about the argument. Sometimes she told Linda way too much. And now Linda threw Guy's high-handedness in her face all the time.

But he'd pissed her off. First, it was so much money. Second, he'd just assumed she could take the time. He was a gym teacher, for God's sake, it was easy for him. He didn't have the responsibilities that she did. She'd been doubly pissed when he told her he'd turned down the principal's job without even consulting her. They were a team. They could have used that extra money for retirement. Why did everything have to be on her? Why didn't he value what she put into her job? He'd labeled her a workaholic instead of appreciating what she'd done to send the boys to the finest universities and give them the best start in life. Dammit, his raise would have at least paid for the extravagant trip he'd planned.

Okay, okay. She was getting carried away. All the anger had been months ago, and she was over it. She'd told herself to savor the luxurious train trip and enjoy Paris and Venice. In preparation, she'd passed things off to her vice presidents, gotten them up to speed. And they'd have Wade, her CFO and second-in-command, to turn to.

If only they hadn't run into this snag with the latest product release, their biggest leap in technology to date. And the anniversary trip was only two weeks away, the middle of May rushing up on her too fast. She didn't know how she'd get everything resolved before she left. And if she didn't get it resolved, there was no way she could leave. She wasn't about to tell Guy yet. There was still hope.

When she'd first asked Guy if he'd bought trip insurance just in case, he'd flipped out, telling her there was nothing she couldn't plan for. But when she'd looked at the itinerary, the tickets, read through all the information, she saw the line item for trip insurance. He hadn't trusted her.

But even with insurance, he'd be angry if she hinted there were issues. So she wouldn't tell him. Not yet.

And she wouldn't tell Linda either.

"I know you mean well, Linda, but honestly, I don't think anything's going on between Sharon and Guy."

Linda raised her hands in surrender. "All right. I won't say another word." She zipped her lips, but that didn't stop her from getting in the last word. "But you know I'll be here if you need me." And she would say it all again the next time they met.

But, despite her protestations, Marnie couldn't help looking at Guy with fresh eyes. His brother's death had been a terrible blow. She'd felt awful for him, and for herself because she'd loved Chris too. She and Guy had been married thirty years, and together five years before that, lovers since they were barely out of their teens. Chris had been like her own kid brother, especially since she didn't have siblings. But Guy had changed after he lost Chris, become more inner-directed, less open and talkative.

Or maybe that's when she'd first noticed the change.

He used to tell her about his kids, as he called his students, about their accomplishments and problems, soliciting her advice with a troubled kid. He'd spearheaded a scholarship program for underprivileged kids who couldn't afford the school's tuition. Working with them was his pride and joy. But when was the last time he'd talked about one of his special kids? Or about any of his students?

And worse, when was the last time she'd asked?

She looked at her watch. It was getting late. Guy hadn't texted to check when she'd be home. He used to text a lot, sometimes just to say hello. But that was before Chris died.

"I better run." She slid out of the booth. "See you next week. Call me if you need me."

"Okay, sweetie. I love you."

With half a glass of wine left, Linda would stay, not wanting to waste it. She was hoping a man would invite himself to sit with her, but it wouldn't happen. At least not tonight, when there were younger women in the bar, single women who weren't scowling. They were the ones the men would go for.

Marnie and Linda both knew that.

Men always went for the shiny new thing. They didn't want old and slightly tarnished.

Is that how Marnie appeared to Guy, slightly tarnished?

God help her, how was she supposed to battle that?

2

A week later, things had gotten so bad at work that she'd cancelled her date with Linda the previous night. The board was breathing down her neck, with the chairman calling her every day for an update, as if he was waiting for her to fail.

And now Marnie didn't have a choice. She had to tell Guy the trip was off. He would go ballistic, but there wasn't much she could do about it.

It was a new product release with significant problems. Last week she'd had hope; this week, everything had gone to hell.

There was no way, as CEO, that she could take off on vacation. No one was taking vacation right now. She hadn't expressly stated that, but the team knew. And as leader, she couldn't suddenly fly off to Europe for a ride on a luxury train.

But Guy would still explode.

She didn't relish the confrontation. Especially since it was her night to cook, and she was late and bringing home take-out. Again.

Yeah, she felt bad about it.

She parked in the garage next to Guy's SUV, gathered the takeout bags, and climbed out of the Audi. When she opened the door into the kitchen, she called out, "Dinner's ready. I got Chinese."

She mostly did takeout when it was her night. And Guy didn't complain. He understood.

But he wouldn't understand this.

He came up behind her as she unloaded cartons onto the kitchen's granite counter. They'd remodeled three years ago, granite countertops, matching backsplash, all new white cabinets that cleaned easily, travertine floor, a big island with a bar and four tall stools, and on the other side, the kitchen table nestled in a large bay window.

His hands on her shoulders, Guy pecked a kiss against her ear.

That was surprising. "Good day?" she asked. She'd already decided she wouldn't jump right in with the bad news. That was how she usually handled things.

She would think of something on the drive home, and immediately she walked in the door, she'd download on him. Had he called the washing machine repairman? Had he fixed that leaky toilet in the half bath? It was like an info dump of everything on her mind while she was driving. But to Guy, it was like hitting him over the head with all the things he hadn't done that day. It was a bad habit, and she tried to be really conscious of *not* doing it. Especially today.

This required a lot more finesse.

He was still standing behind her, his hands on her shoulders, his body pressed close as he said, "Yeah, a pretty good day. That smells good." His breath brushed her ear and sent a shiver of awareness through her.

She wondered how long it had really been since they'd made love. Two months? More? Was it Guy as she'd told

Linda? Or was it her? Sometimes it was just faster and easier to take care of the itch on her own.

She was just so distracted all the time, so busy at work that when she got home, she barely listened to Guy.

She thought about what Linda had said last week, that she had to watch out. But that wasn't Guy, no matter how absent-mindedly she treated him. He would never cheat.

He reached over her for the plates.

He was tall, six-three to her five-seven, and he made her feel petite. He was a hunky football coach, but since losing weight after his brother died, he was now a prime cut. Fifty-five years looked good on him with his thick salt-and-pepper hair and deep coffee-colored eyes.

Guy was deliciously attractive. And not just to her.

With all the containers open, he brought the silverware while she carried the tray of cartons.

They always ate at the table, a habit they'd started with the boys. At dinnertime, there were no cell phones, no texting, no TV. This was the time to check in with each other. The garden lights had come on in the backyard, shining on the flowering bushes, the pool, the hot tub. Maybe they should have a soak tonight.

They sat down, started dishing out, and Guy said, "I had to suspend Randall today."

She stopped, fork halfway to her mouth. "I thought you said it was a good day."

"I consider it good because he's a sneaky little bully. Remember I told you I've known for weeks he's been causing trouble but couldn't catch him at it?" Marnie didn't remember, and she wondered if he only thought he'd told her. "Now I finally got proof."

"What did he do?" she asked around a mouthful of broccoli beef. He hadn't talked to her like this in ages. She didn't want to stop the flow by telling him about the trip cancellation. Not yet.

"He dropped Johnson's gym shorts in the toilet after he'd urinated in it. Then he and his minions were forcing Johnson to put them on." The line between his brow deepened. Guy had zero tolerance for bullying, and it never mattered how important the bully was to the football team. Randall was the star quarterback, but Guy suspended him anyway.

"I'm surprised you actually caught him. Isn't he usually more slick than that?" It was a guess. She couldn't remember what Guy had said.

"Well, I'm sneakier." He grinned broadly, looking like a kid again. "I left in the middle of a staff meeting. Just had this feeling. And I caught them red-handed in the locker room."

"Good for you." It was typical that no one ratted out a bully, not even the kids he tormented.

"After a bit of a tussle because Randall's dad is some big donor, Sharon finally agreed to a week's suspension for him and his little minions."

Principal Sharon Bennett. If his brother hadn't died, Guy would now be principal, making all the decisions, with a very nice salary increase as well. They could use the extra. Ethan, their eldest, was a senior at Harvard, heading for an MBA in the business school, while Jay was a sophomore at Cornell, intending to go into law. And she felt as if the burden was all on her.

But after Chris died, Guy had to rethink his life. He liked working directly with his scholarship kids. He was passionate about helping all his students. He didn't want to spend his time in administration, didn't want the stress. She understood that.

But what about her stress?

She needed to stop thinking about the sneaky way he hadn't told her about his decision until he'd already made it.

They'd had all the arguments, all the days and nights when they weren't speaking to each other. But they'd worked through it. Now she had to put an end to the resentment.

Guy went on as if she were listening. "Sharon agrees that we'll set him up with a counselor when he gets back to school."

He did a lot of "Sharon agreed to this" and "Sharon agreed to that," as if he was making all the decisions and the principal was simply agreeing. Marnie didn't know why he couldn't have been principal, since he was doing it all anyway. But whatever.

"His parents will probably squawk, but Sharon agrees to making it a condition of letting him back come back."

Private schools had different rules. They could make conditions. Maybe it would be good for the boy, but Marnie doubted it. Some kids were just bad seeds.

"What about your day? How's the new product coming?"

The question took her aback. They didn't talk about *her* work problems. That was their unspoken rule. But here he was asking about the product release. Maybe he was trying to feel her out about the trip.

Which meant this was her opening. But Marnie wasn't ready. She wanted to finish her broccoli beef and moo shu chicken in peace. Maybe she'd bring it up while they were putting away the unfinished cartons and doing the dishes, two plates, two forks, and the serving spoons.

"You know." She shrugged. "New product releases."

"Good. I've got a couple of ideas for what we can do on the day we have in Paris, before we board the train."

Her stomach crimped. "Aren't we just taking it easy and getting over jet lag?"

He smiled, as if he was totally happy with himself. "We shouldn't go straight to bed. We need to stay up and get on European time."

She couldn't let him talk about plans for the trip. It would only make it worse when she told him she couldn't go. Then he wouldn't be merely pissed, he'd be livid.

She put her fork down, looked at him as he deftly assembled a moo shu pancake. "I have to talk to you."

He stopped rolling the pancake for three seconds, then continued without saying a word.

She was forced to go on. "This release is really a bitch. We're not as ready as we should be. I've already had Wade increase the returns reserve." Wade, her CFO and right-hand man.

Still Guy said nothing. But the muscles in his jaw tensed as he clenched his teeth.

She had to keep going. "The team is working twelve hours a day, weekends too."

He picked up his moo shu, started eating, not looking at her, not speaking. He had no intention of making this easy. But then she hadn't thought it would be.

So she just said it. "I'm afraid we might have to postpone the trip."

He finished his pancake before finally saying, "We talked about this, Marnie." Each word was clipped, the edges hard.

"And I told you it would be difficult."

"You've had months to plan for all the contingencies."

"Do you think I planned for the product release to go south?" She kept her voice steady. She didn't want a grueling argument, didn't want to shout. She just wanted him to accept.

"Let me ask you this. Do you actually work on the product?"

She put her fork down. She couldn't eat anymore. "Of course I don't actually work on the product. I manage the release."

He tipped his head, gave her a look, his eyes narrowing.

"Oh, so now you're the project manager. I thought you had a project manager."

He knew very well there was a project manager. "We're all part of the team, and, as CEO of the company, I'm head of that team."

He methodically filled another pancake, first smearing a spoonful of sauce, then adding the moo shu. "I understand that perfectly. It's teamwork. But you don't need to be right there on site, overseeing QC or monitoring the manufacturing floor."

He was getting on her nerves, with his tone, his terse words, his questions. He already knew the answers.

"You know damn well I don't," she snapped, then tried to dial it back. "But there's a myriad of decisions that need my input."

He rolled his pancake, looked at her, raised one brow. "Oh, a *myriad*."

She hated it when he mocked her, hated his condescending tone that trivialized her career. She wanted to shout at him, point out that if he'd taken that job when they offered it to him, she wouldn't worry so much about the next semester's Ivy League payments. He'd wanted their boys to go to those schools just as much as she had.

He picked up his rolled pancake, ate it methodically, stopped halfway through to add, "What I'm saying is that you can handle everything with a conference call or a video meeting." He started eating again.

She wanted to scream. She flung out an arm. "We're going to be halfway around the world. There's a time difference. How am I supposed to get back to them with answers right when they need them?"

He didn't even have the decency to look back at her with anger as big as her own. He just looked like... nothing. "It's not halfway around the world. It's a nine-hour time difference."

"But I'll be sleeping while they're working."

He licked his fingers instead of using a napkin, which he knew irritated her. "Eight o'clock Pacific time will be five o'clock in France. Seems to me you can handle any questions at that time."

She was seething. "You're crazy."

"I'm not crazy. But you're a workaholic."

She picked up her nearly empty plate and slammed it down on the tray of cartons. Then she pushed back her chair with a loud scrape across the floor, grabbed the tray, and marched across the kitchen.

"Typical, Marnie," he said without even turning to her. "You don't like I what I say, so you just walk away."

She was so angry she practically threw the tray onto the counter, watching horrified as it slid into the sink, her plate crashing down on top of the cartons she hadn't even closed.

GUY HEARD THE CRASH BEHIND HIM. HE'D KNOWN THIS was coming. It was how Marnie operated. Work always came first, before him, even before the boys. Always had, always would.

He carried his plate to the counter as she was cleaning up the mess in the sink.

She wore her anger on her face, in her hands, and by slamming doors. He wore his anger on the inside. Just like his younger brother. Maybe that's what really gave Chris the heart attack, not the extra weight or the martinis when he got home, but the festering inner hostility.

He wouldn't apologize. He wasn't wrong. The only thing he'd done wrong was not telling her about the job offer *before* he turned it down. But he'd invested his heart and soul in his scholarship kids. He couldn't walk away from that responsibility, no matter how much Marnie wanted him to make a bigger salary. After Chris died, he'd realized his true calling was the kids, not as an administrator, but right out there among his students every day.

He stepped around her, rinsed his plate in the left side of the double sink while she gingerly picked up the spilled cartons. Luckily, the plate hadn't broken.

Keeping his voice reasonable and calm, he said, "We've been planning this trip for months. If we cancel now, we'll lose more than half the money."

"What about the trip insurance?"

"It only covers illness or death, not you deciding work is more important."

"Then what the hell good was it?" Her nostrils flared as she breathed in, and he heard everything she didn't say. That if he'd taken that job, if he made more money, if she didn't have to be the bigger breadwinner, it would be okay if they had to take a hit.

"It isn't just about the money," he said. "It's about your priorities."

She slapped a closed carton down on the counter. "My priorities?" Her voice rose. "Exactly what priorities are those? To work my damnedest so we can pay the mortgage and send our kids to Ivy League schools?"

Yep, there it was. She was all about the money. And she'd forgotten that his job had given the boys a private school education at a fraction of the cost. That he'd done all the running around from one after-school activity to another, from game to game, while she'd been earning the higher salary, as if the money carried so much more weight than his time.

"Actually, I was talking about the homework you didn't

have time for because you were on the phone with your CFO talking about God knows what, or games you couldn't make it to, teacher meetings you missed."

She leaned one hand on the counter, jamming the other on her hip. "We agreed it was easier for you to do all that stuff since they were going to your school."

He'd done all the carpooling, packed all the lunches, checked all the homework, made all the meals because if he'd left it up to Marnie, they'd have been eating takeout every night. He'd handled Jay's tirades when he couldn't figure out a math problem, comforted Ethan when his girlfriend dumped him right before he went off to university, gone to every game they played in, cheered them on. While Marnie conveniently forgot that the boys had received a private school education because of *his* job and *his* career.

But he didn't want to work himself into an early grave, especially doing a job he didn't like. He didn't even want Marnie to work herself to death. He wanted to do a job he loved and have family time as well. And he'd wanted this trip to Europe with his wife of thirty years.

He wanted her to choose him instead of work.

"Yes, we agreed," he said. "And you agreed to go on this vacation."

She gave him a militant, pinch-lipped glare. "You made me agree to it months ago when I couldn't have a single clue what problems were going to come up."

"There will always be problems, always something in the way." He held up his hands in weariness, or maybe just in surrender. "Think about this. I'm going on this trip. It's our anniversary, thirty years, Marnie. And you need to think about what choice you're going to make. And its consequences."

Putting his plate and fork in the dishwasher, he left her to clean up the mess she'd made.

3

Marnie finished cleaning up the mess she'd made in the kitchen sink.

It had definitely sounded like an ultimatum.

She padded down the hall to her home office. The house was large, with a formal living room and dining room, a family room, and a bonus room on the first floor that she'd converted into an office. Of the five bedrooms upstairs, there was their master suite and the boys' rooms, intact for when they came home on holidays and summer vacation. Another was a guest room for either Guy's parents or hers. Her mom and dad had retired to Scottsdale, Arizona, his to Florida. They'd turned the last bedroom into a workout room for Guy. She preferred laps in the pool, although she rarely had time for that. It was easier to work out during lunch in the gym at the office. But Guy liked his home gym. Even now she could hear him on the rowing machine.

She closed the door and collapsed in her comfy chair, where she often read over reports. She'd poured herself a glass of wine, and after a sip, she pulled out her cell phone.

Wade answered on the third ring. She wasn't sure she

could agree to Guy's demands, but she wanted to feel out Wade's thoughts if she did.

"Hey, what's up?" His voice was deep, soothing her fractured nerves. Guy no longer listened to her pour out her problems. But Wade had turned out to be a good sounding board.

"I'm not disturbing you, am I?"

Divorced, his three kids, all teenagers, stayed with him every other week. "No, just watching TV."

"You know this trip I had planned, we're supposed to leave next week," she reminded him.

"I remember."

"I'm back and forth on this. A huge part of me knows I need to stay here and keep my eyes on the release. But I was just talking about it with Guy, and it looks like we'll lose at least half of what we paid if we cancel now."

"I thought you had trip insurance?"

"We do. But it only covers unforeseen events like illness or a death in the family."

"What if you just postpone?"

"I think it's the same deal." She wasn't sure. Maybe Guy was wrong. Maybe he hadn't read the fine print well enough.

"It's your anniversary, right?"

He knew it was. She wasn't afraid to talk about personal things with Wade. When there'd been trouble with the boys, she'd often bounced things off him. And sometimes, if she and Guy had a fight, she'd subtly ask Wade's opinion. That didn't happen often, only a couple of times, like when Guy had shut her out of the decision about the principal position. Wade agreed that Guy should have consulted her.

She wondered if she should tell Wade that they hadn't merely discussed the trip, that Guy had damn near issued an ultimatum. But no, she wouldn't even tell Linda that.

"You've got international calling, and there's email and texting. If we absolutely need you, we can get hold of you."

"Yeah, but there's the time change to consider. They're nine hours ahead."

"But our morning is only suppertime over there. Don't the French eat really late? And you'll be living it up every night." He chuckled, because really, when had she ever lived it up? She'd sometimes texted him at midnight when something struck her. Wade was a night owl too.

"I'm not sure about this. What if the release falls apart?" Even worse than it already had.

He was silent a second too long. "I know all this stuff as well as you do. I can handle any questions."

"I didn't mean it like that, as if you're incapable."

"I know," he murmured. "It's only ten days, Marnie. You and Guy need this time to mend a few fences now that the kids are out of the house."

She wondered how much she'd actually told him, since he seemed to think she needed some fence-mending. Obviously more than she'd realized. There were those late nights, especially when they were preparing for a board meeting, when she was tired and sometimes let out a bit of her frustration. Linda was great to chat with over dinner or drinks, but for the past year, since she'd caught her cheating husband, they'd talked mostly about Linda. Or about how Marnie needed to make sure Guy wasn't cheating.

Wade was a better listener.

"You need this, Marnie. Go for it. You'll only be a text away."

"But what if the board freaks out that I'm not there during a crisis?" They would ream her a new one. They were always looking for something she hadn't done right. As if, just because she was a woman, she didn't have her priorities straight.

"It's not quarter end, there's no board meeting coming up. They won't even know you're gone."

Could she really go on this trip? She'd have to explain to Guy that she'd need to check in a lot. In fact, he'd mentioned that himself. And Wade was good. She trusted him, valued him. If she ever left—or worse, the board ousted her—he could take over in a flash.

She felt breathless, but she said it anyway. "You're right. We can handle just about anything by phone. Let's set up the daily project meeting for ten in the morning. That'll be seven in the evening in France. I can handle that."

He laughed. "I'm not looking forward to Guy coming after me if I schedule a meeting you have to attend every night at seven o'clock. No. We'll call you if we need you. Just enjoy your vacation. You deserve it."

And Guy would have a fit if she scheduled a meeting every night at dinnertime. "Okay, okay. I hear you. Just text me any questions so I can tackle them first thing when you guys get in." Then she changed the subject completely. "What are you watching on TV?"

He didn't miss a beat. "I'm binging an Australian show called *Rake*. It's about lawyers. It's pretty hilarious."

"I'll have to try it."

"All right, see you tomorrow. Night, Marnie."

"Night, Wade."

Okay, she felt better. Wade was on her side. It was a different dynamic than usual, the woman in charge, the man working for her. Guy didn't understand, even though he now worked for a woman. He was in the education system. Business was completely different. As a woman, she always had to prove herself, and it was getting harder now that she was in her fifties, as if she had two strikes against her. Some men thought menopause was a form of female dementia. More and more lately, the board was second-guessing her decisions.

That's why this product release was so important. She had to make it work. If it didn't, it could be one more nail in her coffin.

Marnie walked upstairs, heading down the hall to the rhythmic sound of the rowing machine. She hung in the doorway, bracing herself on the doorjamb with both hands.

Guy wore only shorts, his chest glistening with exertion, his muscles bulging. He could still take her breath away as she felt a sweet, hot quiver of desire.

She must have made a noise because he looked. But she couldn't tell him what was on her mind. Couldn't beg him to drag her into the bedroom or down onto the floor of his workout room.

Instead, she said, "I just talked to Wade. We think that between us, we can work it out for the trip."

He went back to his rowing, whatever might have been in his eyes gone like a flame in the wind. "Oh, so the mighty Wade says it's okay."

She wanted to snap at him, but she kept her cool. "*He* didn't say it was okay. We worked it out together." Despite all good intentions, her voice was sharp. "He can text any questions. I can handle it all once a day, maybe just one text."

He grunted as he pulled on the machine. Or maybe it was a snort of disgust. "I suppose you moved your project meeting to earlier in the day so you could attend."

She didn't want to admit that she'd suggested it and Wade vetoed. "No, we didn't. He'll brief me when he gets there in the morning and I can deal with anything at that point." Then she added snidely, "That should make you happy."

He looked at her, never breaking his rowing stride. "You have no idea what would make me happy."

It felt as if he'd driven a knife in to the hilt. And that made her think about everything Linda had said. His weight loss, how much he was pumping iron, a midlife crisis, an affair. She'd been telling herself Guy wouldn't do that. They were just empty nesters, adjusting to being alone together. But maybe Wade was right. Maybe there were some fences to be mended on both their parts.

Maybe they really needed this anniversary trip, just the two of them, no work, no school.

Maybe it could change everything.

THE LAST WEEK HAD BEEN A STRUGGLE. MARNIE HAD worked late almost every night, gone in on the weekend, and since the flight wasn't until late afternoon, she'd been at the office that morning as well.

Guy ended up doing her packing for her. He'd arranged for someone to water the plants, stopped the mail, ordered a car to take them to the airport, checked them in for their flight. She felt guilty leaving all the arrangements with him, but there was so much to do at work. She'd made her concession when she hadn't canceled the trip. Wade's contention that the board would never even know she was gone hadn't panned out, and they were breathing fire like a pack of dragons, wondering why the hell she'd take off for ten days with the product release in jeopardy.

But the decision was made, and they were on the way to the airport.

"Do you have the passports?" She sagged against the seat. She'd sleep on the plane. It would be good to relax. She just had to turn off her thought treadmill and not worry about work.

"Didn't you pick them up?" Guy asked.

She jerked straight up, her neck cracking painfully. "No. I asked you to get them out of the safe. I thought you'd taken care of it."

"I followed all your instructions," he drawled. The edge of irritation in his voice was almost constant now. "I got the passports out of the safe. I called all the credit card companies and let them know we'd be out of the country so they wouldn't hold any of the cards if they saw strange charges. I thought you saw the passports on the table."

"Shit," she muttered under her breath. "When I asked you to get the passports out of the safe, I thought that meant you were bringing them with you."

She leaned forward to tell the driver they had to turn around. God, they'd be late. Would they miss their flight? She didn't know if their luggage would even make it onto the plane now. She should have left work earlier. But then she couldn't leave any sooner. Her day had been crazy. While Guy had taken the whole day off.

"Just have Aubrey drop by the house and bring them to the airport," he said nonchalantly, as if the trip wasn't suddenly in jeopardy, especially after all the fuss he'd made about work getting in the way.

"My admin?" she repeated incredulously.

"Yeah. Why not?"

Honestly, she didn't know why not. She'd had Aubrey run personal errands before, and she had a key to the house for emergencies. "All right. I'll call her. But it's going to be tight. We won't be able to hand in our bags until we have those passports."

He sighed, deeply, heavily, as if Atlas had dropped the world on him. Or as if he was fed up with her. "Let me just check my bag one more time."

The computer bag was on the floor in front of them, and he leaned forward, opened the front flap, rummaged inside. Then he pulled out the two passports. "Oh, look, I must've done it without thinking."

She could only stare at him for long, raging moments.

"You did that on purpose," she said in a whisper, mostly because she couldn't believe it.

He gazed at her without a single expression on his face. "It just slipped my mind."

But she knew he'd done it on purpose.

She wondered how bad this anniversary trip was going to be.

THE PASSPORT THING HAD PASSIVE-AGGRESSIVE BULLSHIT. But Marnie had been issuing orders for a week as if he were an idiot who couldn't take care of anything without her. Hold the mail, find a plant sitter, pick up the dry-cleaning. And she couldn't even get home in time to do her own damn packing. If Guy hadn't put in this thing or that thing she wanted, he'd sure as hell hear about it when they got to Paris.

But he still shouldn't have freaked her out about the passports. He honestly wanted this trip to be a good one, like a renewal. He didn't want to be angry or to push all her buttons and make her angry. The lie had been a momentary lapse.

Now he picked up her hand. "I'm sorry." Raising her knuckles to his lips, he kissed her. "Let's not fight. We've got our passports. We're on our way. Let's just enjoy."

But he wondered how much she'd make him pay for being a passive-aggressive asshole.

✦ 4 ✦

Marnie was sure Guy had known the entire time that those passports were in his bag. But they were in Paris now, and she was determined to stop thinking about it. Besides, maybe he had a point. A small one. She had left him to take care of all the arrangements, writing him a list as if he were a child who couldn't figure out what to do on his own. And to top it off, she'd relentlessly interrogated him to make sure it all got done.

She hadn't even given him a chance to screw it up. She'd just assumed he would. It was nothing against him. He was just a man. And men weren't detail-oriented.

But she supposed he deserved that little dig with the passports.

Besides, who wouldn't forgive a man who'd booked three months in advance for a romantic dinner at the Jules Verne Restaurant in the Eiffel Tower?

Guy raised a glass. "Happy anniversary, sweetheart." He was smiling without even a hint of sarcasm.

She didn't add any sarcasm of her own. "Happy anniversary, darling."

They clinked glasses and drank. She was only a little tired right now, having slept well in their first-class seats. She hadn't even resented the extra money. The comfort was worth it.

They'd landed in the early afternoon and breezed through customs. Guy had booked a hotel in the heart of Paris from which they could actually walk to the Eiffel Tower. There was still a line to get into the tower itself when they arrived, but the restaurant had a separate entrance. And the view of Paris from the second floor was magnificent.

She sipped her champagne. "This is delicious."

"Only the best for you."

Was that sarcasm? How long had she been wondering if everything Guy said to her was sarcastic and everything he did was passive aggressive?

Maybe it was just since she'd forced him to make that ultimatum about the trip. But she'd already decided to stop thinking about it. No more negative thoughts.

He'd packed a classic black cocktail dress for her, probably with this night in mind, and a mouthwatering dark suit for himself.

She took in the marvelous view, the green lawns of the Champ de Mars, the trees and old buildings surrounding it, the church spires rising above everything else. This looked like old Paris, with the skyscrapers rising only in the distance. "Isn't Paris amazing?"

Guy nodded. "Here's to thirty years of wedded bliss," he said, gazing out over the magnificence that was Paris before the sun went down, the light bathing the streets and buildings in red and gold.

She would have felt better if he'd looked at her when he said that. "Thank you for this wonderful surprise. How many people get to have their anniversary dinner in the Eiffel Tower?"

He looked at her, finally. "You're not jet-lagged?"

She shook her head. "Not really." She gave him kudos for the flights. "It's incredible what first class will do for you. Thank you."

Guy grinned. "I didn't want to sleep through an entire day when we arrived."

"It's perfect."

Their waiter appeared, having given them an extra fifteen minutes to enjoy the champagne before ordering.

The restaurant's color scheme was silver, white, and gold, the pedestal tables bare of tablecloths and elegantly set, all the chairs facing the view no one wanted to miss. The waiter fit right in with a short white jacket and black pants, his bald head shiny.

His English was excellent. "Madame, have you decided what you would like? If I may make any make recommendations, please let me know."

She smiled. During the week, the chef offered an a la carte menu in addition to the five- or seven-course tasting menu. Both she and Guy had opted for a la carte. "I've decided, thank you. I'd like the ravioli starter, the duck for the main course, and the choux puff for dessert." The cream-filled pastry had looked delectable on a passing tray.

"Excellent choices, madame." Smiling, his teeth gleamed white as he turned to Guy. "And for you, monsieur?"

"I'll have the salmon starter, the fish, and the pear."

"Another excellent choice. Exactly the opposite of madame. That way you can share." Then he turned, his heels tapping together in military fashion.

Obviously, sharing wasn't frowned upon. The buzz of conversation was low. It was probably early for dinner here in France—she'd heard they usually sat down between eight and nine—but there were no empty tables.

"Shall we call the kids?" She smiled widely. "Tell them

we're in the Eiffel Tower?"

He twisted his wrist to read his watch. "They're in class right now."

"You know their schedules?"

Of course he did. Guy just smiled, and she knew what he was thinking, that she didn't talk to them enough, that he carried the responsibility for the two of them. "Let's call them when we get back to the hotel."

That made her think about work. She should have called Wade before they left for dinner, but there hadn't been time. And Guy would have been angry if she'd made them late for their dinner reservation.

Maybe she could sneak a call in after Guy fell asleep.

"What have you got planned for tomorrow before we catch the train?"

Guy had arranged everything, and the train didn't leave until late in the afternoon. They would have most of the day to wander Paris.

"Another surprise." He smiled again.

Her husband had a beautiful smile. He was a gorgeous man, totally in his prime at fifty-five, while a woman of fifty-five was over the hill. But that was Guy, stunningly, beautifully prime. Especially since he'd lost weight and started working out more. Not that Guy had ever been totally out of shape. He was a physical education teacher. He couldn't go to rack and ruin if he wanted his students to get the message about keeping a body healthy.

She smiled in return. "I'll love the surprise."

They weren't exchanging gifts. The trip was their present to each other. And while she'd been manic preparing for the time away, now she could relax.

They shared their starters, the ravioli and the salmon both melt-in-the-mouth. And her entrée, the duck, was to die for. "Oh my God, you need to try this."

She cut a slice, but when she would have handed Guy the fork, he reached across the table, guiding her hand as if she was feeding him.

Surprising and deliciously sexy, the gesture reminded her again of how long it had been since they'd made love, how she missed the physical intimacy, a fact she'd forgotten in their hectic daily life.

Maybe that's what this trip was all about, reconnecting and rediscovering their sensuality.

"May I try yours?" Her thoughts came out in the low, sultry timbre of her voice.

When he slipped a piece of fish on his fork, she guided his hand to her mouth, taking exquisitely long to draw the flakes from the tines and savor each flavor, butter, fennel, sesame.

She closed her eyes. Groaned. "Oh my, that's good."

Lord, she was seducing herself too.

If only she'd had time to buy new lingerie before they left. The worst was that she hadn't even thought about it. The last dazed week had been all about work, about everything that could fall apart, about the board's wrath if it did.

But this what she needed to concentrate on, romantic Parisian nights with her sexy husband.

She said exactly what she was thinking. "This trip is going to be all about us." She smiled at him. "No work intrusions except emergencies."

Guy snorted. It wasn't a good sound, almost derisive. "I won't hold my breath just in case I turn blue and die."

Her mood plummeted. All the sexy feelings died a cringing death.

She was suddenly close to crying. It wasn't just hurt. It was guilt. He was right. But he didn't understand the pressure she was under. She could never make him see that.

But she absolutely would not let it ruin the night, and she tried to smile flirtatiously. "Well, I did tell you I might have to do some work while we're here." She reached for his hand. "But there'll be plenty of time to enjoy ourselves."

He ate methodically, concentrating on his meal, not offering her another bite. And she didn't offer another bite of hers.

"Don't make promises about not working," he said.

"I wasn't making a promise. It was just a thought."

She could feel the potential for an argument growing. It always did when they talked about her work or money or the principal's position.

She didn't want to argue right now, not when they were in the Eiffel Tower, in Paris, the city of lights, and it was their anniversary, the actual day, and they were on a trip that Guy had planned just for her.

Even if she hadn't really wanted it.

Not that she'd ever tell Guy that.

THE VIEW HAD BEEN SPECTACULAR, AND THEIR MEAL HAD taken over two hours as they savored each course, topping it off with coffee, the negative vibes between them finally bleeding off.

Since they couldn't get into the rest of the Eiffel Tower from the restaurant, they took the elevator back down. But Marnie had seen what they'd come for, the Paris skyline lit up at night after the sun set.

As they exited the door, she linked her arm through Guy's. "Thank you. That was amazing." She didn't even feel the jet lag catching up with her.

Guy smiled, leading them across the concourse. "No better way to spend our anniversary." He stroked her hand. "Except if the restaurant had been at the very top."

"It was perfect just the way it was."

They laughed together as they crossed the concourse, the bright lights and calliope music of a carousel calling to them. She walked faster, pulling Guy. "Let's do the carousel. That would be so much fun."

It was disgorging riders as they reached it, and Guy handed over a couple of bills to the attendant, who waved them on.

"I can't remember the last time we were on a carousel." Her voice sounded dreamy. Maybe it was jet lag.

"It was when we took the boys to Six Flags in Vallejo." Guy remembered everything.

Had she actually been with them? Yes, she remembered now. "They didn't want to go on the carousel because they said it was for kids." She smiled. "They just watched while Mom and Dad acted look fools."

While their teenage boys had groused about the carousel, they'd actually been smiling as they watched their idiot parents. It had been a special day. And far too long ago.

This was a second chance. They climbed on two brightly painted wooden horses, giggling like children as the carousel started moving. She suddenly realized how much she'd missed over the years. She was always work, work, work. She never slowed down. That day at Six Flags, she'd been on the phone at least five times. Even then, she couldn't take a day off without checking in, frantic about this project or that project. She wasn't CEO yet, just controller. But she'd wanted to climb that ladder to the very top. As her horse climbed to the top of the pole, she wondered if climbing the ladder had been worth it.

She was glad Guy hadn't let her weasel out of this trip.

When the ride ended, the attendant held out the automatic photo. They were both laughing, Guy's head tipped back, her gaze on him as if he dazzled her.

When Guy would have waved the man away, she took his arm. "Let's get it. It's such a lovely photo."

He forked over the euros then tucked the picture into his pocket. It was their anniversary, and the photo would commemorate it.

The lights on the Eiffel Tower started to change then, and the crowd still thronging the concourse gazed up in wonder.

Guy leaned down to whisper to her, "It's a light show for our anniversary."

She pulled back, looked at him. "You're kidding."

She wondered how much it cost. It was probably astronomical.

Then he laughed at the look on her face. "They do it every hour at night, sweetheart. Don't worry, I didn't spend any money on it." He looked up at the lights, then back at her. "But I'm very pleased you didn't ask how much the dinner cost."

She could have gotten mad, but it wasn't worth it. They always argued about money, but she didn't want to fight now. "I would only expect the best dinner on our anniversary."

As they watched the lights, she wished he hadn't told her they were a regular thing. She would have liked to think he'd requested the special light show just for her, no matter the cost.

DINNER HAD BEEN GOOD. SO HAD THE CAROUSEL RIDE, THE memories of the kids, and walking hand in hand with Marnie. He'd even felt a spark of heat between them as they fed each other delicacies. But somehow that candid photo of them on the carousel had bothered him. It wasn't how they really were together. In a way, it was a lie. They weren't that happy.

Guy had hoped Marnie could stop thinking about work

and money on this trip. But that was impossible. Work and money bled into everything, tainting even their anniversary.

He'd shoved the photo into his computer bag. Marnie would be pissed if he threw it away.

And now he stood beneath the shower spray, letting the water beat against his neck and back. Jet lag would catch up with them eventually, despite having slept on the plane.

Marnie was in bed, and he'd thought a shower would relax him. He'd fallen in love with her because she was driven and ambitious. She was confident and smart and knew exactly what she wanted. He'd been silent witness to his parents' marriage, his mother's neediness, how she couldn't make a decision without his father's approval. When he was away on business, she was like a ghost. Guy swore he'd never live like that.

Yet all these years later, he realized he wanted to be needed. Not like his parents' codependent relationship, but he'd like to know that if he was gone for a month, Marnie would miss him for more than putting dinner on the table or picking up the dry cleaning or reminding her to call the boys at least a couple times a week. He wanted to mean more to her than the tasks he accomplished.

He'd planned this trip because they'd watched a PBS show about the famous train. And because Marnie had said it would be fun. He'd believed that with months to plan, she could make the time. Except she hadn't. She would have backed out if she could. But he hadn't let her.

God, he was tired, the jet lag catching up to him in a single moment. Or maybe it was just his maudlin thoughts. He shut off the water, grabbed a towel, stepped onto the mat to dry off.

And he heard her soft voice.

She couldn't wait to get on the phone with good old Wade. It was like Wade shared their bed. If she had an idea, something important about a project, no matter how late, she'd have to text Wade before she forgot. And good old Wade always answered. It was no wonder his wife divorced him.

It wasn't an affair. It was like the weird codependency his parents had. Neither of them could do anything without the other's approval. But they weren't having an affair.

Or maybe he was just lying to himself.

He towel-dried his hair, and with his eyes closed, he thought about Sharon.

He had no idea what he was going to do about her.

GUY WAS IN THE SHOWER. IT WAS THE OPPORTUNE moment, even if Marnie was feeling the time change dragging her down.

She called Wade, snuggling down into the covers, pulling them to her throat.

"How's the trip?" Wade said, his voice husky in her ear.

"Great so far. Guy took me to the five-star restaurant in the Eiffel Tower."

"Oh yeah, happy anniversary."

She wondered if she detected a little sarcasm. She couldn't be sure. But this was Wade, and they could say anything to each other.

"The food was amazing. Just as good as the view."

He laughed softly. It felt cozy to be lying here talking to him when she was in bed. Usually, if she talked with Wade late at night, she took her phone down to her office. And this suddenly felt a little too intimate. Maybe even sexy. And it most definitely was not. "So tell me what's happening. How much did I miss in two days?"

"It hasn't been two days. You're just nine hours ahead of

us. There's nothing new." He recapped the daily meeting, and oddly, she found it boring. As if flying across the ocean, eating a five-star meal with the view of Paris laid out before them, then riding on the carousel and watching the Eiffel Tower sparkle, had helped her step away from work as well.

When he was done, she said, "It sounds like everything's good."

"Yeah. Are you tired yet?" he asked.

"We slept on the plane. But yeah, I'm a little tired. It'll be good to sleep."

"What time does the train depart?"

"Late afternoon. We have almost the whole day in Paris." Her eyes were closing, and she felt herself drifting. "I'll call you before we get on the train. I'm not sure what kind of reception I'll have while we're on it. Or if they have Wi-Fi."

"It's a luxury train, Marnie," he said with a slight drawl. "Everything will be at your fingertips."

"I guess you're right." She snuggled deeper into the covers. She almost thought his voice would follow her into her dreams.

Marnie only realized she'd fallen asleep when Guy took the phone from her.

"He's already gone." There was a harshness in his tone. He didn't even ask if it was one of the kids.

She hadn't even tried to call them. She'd called Wade instead. But Guy knew she had to check in daily with work.

She didn't bother to sit up. "Do you want to call the boys?"

He leaned over, sliding her phone onto the bedside table. "No. I'm tired. Let's go to sleep."

It was only as a last thought before she fell into dreamland that she realized they hadn't made love on their anniversary.

5

Bad thoughts always assaulted Marnie in the morning. She'd wake up tormenting herself with worry. The first morning in Paris, the bad thought was that they hadn't made love on their anniversary.

Could it be that Guy didn't want her anymore?

Worse, could it be that he didn't want her because he was having an affair?

No. Linda was wrong. Marnie just needed to step up her game. She'd been so caught up in work that she hadn't bought a single piece of fancy lingerie for this trip. She'd let Guy do her packing, for God's sake. He would have grabbed the everyday wear from her lingerie drawer.

The thoughts still plagued her as she stood under the hot spray of the shower, giddy with fear. Through the misty glass, she saw Guy shaving in front of the bathroom mirror.

He'd done her packing, but he hadn't picked out any sexy lingerie. Did that mean something?

There was nothing else to do but go shopping today for some sexy French lingerie. She'd just have to figure out how to do it without Guy noticing. Lingerie needed to be a surprise. She also didn't want to look desperate.

The train would be the perfect place to deploy new lingerie.

Since they weren't boarding until late afternoon, they did a walking tour of the sites around their hotel. The impressive Arc de Triomphe, the beautiful Tuileries Garden, the Place Vendôme with its expensive jewelry stores and hotels. Then there was the Champs-Élysées, the most famous shopping street in Paris, where Marnie got Guy to wander through Ralph Lauren.

"I'm really not interested in shopping," he told her.

"Find something for the boys." She pushed him lightly in the right direction.

"They can get Ralph Lauren at home. Shouldn't we buy something they can only find in France?"

She could swear he actually rolled his eyes. She wanted to growl at him. *Just do it.*

Of course she didn't say that. "Wander for half an hour. We'll meet up again right here."

As soon as Guy disappeared inside the store, she race-walked two doors down to the lingerie shop she'd seen. When the salesgirl wanted to help her, she smiled politely and waved her away. She hadn't shopped for lingerie in years. She had her favorite brand and when she needed new, she just ordered the same style and size online.

Maybe that was part of the problem. She wasn't putting any effort into it. But there were so many choices, from sexy thongs to see-through lace to tap pants to boy shorts. She'd need more than half an hour. Since she worked out in the gym on the fifth floor, she was in good shape. It was when she did her best thinking too.

That was another double standard in the workplace. A man could get a paunch, but as soon as a woman gained a few pounds at her age, they said it was menopause, that she was off her game.

She could buy a thong. She'd probably look good in it. But in the end, she chose a lacy pair of tap pants, a matching brassiere that would show the dusky outline of her nipples, plus a pretty lace camisole that opened down the front. Very sexy.

Would Guy would like it? That's how out of touch she was. It was actually kind of sad.

Along the way, they'd bought a box of French macarons, and when the saleslady wrapped up her purchases, Marnie lifted out the box of macarons and put the lingerie in its tissue paper at the bottom of the bag.

Done. With five minutes to spare.

GUY DIDN'T FEEL LIKE SHOPPING, NOT FOR HIMSELF, NOT for the boys. He'd look for something else, something very French. Leaving the store empty-handed, he decided to tell Marnie he'd found nothing.

People watching and window shopping, he strolled the wide esplanade with its designer store fronts and outdoor cafés enclosed by banks of potted flowers. Smartly dressed women passed him, weighed down by bags in both hands. Teenagers on scooters wended their way through the crowds. Passing a lingerie shop with mannequins draped in lacy night-ies, he saw the flash of a beautiful woman beyond the glass.

Marnie.

So that's what it was all about, getting him inside Ralph Lauren so he wouldn't see where she went. He should have thought about buying her something sexy for their anniversary, but they'd said no presents. Still, he could have splurged on some lingerie. He just didn't think she was particularly interested. She always wore the same brand, probably because it was easy to get on the internet.

His phone pinged with a text, and he stepped back from the front window, not wanting Marnie to see him. Checking, he saw it was Sharon. Again. He'd put her texts in timeout. He'd have to deal with them eventually, but after what had happened between them, he wasn't sure how to make any of it work.

He glanced at his watch, retreating down the Champs-Élysées, looking at the window dressings. Marnie left the lingerie shop, turned right and walked away toward Ralph Lauren.

Guy followed. Even in jeans, a loose-fitting blouse, and tennis shoes, she was sexy, her rear swaying seductively as she walked. Heads turned, mostly older men. Older men knew how to appreciate a woman in her prime.

He needed to learn to appreciate Marnie. That's what this trip was about. Learning to appreciate each other again. They both seemed to have forgotten how in the last few years.

THEY'D COLLECTED THEIR BAGS FROM THE HOTEL AND taken a cab to the train station. At the check-in counter, Guy had pulled out their passports and his printed confirmation.

And everything went to hell.

"I'm sorry, monsieur, but we have no record of your reservation." The agent sat behind an old-fashioned counter made of marble and polished wood, the accents in gold. She tucked an errant lock of hair behind her ear, hiding her nerves. People were stacking up behind them in line, and a kindly clerk opened another booth.

Marnie wanted to scream. How had Guy screwed this up? They'd been arguing with the agent for the past twenty minutes. She should have checked what he'd done. But at the time, she hadn't wanted to look at the credit card because the cost of this trip would have started another argument. She'd agreed to it, she couldn't argue with him, so she hadn't looked.

But now she saw what an idiot she'd been. How could she have left something like this for him to handle alone?

"I've got my confirmation right here," Guy said. She could hear his teeth crack as he ground them together. She wanted to grab the confirmation out of his hand and figure out what he'd done wrong.

She should have known. Each word sounded off in her head like a separate sentence.

"Maybe our names got misspelled," she suggested.

Guy growled. "I did not misspell our names."

The agent, a flustered pretty young French girl, looked over their confirmation, tapping on the keys at the same time.

"Maybe we've got the wrong dates," Marnie offered.

She could almost see enamel flying off with each gnash of his teeth. "I didn't get the dates wrong."

Typical. He couldn't even handle it if she made a suggestion. Guy could never be wrong about anything. Except when he was wrong about everything.

She leaned into the window. "Perhaps we could talk to a supervisor," she said politely to the clerk.

Guy glared at her. "I can handle this." Then he said, just like she'd wanted, "It would be good if we could speak to a supervisor."

The supervisor was a tall, elegant man with white hair teased to give it volume. "I am Monsieur Gateau. Let me see how I can be of assistance." The supervisor and the clerk spoke in rapid-fire French, then he meticulously perused Guy's paperwork, examined their passports, studied the screen again. He leaned over the girl to type one-handed on her keyboard.

Then he looked at Guy. "I'm sorry, monsieur, there's been some sort of confusion. Unfortunately, we have no record of you on this train."

Guy took two deep breaths, his nostrils flaring. "There has to be a record."

Marnie felt the eyes of other passengers stabbing her in the back. "Perhaps we could log into our credit card account and show you the payment," she proposed.

Guy glared again. As the old saying went, if looks could kill, she'd be a bloody mess on the station floor.

She gave him her own telling look right back. *You screwed it up, you fix it.*

Then she sauntered to the coffee bar at the other end of the station and ordered a latte. When the barista gave it to her, she sat in a comfy chair watching other passengers checking in while Guy continued to grind his teeth. She looked at her phone, the time tick-tick-ticking away. They wouldn't make it. That train would depart soon. Without them.

It was all Guy's fault.

GUY ACTUALLY SAW A RED FRINGE AROUND HIS VISION. That's how pissed he was. He was even more pissed when they agreed to Marnie's suggestion about looking at his credit card.

"Yes, the charge appears to be correct." Monsieur Gateau's cultured French tones still seemed to say that Guy was an idiot.

No shit, he wanted to say. He had the charge, he had the confirmation, and he would damn well stand here all night until they found his reservation. It wasn't just the money, though that was a hell of a lot. It was the principle.

They all spoke in French, the supervisor, the clerk, and a third woman who'd joined them. They gestured at the screen, tapped the keyboard, pointed. Monsieur Gateau nodded his snowy head. The clerk nodded gravely. The newcomer nodded with her whole body, rocking heel to toe.

What the hell did all the nodding mean?

Guy imagined his head exploding, his gray matter splattering the floor, the walls, the clerk, the supervisor, and the woman who hadn't introduced herself. This holiday was supposed to be easy, a vacation where they could reconnect. But it felt like everything had gone to shit from the moment Marnie told him she didn't think she could get away from work.

He could hear her voice even though she hadn't said it. He'd screwed up again. She couldn't depend on him to get anything right.

How the hell had it happened? Not the debacle with the reservation, but that they'd once been a couple who believed in each other, supported each other, and raised two great kids together only to end up as adversaries rather than lovers.

Monsieur Gateau went on gesticulating, speaking in fast, agitated French.

Outside the station's window, the train was still sitting by the platform even though its departure time had passed fifteen minutes ago.

Were they holding the train for him and Marnie? If so, it was a good sign.

Then, as if his thoughts created negative energy, the grinding of gears and metal wheels and the chug of the enormous engine drowned out everything else as the train pulled away. Stranding them in this opulent and empty station.

He hadn't seen or heard her move, but Marnie's hand was

on his arm as she whispered in his ear. "It's leaving without us." As soft as her voice was, her recrimination sliced like a knife.

He would never live this down.

Outside, the platform was empty except for a couple of porters returning baggage carts.

The Frenchman said, "Monsieur, I believe we have discovered the problem. It is very technical. A migration glitch."

Guy didn't care enough to ask exactly what a migration glitch was. He was tired, and he'd gladly fly back home right now. But they had to get to Venice to catch their homeward-bound flight.

And their ride had just left the station.

"What does that mean?" Marnie asked almost sweetly. But she didn't have to wear the mantle of failure on her shoulders.

Monsieur Gateau pointed at the computer screen as if they could see it. "We migrated our booking system a few months ago. Unfortunately, there were minor glitches. As always happens with a project this large," he added defensively. "I'm afraid your reservation was caught in the glitch."

Guy didn't even feel vindicated.

"But what *exactly* does that mean?" Marnie pressed.

"We have found your reservation, but unfortunately it didn't migrate. When it was manually entered, the digits were transposed. It went into the system for December rather than May." His hands came together as if he wanted to applaud their discovery.

Marnie choked back a shocked laugh, her hand over her mouth. She flung her arm out toward the platform. "So we have a reservation. But you just let the train pull out of the station." She glared at the man. "Without us on it."

"I apologize, madame. But unfortunately, there were no more sleeping berths available on that train. I did not imagine that you would want to sit up all night in the club car."

Marnie growled like Marge Simpson. Guy just wanted to laugh. None of it made sense. He was no techno-wizard, but why would anyone key anything in by hand during a system migration?

"No, I do not want to sit up in your club car. What I want to know is how you're going to make this right," Marnie said in her best CEO how-do-you-plan-to-fix-this tone.

She was in executive mode, and it actually turned him on. Except that, yet again, she was taking over as if he was incapable.

As if she couldn't depend on him.

Monsieur Gateau smiled. "Madame, let me tell you how I'm going to make this right, as you say."

And he did.

6

Marnie stood at the window of the luxurious suite with a magnificent view of the Trocadéro Gardens and the Champ de Mars with the Eiffel Tower between them, while barges and boats floated along the Seine.

She turned to Guy. "What do you think?"

Their suite was on the top floor of one of the best hotels in Paris. Though decorated in French provincial furniture, the sitting room was extremely comfortable. The marble fireplace matched the bar along the wall. French doors opened onto a balcony with two chairs where they could watch the sunset. The bedroom lay through a set of tall double doors, and the bed was massive, covered in a thick counterpane that felt like silk. A fruit basket sat on the bar along with a plate of hors d'oeuvres and a bottle of superb French champagne, compliments of the stuffy Monsieur Gateau.

"It's pretty nice," Guy said.

She buffed her fingernails on her blouse. "I done good, didn't I?"

It was a pretty damned huge mistake the company had made, and she and Guy deserved this luxurious suite.

"Yes, sweetheart, you did good." Yet Guy didn't seem happy about it.

There had been no open cabins for two days. But Monsieur Gateau had reserved the next one available, and he was putting them up in this deluxe hotel for two nights, compliments of the company, all expenses paid, their meals and even their drinks carte blanche. He'd also thrown in tickets for the Louvre.

"When he said he'd make it right, he sure made it right." She was exceptionally pleased with herself. Yes, Monsieur Gateau would probably have done the same thing for Guy, but would Guy have been as assertive? What the heck, it didn't matter. They were here. "Let's open the champagne and celebrate."

But he was already pulling out his phone. "I have to call the hotel in Venice and cancel the first two nights we were supposed to be there."

"Just make sure there's no cancellation fee, since this isn't our fault."

He gave her a blank look, like he didn't get what she was saying. Or that he was giving her no expression at all to hide everything going on inside. Passive aggressive again. He wouldn't say anything now, but he'd stick it to her later. She didn't care, because even on her salary, she never would have booked a suite like this in the middle of Paris. And she *had* done good getting it for them.

She poured the champagne and drank it while Guy was on the phone.

Since they were supposed to dine on the train, they hadn't eaten, and after he took care of the Venice hotel—there was no extra fee once Guy explained the circumstances—she had

Guy call down to make a reservation in the hotel's five-star restaurant.

She was tired, still a bit jet-lagged, and it was actually a good thing they were taking the train two days later. She'd be better able to stay up late, enjoy the club car, and savor every moment of the trip.

They video-chatted with each of the boys, showing them the fabulous view from the balcony, and explaining that they'd be taking a later train. Then Guy took a shower before dinner, and she called Wade.

"You're calling me from the train?" he asked before she even said a word.

She'd given him the itinerary. "No." She wanted to crow about the suite, but first there was the explanation. "The reservation with the train got screwed up."

"Jesus. What did Guy do?"

"It wasn't Guy's fault this time." Then she wished she hadn't added "this time." Sometimes she used Wade as a sounding board for personal matters she should keep to herself, like making it seem as if Guy were a screw-up. And yet she felt as if she needed someone on her side.

"Tell me what happened?"

"There was some sort of migration glitch." She said it as if she were using air quotes.

Wade laughed. "What the hell is a migration glitch? That sounds like the time you made up the term 'accounting arti-fact' to describe the huge mistake my predecessor made."

The "accounting artifact" had gotten the man fired. And she'd brought in Wade.

"They lost some data and had to key it in manually." She told him the story—except the part where she'd been sure Guy had screwed up the whole thing—and how they were now staying in a five-star hotel for two nights.

Wade said, "Ya done good." Which is what she'd hoped Guy would say. But he hadn't.

"Thank you. You should see this suite. The bed is massive. You could fit six people on it." She laughed self-consciously. "Not that we're going to have six people on it." But that somehow made it worse. She shut her mouth.

"Sounds amazing. But how does this affect your Venice trip?"

"Guy canceled the first two nights. I made sure he didn't let them charge us a cancellation fee." Though Guy handled it brilliantly, she wasn't sure what he would have done if she hadn't reminded him. "It turned out great. Two more days in Paris. A luxury hotel. Five-star wining and dining."

Wade chuckled. "You're amazing, Marnie, always getting the extra mile, just like you do on the job."

She liked Wade's praise. That's what they did for each other, in the business sense, of course. They built each other up.

"Okay, enough about this trip. What was Kelly going on about?" She'd gotten a couple of texts she hadn't been able to answer during the reservation debacle.

Wade let out a sigh. "We had our own glitch here."

Marnie groaned. "Just tell me it's a glitch where everything's going to be even better than we planned."

He chuckled. "It's nothing we can't handle."

They went over the details for the next fifteen minutes. Until Guy left the bathroom, giving her the windup signal and pointing to his watch. She realized they'd be late for the reservation in the hotel dining room if she didn't cut off the conversation now.

"Gotta go," she said. "Keep me informed."

"Will do."

"Telling Wade all about how I screwed up the reservation?" Guy asked, his eyes narrowed.

"No," she said, keeping her voice light as if she didn't see his scowl. "I told him all about our fabulous suite and two extra days in Paris."

"Good old Wade," he muttered as he followed her out the door.

She should have hung up before Guy finished dressing. She could only hope they'd still have a pleasant dinner.

❦

THEY ENJOYED ANOTHER SUMPTUOUS FIVE-STAR MEAL. Marnie dined on sea bass in a caper *rémoulade*, and Guy had beef *tournedos*, the meat so tender it almost melted in the mouth.

And now, while Guy was in the bathroom of their luxurious suite, Marnie decided it was the perfect time to deploy the sexy tap pants and bra she'd purchased today. She'd save the camisole for another time. She was gathering the ensemble from beneath her other clothing in the bureau when Guy's phone on the bedside table pinged with a text.

Thinking it was one of the boys checking in, she walked over to look at the first couple of lines on his lock screen.

But what she read turned her blood to ice, blocking her veins from sending life-giving oxygen to her brain. She felt dizzy even as she told herself she wasn't reading it correctly.

She looked again before it disappeared behind a blank screen.

Sharon. So, he called her Sharon, not Ms. Bennett or Sharon Bennett or Principal Bennett. But Sharon.

I really hate the way we left things. Please call me. We really need to talk.

She'd read it correctly. And it sounded like the text from a woman who'd had a fight with her lover before he left on his anniversary trip with his wife.

Marnie imagined all sorts of scenarios. That Sharon had demanded Guy tell Marnie he was leaving her. That she'd begged him not to go on the trip. That she'd threatened to tell Marnie about the affair.

She had her first coherent thought. *That bitch.*

Wives always blamed the other woman, as if their husband had nothing to do with his own seduction. And she reversed the thought. *That asshole.*

Finally, when she could breathe again, she told herself all the other things the text could refer to. There was nothing inherently salacious. It hadn't been a sext. It was rather innocuous. It could have been about Randall, the boy Guy had suspended. Maybe they'd had a disagreement about how to handle him. The text could have been about anything. It didn't have to be a love affair.

She knew Guy. He wouldn't have come on this trip with her if he was having an affair with Sharon. Right? *Right?*

But maybe he planned to tell Marnie about his affair on the last day or on the flight home. Or maybe he didn't plan to tell her at all, and that was the problem Sharon had. She wanted something more permanent, something out in the open.

Marnie had to see more. She had to see the whole text string. She had to *know*. And she was just about to pick up his phone and enter his passcode—they knew each other's codes, nothing to hide, right?—but the bathroom door rattled, and Marnie flung herself across the bed a moment before Guy stepped out of the bathroom.

Stupid, stupid, stupid. Why hadn't she picked up the phone when she'd first seen the text? Now she'd lost her chance.

She was still in her pajamas. She'd forgotten all about the sexy underwear. It sat in its box on top of the bureau. But Guy didn't even look.

She'd already scrambled beneath the covers when he asked, "Was that a text I heard?"

His ping being a unique sound from hers, he wasn't upset this time. And, her voice unbelievably normal, she answered, "Yes. Is it one of the boys?"

He picked up the phone, tapped in his code.

First, he frowned. Then his jawline went rigid. He swiped again and set the phone on the bedside table.

"Just work stuff," he said. "I told them not to bother me while I was gone." He looked at her as if she was the one who'd committed a carnal sin.

She waited for him to fall asleep. She couldn't get that text out of her mind, and she knew she'd never sleep. When his breathing fell into a soft, even rhythm, and he let out a gentle snore—Guy never snored loudly—she grabbed her phone off the bedside table. She thought about taking his phone, but she was afraid he'd wake up and find her snooping.

The suite didn't have a bedroom door, it was a wide arch-way. So she glided silently into the bathroom, grabbed a fluffy robe, and wrapped herself in it. There were even matching slippers. And she let herself out onto the balcony.

Below, the dinner cruises meandered along the Seine, their music playing across the night. The Eiffel Tower had started its light show. Paris, the city of lights, glowed before her like a carpet.

It wasn't cold, but it was definitely cooler, and she tugged the robe tighter.

She had to talk to someone or she'd go crazy. Wade was out, of course. No way could she talk about *this*. But instead of calling Linda, she texted. It would minimize the damage, and she could still get her thoughts off her chest.

She sent the text before she could rethink it. *I saw a strange text from Sharon on Guy's phone.*

It didn't take even five seconds for Linda to speed-write back. *What did it say?*

Marnie answered, though not as quickly. *It said something about how she didn't like the way they'd left things and that she needed to talk.*

The words *Oh my God* came back, and Marnie could almost see Linda's head sagging on her shoulders as she added, *That's really bad. He must be having an affair and this was a lover's quarrel.*

Marnie had known that's what Linda would say. That had been Marnie's immediate thought too. But she wanted to hear Linda's arguments and come up with a reason why those arguments couldn't be true.

It could be a work thing, she typed. *Guy said he'd told them not to bother him on this trip and he didn't even answer it.*

Linda must be dictating, because she came back way too fast to have typed everything out. *He didn't want to answer it in front of you. Because it's incriminating and he didn't want you to see what he had to say. You've got him on the run. I told you this would happen. You should have been more careful.*

Marnie felt a flash of irritation. How was she supposed to be more careful? By searching his pockets and going through his email and peeking into his phone? That wasn't in her. And besides, if she saw anything, that would mean it was already happening. There was no way to have nipped it in the bud at that point.

This time her fingers were on fire as she typed. *The text didn't say anything about love or sex or an affair. It was actually pretty meaningless.*

But to Linda, nothing was meaningless. *It's obvious they had a fight if she wants to talk about it. And you don't fight with cowork-ers. You fight with lovers.*

Oh God. That was true. Marnie's stomach cramped. She tried to explain the feeling away in her reply. *He's had trouble at school with a student. He had to force Sharon to suspend him. They could've been fighting about that.*

But Guy had used the word *tussle*, not a big fight, and everything had seemed settled.

Linda was right there again. *She's the principal. Why would she have to fight about it? No, it's a lover spat.*

That's when Marnie started to feel the reversal she'd been seeking. *No, I don't think so. This just doesn't feel personal.*

Linda wasn't buying it. *It's a text, how would you know if it's personal? Marnie, you have to jump on this right now. Find out what's going on before it's too late.*

The more Linda went on about it, the calmer Marnie became. She'd been battling Linda's suspicions for months. Guy was always where he was supposed to be when he said he'd be there. Marnie was the unreliable one. When she called him on his phone, he always answered. There were no stray panties under the bed, not that she actually looked, but her housecleaner would have shown them to her, she was sure.

No, there was nothing incriminating except a text. And that text could mean anything. She typed back before she could change her mind. *I'm going to give him the benefit of the doubt.*

Linda was just as quick. *Then you better confront him about the text. See what he says. Decide if it sounds reasonable. But you aren't doing yourself any favors by ignoring this. I know from experience.*

But Linda hadn't found any texts or emails or strange receipts or panties under the bed. She'd had no warning at all. At least not that she'd ever admitted. That was one of the reasons Marnie felt so bad for her, because she'd been blindsided. It was tragic, really, and she completely understood Linda's mindset.

That didn't mean one odd text was proof of an affair.

But Linda had a point. Marnie needed to ask Guy. Otherwise, she'd spend this entire trip fuming about that text. She typed back one last time. *I'll ask him. But now I have to go to bed. Thanks for listening.*

She'd gotten just what she wanted out of the conversation. Perspective.

Guy was still sleeping when she crawled back into bed, setting her phone on the bedside table. She turned it off so it wouldn't buzz if Linda texted back. And if the boys couldn't get hold of her, they'd text Guy. In fact, they'd text him first before they tried her.

She decided not to think about the text, at least not for the rest of the night or tomorrow. They had a whole day to wander Paris, and she didn't want to ruin it right from the beginning by fighting about a text that probably meant nothing.

But rolling over in bed, her back to Guy, it took her hours to fall asleep.

7

In the morning, they ordered room service and ate on the balcony, dressed in the fluffy hotel-provided robes, watching the tugboats and ferries and tourist boats chugging up and down the Seine. Everything was bathed in the beautiful morning light, and Guy could make out the lines already forming at the Eiffel Tower.

He poured more coffee for both of them. "You look tired." He waved a finger at the dark circles under Marnie's eyes. "Jet lag? Didn't you sleep well?"

She changed then, almost like a switch had turned on. Or as if she'd made her mind up about something. "No, I'm fine," she said. "Last night's dinner was perfection, wasn't it?"

Guy patted his flat stomach. "I'll have to walk it off in the Louvre today. Including that breakfast we just ate."

They'd indulged in meats and cheeses and fruit and French pastries.

"I was thinking that we'll be saving money because we got two nights free lodging and we don't have to pay for food." She grinned at him.

She acted as if the hotel was all her doing. As if he

couldn't have gotten the same thing. Whatever. He didn't want to fight. And she was a good negotiator.

He reached into the robe's pocket. "I made a list of all the things we need to see at the Louvre. The *Mona Lisa*, of course. The *Venus de Milo*."

"I expect nothing less than a list from you, darling."

"And," he said, holding up a finger, "those tickets Monsieur Gateau gave us will get us in a special entrance door where we don't have to wait in line."

She laughed. "No wonder you aren't rushing me out the door this morning."

It was a good day. They didn't have a single fight, though it seemed that lately they were always on the edge of an argument. But today, they were both trying.

Despite not having much of a line to get into the Louvre, the crowds inside were vast. It took them almost fifteen minutes to make their way through the throng around the *Mona Lisa* to get a closer look. Everyone wanted their chance, and some people took too long at the railing.

Marnie leaned into Guy and whispered, "It's so much smaller than I thought."

"But the eyes do seem to follow you no matter where you are." It was truly an amazing work of art. Guy felt the wonder as he gazed at it. But then he experienced that same sense of wonder all day in the Louvre, the way you could move from the small but no less amazing Da Vinci masterpiece to the huge spectacle of *The Coronation of Napoleon* by Jacques-Louis David. Up close, he could study each minute detail of every figure. But he had to stand back to take in the full glory of the massive work.

While the *Mona Lisa* was smaller than he'd thought, the *Venus De Milo*, the work of ancient Alexandros of Antioch, was far larger than he'd imagined.

"What do you think she was doing with her arms before someone lopped them off?" Marnie mused.

Guy had read the guidebook. "They think perhaps she was holding a shield."

"She's still stunning, even armless."

Guy felt the shared moment between them and relished it. Those moments seemed so few these days.

In fact, the day was one long shared moment, as if they'd put down their weapons and agreed on a truce after yesterday's battle over the train. He still wasn't sure she accepted that it wasn't something he'd done wrong, that he'd once again fallen below her expectations. But then he hadn't lived up to her expectations in years.

They marveled at the slaves by Michelangelo, two statues which were supposed to have graced the tomb of Pope Julius II. And the ancient Greek statue *The Winged Victory of Samothrace* at the top of the grand Daru staircase.

"It's really too bad she lost her head," Marnie said.

"But look how alive she seems, as if the wind is blowing through her skirts." The magnificent statue had survived five thousand years of history, even if she had lost her head.

"I think this is my favorite," Marnie said of *Pysche Revived by Cupid's Kiss*.

"Even more than *Venus de Milo* or *The Winged Victory*?"

"It's so romantic." She looked at him, her eyes almost shining, as if the beauty of the sculpture brought tears.

He looked at the entwined figures. Cupid wasn't the chubby boy of Valentine's Day, but a magnificently rendered man. Even he could feel the romance, the sensuality, the beauty. "You're right. They're exquisite together."

Marnie slipped her hand in his. It felt like... a moment. After thirty years of marriage, they had so few moments like this. Connected. Sharing rather than arguing.

Of course, they weren't *always* fighting. It was just that the arguments were what stuck in his mind.

He swore to himself he'd remember this moment of connection.

There were so many wonders they seemed to connect over. The great Sphinx, supposedly the largest outside of Egypt, was mostly intact, especially the head.

Marnie wanted to see the French crown jewels, and Guy had to admit they were spectacular.

By the end of the day, they were on overload, and though they'd eaten in the café, Guy was starving. "Let's get some dinner. There's time to come back tomorrow before we leave for the train." It had been such a good day.

He wanted tomorrow to be even better.

THEY LEFT THE LOUVRE TO WANDER AROUND THE FAMOUS pyramid. It was huge, an engineering spectacle. Marnie wondered what really lay in its depths, especially after having seen *The Da Vinci Code*.

"Let's get a selfie." Guy wrapped his arm around her, pulling her close. "For the boys."

They both smiled into the camera with the pyramid behind them. They had tons of selfies with the boys, then suddenly, as if life as a family or even a couple ended when the kids left for university, she'd taken barely any photos at all. It was a crazy thought. Life hadn't ended, it had only just begun, and they could both attain their new goals without distraction.

Yet a little voice whispered that perhaps she'd lost something else in the ensuing years. Perhaps she'd lost her husband.

"You want to walk or take a cab back?" Guy asked, dragging her out of her ruminations.

If she was really suspicious, Linda would tell her to hack into his phone and take a look at his messages so that she'd know if something was going on. That way she'd be armed.

Though she might be considered a shark at work, she'd never considered herself that in her marriage. But, Linda seemed to be whispering, this was a whole new battlefield.

"The hotel's only a couple of miles from here, right?" When he nodded, she said, "Let's go for it. I've got the right shoes." She pointed down at her walking shoes.

They set off. In days of old, Guy would have grabbed her hand. But those days seemed long past, and they walked while he studied the guidebook's map.

"We could pass by the Palais Garnier, the opera house, if we go this way." He trailed a finger along the map.

"Isn't that the one in Phantom of the Opera?"

He nodded. "The guide book says there's actually a lake underneath just like in the musical."

The route took them off the main thoroughfare along cobble-stoned back streets. Planters hung from balconies, the flowers growing over the balustrades. For a moment she could imagine they were walking through old Paris, the façades of the houses stained by years of pelting rain and oxidizing iron.

Guy directed them onto a wider street with slightly more foot traffic and more cars on the boulevard. Businesspeople rushed by, heading down into the subway station. Standing still for a moment, she could almost feel the rumble of the metro beneath her feet.

The bustling crowd parted a moment, and she spied a little old lady sitting on her walker against the wall, her head lolling as if she was taking a nap. Marnie dodged commuters, finding herself separated from Guy until she heard him call her name.

Turning back, she realized he'd stopped by the old woman. Leaning close, he was saying something to her, and Marnie wondered why he didn't just let the poor thing sleep?

By the time she made it back to him, Guy was hunkered down beside the lady. "Are you all right, madame?"

The lady looked at him, her eyes bleary, and Marnie made out tear tracks down her ancient, wrinkled face. She wore a kerchief tied beneath her chin, a buttoned-up coat that reached far below her knees and her feet encased in sturdy walking sandals that barely touched the sidewalk. She said something in French that neither Marnie nor Guy could understand.

Then her face puckered in a new bout of tears that filled the fissures of her skin, her nose running. Marnie reached into her bag for a tissue, handing it to the woman who dabbed at her nose.

"How can we help you, madame?" Guy asked again.

"That's kind of useless," Marnie said softly. "She obviously doesn't speak English."

Guy pushed himself to his feet. "You're right." He blocked the way of a man scurrying toward the subway station. "Excuse me, do you speak English?"

The man shook his head, and said, "*Oui*. But I'm in a hurry, monsieur."

Guy didn't move. "I'm sorry to bother you, but this woman needs help, and unfortunately I don't understand French. Could you ask her how we can help?"

The man was young, his eyes dark, his nose aquiline, his bearing haughty, and for a moment, Marnie thought he'd simply step around Guy. But then he turned to the old lady, speaking loudly in French. The woman answered, and the young man turned back to them. "She said she's lost. She doesn't know where she is or how to get back home."

"Can you help us?" Guy asked.

The man shot his arm out of his jacket sleeve to look at his watch. "I'm going to miss my train. All you have to do is find a gendarme to help her."

"Where would we find a gendarme?" Guy wanted to know.

"They're on the big streets. I'm sure you'll find one." Then he took off as if his duty was done.

Marnie held Guy's arm. "Let's find a main road, and someone can direct us to a gendarme from there. We can send them back for the old lady."

Guy gave her a look, narrowed eyes, a grim set to his mouth, as if he couldn't believe she'd suggest leaving the woman.

But she was quick to add, "It's really the only way we can help. We have to find someone who can talk to her and figure out where she belongs."

Guy's dark eyebrows drew together. "I can't leave this old lady sitting here all by herself. She's crying, for God's sake."

She felt a moment's irritation. What else were they supposed to do when neither of them could understand her? But this was Guy, Sir Galahad. And in the next moment she realized how right he was. The lady could wander away and the gendarmes wouldn't be able to locate her. Especially if it took several minutes to find help.

"All right, we'll take her with us."

Together they hunkered down by the old woman. But then how were they supposed to explain what they wanted to do?

Guy pointed a finger to the big intersection they could see a block and a half away. "Gendarme, gendarme." Guy said it twice, hoping she would understand.

Rising, he took the little lady's arm, but she grabbed the handles of her walker, refusing to stand.

"Gendarme," Marnie tried. "We will look for a gendarme."

She pointed down the street but all her words and gestures accomplished was to make the little lady hold tighter to her walker.

Marnie looked up at Guy. "Maybe she thinks we're trying to take her to jail."

He stepped into the sidewalk again, this time stopping an older woman, streaks of gray in her perfectly coiffed hair. Wearing an expensive suit, she was probably a businesswoman.

"Excuse me, madame," he said. "Do you speak English?"

The woman shot him a disdainful look. "Of course," she said in a clipped French accent.

Guy pointed. "This elderly woman is in trouble. She's lost. But she only speaks French, and my wife and I can't understand her. Could you help us find out where she belongs?"

The woman snapped out, "You need a gendarme."

"I realize that. But I don't feel comfortable leaving her alone while we look for one. I'm not sure she'll be here when we get back."

The lady looked at Marnie hunkered down by the old woman. "Perhaps you should split up then," she said, her lips pursed as she looked from Guy to Marnie as if they were stupid Americans.

"If nothing else, we'll try that. But we thought perhaps you might find out where she lives, and we could take her there."

Her face a mask of annoyance, she moved to the elderly lady, bending at the waist. Her hand gentle on the woman's arm, she spoke in French, her words coming fast.

But she suggested helpfully, "Perhaps she has a phone and we could call someone. She might have a family member in her contacts." She didn't want to run through the back streets of the city trying to find a place the old lady probably didn't even remember clearly.

"She does not have a phone. I doubt she'd even know how to use one." There was more French between them, the woman's voice, smooth and cultured, the elderly woman's fractured and hoarse.

Marnie stepped back to whisper in Guy's ear. "Maybe we should just leave it to this lady. At least she understands her. What are we really supposed to do?"

Guy looked at her, and she wanted to recoil, the heat in his eyes making her feel guilty and small.

Then, his voice hard, he said, "We need to make sure she gets home or to a gendarme. How do we know this lady won't just abandon her as soon as we leave?"

She glanced at the woman, hoping she couldn't hear his harsh whisper. Because that woman was the only hope they had unless they wanted to stop every passerby on the street.

The aristocrat—that's how Marnie thought of her, especially once she'd recognized the woman's suit as an expensive St. John's—rose to her full height and looked both Marnie and Guy up and down. "I suggest you find a gendarme. However, the lady says she lives on *Rue du Sacré*. I'm not familiar with it, but I'm sure that if you find a map—" She pointed at the guidebook in Guy's pocket. "—you'll be able to figure out where it is. It can't be far. She's old. She couldn't have come a great distance."

Guy wasn't about to let her go. "Could you help us find it?"

She held out her hand imperiously, and Marnie realized she wanted the guidebook at the same moment Guy pulled it out of his pocket, opening it to the map.

She studied the map before finally saying, "I'm afraid it's too small for me to read." She handed the book back. "I'm sorry. I wish I could help you more. If I see a gendarme, I will send him this way. But unfortunately, I have an engagement I cannot be late for. By the way, her name is Madame Colbert and she is one hundred and three years old. Once you find the correct street, I don't believe it will be hard to find her family."

Marnie gasped, covering it with the sound of a cough. One hundred and three? And the family actually let her out of the house on her own? It was unconscionable.

Guy said, "Thank you for your help."

Then the lady was off on her round-heeled pumps.

"She's got a good point," Marnie said. "We need a gendarme."

Guy shook his head. "We've got the street name. Let's take her there. If we still can't find her people, we'll look for a policeman."

He wasn't going to let this go. And once again, Marnie felt churlish. If this was a lost child on the street, would she have walked away? The answer was absolutely not. Was a little old lady any less vulnerable?

And that was Guy, always there to help, his scholarship kids, his students, and now little old ladies. She was ashamed that she wasn't as generous. She was like that aristocratic woman, on her way to an important meeting, too busy to help.

Guy said to the old lady, "We'll look for your street," and pointed to the map. Then he leaned against the wall, studying the guidebook.

Standing close enough to smell his woodsy aftershave—her favorite—Marnie scanned the map with him. "Let's see if it's in the index."

Guy grimaced. "Unfortunately, there's no index."

Then he held the book close, turned it slightly, and finally looked at her with a smile as big as the Eiffel Tower. "I think it's right here." He held out the book. "It's not exactly the same name, but similar. *Rue du Sentier*."

He hunkered by the old lady and pointed on the map. "Here?" She gave him a blank look.

Marnie wondered if they were on wild goose chase. At a hundred and three, maybe she didn't even remember where she lived. *Rue du Sacré* might have been a place from her childhood.

Guy stood, his lips tipped in a smile as he pointed from the map to the street. "This way."

He turned them in the opposite direction of the main intersection where they might actually find a gendarme. He was on a roll now as he tapped the handle of the lady's walker, then put his fingers under her elbow, indicating she should rise.

Guy never gave up. She'd always admired that about him.

So when had it become irritating?

8

Marnie thought they'd be in for a fight again, but the old woman rose laboriously, undid the brakes, and pulled her walker away from the wall. She didn't walk fast, but gripping the handles, she seemed quite steady, though her shoulders were so stooped, she had trouble lifting her head. Marnie wondered if that's how she became lost, because she couldn't see where she was going.

"Two blocks, then we turn right." Guy directed.

They turned down a narrow cobblestoned road. Shop windows on the buildings' lower levels drew patrons in with brightly colored clothing or deliciously scented baked goods. Second- and third-floor apartments had their windows thrown open to the late afternoon air, the day's washing hanging from balconies, next to flower boxes draping geraniums. Everything seemed so close, voices floating down, making the atmosphere cozy, the way life might have been a hundred years ago.

They strolled two blocks, and Guy pointed to the street sign attached to the side of the building ahead. Holding the map out to the old woman, he asked kindly, "Is this the street?" Then he added, "*Rue du Sentier?*"

The woman raised her head with difficulty, turned slightly left and right, gazing each way down the narrow street. Then she sniffled and shrugged.

Marnie's hopes fell. They would never find a gendarme on these minor streets. They were narrow, filled with parked mopeds and scooters, occasionally a tiny car pulled onto the sidewalk.

A boy in his mid-teens parked his scooter, and Guy was on him in two seconds. Pointing, he asked, "Do you know this woman?"

The boy shrugged as if he understood Guy but had no idea who the woman was. Then Guy was back, decisive. "We'll walk down to the left for two or three blocks. If we don't find anyone, we'll come back and head to the right."

Once more he squatted next to the woman so she could see his face as he explained his plan. Not that she understood. He was so kind, so gentle, never even the hint of impatience in his voice. Marnie was struck again by how different they were, how good he was, how empathetic. While she was just... an impatient, annoyed bitch.

The knowledge didn't sit well. Was it all her years in the business world while Guy had worked with kids his entire career? Maybe she'd forgotten how to be compassionate. She no longer suffered fools easily. Yet this lady wasn't a fool. She was just elderly and helpless and lost. Marnie considered what it would be like to be that old, unable to walk without help, unable to even lift her head to see where she was going, unable to remember where she'd come from. She didn't want to think about losing her faculties.

But she also didn't want to think about what it meant to be self-centered and constantly annoyed when people didn't do things the way she thought they should.

She told herself she wanted to be more like her husband, to have compassion.

There were even fewer people about on this street. It was late in the day, and most of the shops were closed so they couldn't stop to ask. The few kids or teenagers or even young adults on scooters motored by too fast to even stop them.

Guy found an old man just past the street corner, but he shrugged the same as the teenage boy had.

No one along those three blocks knew the old woman, and she recognized nothing. She was also slowing down, the last block taking five minutes to navigate.

"I'm not sure she can make it three blocks back and then another three blocks the other way," she said softly to Guy.

"We have to try, but let's split up this time. One of us can walk fast and cover those opposite three blocks and ask anyone we see. The other can just walk slowly with her and keep checking if she recognizes anything."

That seemed fruitless. "Maybe we should just call emergency."

"How do you even call emergency in France?"

Marnie shrugged. "Is it in the guidebook?"

Guy scanned the table of contents and shook his head. "Nothing here. But this isn't an emergency anyway."

It would be once it got dark and the lady was all alone. She was about to take her phone out and see what the internet said when she laughed. "For two high-powered executives, we are so useless."

Finally, Guy laughed with her. "You're the high-powered executive. I'm just a lowly PE teacher. Besides, you're the world traveler, you should have it all figured out," he added with a smile.

Not that Marnie did all that much traveling in Europe. Most of her business trips were in the US and Canada. "All right, I agree, it's not an emergency *yet*," she emphasized. "And since you have a better rapport with her, I vote to jog the next three blocks asking anyone I see if they're missing an old lady."

"Deal." Guy bowed down to the woman who couldn't understand him and said, "My wife will search ahead and see if we can find your family."

Her heart wrenched watching him with the old lady, and the inspiration struck deep inside that there was no way this kind, caring man could be having an affair.

Except that Linda had thought her husband was kind and caring too.

Marnie shrugged off the thought. She didn't want to believe that text was evidence of an affair, no matter what Linda said.

When he stood, she kissed him on the cheek, and before he could react, she took off at a fast clip.

She asked a young woman, a couple walking hand in hand, and a businessman. No one had lost their grandmother. She found an elderly lady who didn't speak English. Marnie pantomimed using a walker, hunched over like a lost old lady, but she couldn't get the message across. The woman threw up her hands and walked away.

As she got closer to the main boulevard, she saw more teenagers, more couples, especially now that it was getting closer to the dinner hour. She asked a woman with a baby stroller, the child fast asleep, bubbles blowing out its cupid's bow lips. No one knew anything. What had she really expected? That someone would rush up to claim the old woman, throwing their arms around Marnie to thank her for finding their grandmother?

She reached the end of the third block and scanned the boulevard for a gendarme but saw none.

Seriously, when would the situation become an emergency

that necessitated calling the police? Maybe the problem was that Guy just couldn't admit defeat.

She turned around, making it the full three blocks to meet Guy. She sighed her dissatisfaction and shook her head at him.

Once again, he squatted down by the woman's side. Amazingly, even as slow as she walked, she didn't seem tired. Maybe it was all the rest stops on the seat of her walker.

His hand over the lady's on the handle, Guy said, "My wife couldn't find your family. It looks like we're going to have to walk a little farther. Can you handle that?"

As if the woman actually understood, she rose from the seat, grabbed the handles, and determinedly marched on.

Until half a block down when she collapsed onto the walker again.

Marnie knew they had to give up. The woman couldn't go on anymore.

Then a scream rent the air, and from above, someone shouted, "Grand-mère," followed by a flurry of French.

Marnie heard the pounding of footsteps down an interior stairwell. The narrow door by the front window of a closed bakery flew open and a large matron barreled into the street. She stopped in the middle of the cobblestones, her hands to her mouth. Then she ran the rest of the way, falling to her knees in front of Grand-mère's walker with a thump that must have hurt. The two chattered in fluid French, the old woman's voice gravelly, the younger woman's, who was probably Marnie's age, high-pitched and filled with tears.

The old lady pointed to Guy, as the younger jumped to her feet despite her bulk and grabbed his hand in both of hers. "*Merci, monsieur*. I didn't know she was gone. I haven't seen her since *déjeuner*, and I thought she was resting in her room until just two hours ago. I've been *frénétique* ever since. You are so kind. I don't know how to thank you." She swiped at the tears on her cheeks. "My husband and all the children have been out searching. He even called *la police*." Her English was peppered with French.

Guy explained to the middle-aged woman, "We were looking for a gendarme. Someone told us they were on almost every street corner, but we walked several blocks."

The woman just waved her hands and rolled her eyes, made a gesture, and burst out with, "Whoever told you that must be *cinglé* to think there's a gendarme on every corner." She bent to hug the old woman then stood again, spreading her arms wide to encompass both Guy and Marnie. "I don't know how to thank you. May I call my *famille* and let them know we have found her?"

Before either Marnie or Guy could agree, she pulled out a cell phone, punched a button, and began chattering in French. She looked from Guy to Marnie, saying, "*Oui, Oui.*"

Hanging up, she said, "My husband is gathering everyone. They will be home soon. I would like to invite you for *dîner*." She laughed. "The cassoulet might be a bit overcooked. But cassoulet is good a little overdone. We would be *honoré*."

"Oh no, we couldn't take advantage," Marnie said before Guy could open his mouth.

"It is no bother," the woman said. "And we must do something. You were so kind. And everyone would like to meet Grand-mère's *sauveur*."

Then she leaned down to say something to her grandmother.

Marnie subtly touched Guy's arm. "We have that five-star dinner at our five-star hotel."

Guy shook his head. "We can't ignore her hospitality. And besides, when are we ever going to get the opportunity for a real French dinner with a real French family? Come on, Marnie. We can't disappoint them."

His words made her feel churlish all over again, as if she

were implying their five-star meal would be better than anything these people could offer. And she nodded. "Of course. You're right."

This might actually turn out to be a once-in-a-lifetime experience.

The Colberts treated Marnie and Guy as if they were family they hadn't seen for years who'd flown in for a wedding. The apartment above the shop, a bakery which the Colberts owned, had a massive family room, dining room, and kitchen on its first level and bedrooms on the two levels above. There were too many Colberts for Guy to remember all their names, and he realized only as the scent of a delicious casserole filled the air how famished he was.

Papa, the youngest son of Grand-mère, was seated at the table's head, a big gregarious man in his seventies, his smile wide beneath his thick beard, his wiry black hair only slightly peppered with gray. Guy never learned his name, or if someone had said it, he didn't understand. If there was a Mama, she wasn't here. Jeanette, his daughter, the woman who'd rushed down to the street, and her husband Robert—said without pronouncing the *t*—had two strapping sons in their thirties, both married, with children that seemed to come out of the woodwork.

As the family rambled back to the apartment after the

search for Grand-mère, Guy could no longer keep up with all the names. He and Marnie were the recipients of heartfelt hugs and kisses on both cheeks. Jeanette bade them sit while a daughter-in-law set down a large bowl of beet and carrot salad to start.

The chatter was half French, half English, everyone trying to include the visitors, even Papa who didn't speak much English.

"I am surprised no one saw you on the streets while they searched," Jeanette said. "But Grand-mère is like a little child. Always wanting to escape." She looked at her husband. "We should never have put in *l'ascenseur*." Which, in context, Guy realized was the elevator.

She leaned forward, chattering at Grand-mère in French, the old lady grumbling back until Robert laughed gustily, saying, "She says she is good on her own and doesn't need her —what did you call it, a walker? And that the stairs are no bother to her. She didn't need *l'ascenseur* at all." At which point everyone laughed.

Then Jeanette added, "She thinks she is Wonder Woman and can do anything. I am terrified she will fall one of these days. But we all thank you for finding her." Then she pointed at one of her teenage grandchildren, a pretty girl with long, dark, curly hair, perhaps sixteen or seventeen. "It was Char-lotte's turn to look after Grand-mère and take her for her daily walk, but she was off with a handsome boy."

The girl blushed.

And Robert patted Jeanette's arm. "Do not shame the poor girl in front of our guests," he chided, though when everyone laughed, Guy realized it was probably a standing joke. Grand-mère most likely escaped often and sent the family off on a wild chase to find her, almost as if it was a game.

Although Guy was sure the old lady's tears had been real.

The plates were removed by the daughters-in-law, along with the now empty salad bowl. The beet and carrot salad in a light vinaigrette had been delicious. They returned quickly with two huge Dutch ovens, the lids removed to reveal a crusted casserole. Guy's stomach growled.

Jeanette laughed. She was probably his age and yet still she seemed like the matron of the brood. "You have worked up quite an appetite in your good deeds." She pointed at the huge casserole. "Please, you both must go first."

The daughter-in-law had set one of the pots in front of him and Marnie, the guests of honor.

"It is cassoulet," Jeanette explained. "Chicken and pork and beans which take all day to get the perfect crust on top. While baking, it must be turned regularly and turned just so," she added, making an O of her finger and thumb.

"Mama makes the best cassoulet crust," Robert said with pride.

Jeanette beamed with his praise as she held out a big spoon to Marnie. "You break the crust."

"Thank you," Marnie said, obviously understanding it was an honor. The steam wafted up in a mouthwatering vapor of scents as Marnie punctured the crust and dipped the spoon in for one of the chicken quarters. Everyone clapped.

Guy counted fifteen at the table, and he figured the casserole dishes would be scraped clean by the time they were done. Yet no one broke the second crust until he and Marnie had served themselves.

"This smells delicious." Marnie closed her eyes, breathing deeply.

Jeanette smiled, and Papa broke the crust of the second pot.

A daughter-in-law passed a bowl of green beans that looked straight from the garden rather than something out of a can.

"Eat, eat," Jeanette encouraged, waving her hands expansively. "Before it gets cold."

"Thank you so much for having us," Guy said, Marnie echoing the sentiment, while Jeanette waved away the thanks.

"You all live here and work in the bakery?" Marnie asked.

Guy wondered if the question was rude, as if, being Americans, they thought there was something wrong with a family living together in one big apartment.

But if Jeanette was offended, she didn't show it. "Oh no, Jacques has a *boucherie* three doors down, with an apartment above." She pointed to one of the sons, the two of them so alike they could have been twins. And Jacques leaned close to say, "Butcher shop," in case they hadn't guessed.

"And Matisse," Jeanette went on with pride, "is *le charpentier*." One of the daughters-in-law whispered, "Carpenter," though Guy had figured that out.

"They have an apartment next door. And this lot—" Jeanette waved a hand at the passel of children. "All the younger ones sleep in whatever house they end up in. But I insist on dinner together." She slapped the table and smiled.

"That's wonderful." Guy patted Marnie's hand. "Marnie always insisted on dinners together when the kids were growing up."

"How many children do you have?" Jeanette said with keen interest.

"Two boys," Marnie told her. "They're both at university now."

"And what are their names?" Jeanette had to know.

"Jay and Ethan," Guy told her.

"Where are you from in America?" Matisse asked.

"San Francisco, or at least a suburb near there," Marnie supplied.

"San Francisco," one of the boys piped up in an excited

cry. Dark hair and dark-eyed, he was probably about twelve. "The Golden Gate. Alcatraz."

"That's right," Guy said, smiling. The boy was bright and animated.

"He loves all things America," Jacques said, obviously his father.

"These fresh green beans are amazing," Marnie said, and Guy wondered if she was uncomfortable talking about themselves, as if there was something dangerous in revealing any information.

But Jeanette seemed ecstatic with the question. "I grow them myself." She patted her hand to her chest. "I have a garden up there." She elbowed her husband, but it was Jacques who added "A rooftop garden."

"The vegetables we get at the store can't compare," Marnie marveled.

The meal went on like that, compliments about the food, the children peppering them with questions about what it was like to live in America. They were kind people, filled with joy and happiness and love.

Which made Guy think about his own family. Yes, Marnie had made them sit down to dinner together, but she was often late, rushing in after he'd already dished out. Everything about their lives had seemed rushed, as if there was so much to do and not enough time to do it. It was nothing like this, which was joyful chaos, everyone talking over each other, toasting with wine for the adults, a flurry of French and English, some of the threads translated, others not, but it didn't matter. Grand-mère, smiling as Jeanette cut the chicken off a bone for her, even sometimes joined in the conversation.

With the cassoulet demolished, the daughters-in-law brought out a cheese board and the red wine was switched for something white and sweet. They all cut into the soft cheeses, smearing them on small slices of baguette, the scent of them fragrant and delicious.

"Oh my God," Marnie said with her hand over her mouth as she tasted a reddish-orange cheese. "That's so good. What is it?"

Jacques rattled off a French name that Guy didn't understand.

Marnie followed the bite with a sip of wine. "And the wine is absolutely meant to be with that cheese."

There was laughter and smiles as Jeanette held up a bunch of green grapes.

"Now you must have a grape as well. The mix of flavors will burst on your tongue."

Marnie, eating the grape along with the cheese, groaned with pleasure. She pointed at Guy. "You've got to try this."

There was a sudden silence as everyone waited for Guy's verdict. The taste was good enough to swear over. "I've never tasted anything quite so delicious." He smiled. "Except your cassoulet."

Everybody clapped, and just as he thought the meal was over—and he couldn't manage another bite—the daughters-in-law brought out coffee and dessert, individual pastries, something Jeanette called *canelés*. They were probably made in the bakery downstairs, a small pastry that looked like a mini-Bundt cake with a caramelized crust and custard inside with hints of vanilla and rum.

"Mama's specialty," Robert said, once again with pride. "They come from miles around for Mama's *canelés*."

The coffee was fragrant and rich and strong, and it was sure to keep him up all night. But the meal was absolutely worth it. And so was the company. "It's scrumptious." They might not know the word, but they knew the meaning, and both Robert and Jeannette beamed.

While the younger generation cleared the table and set

about doing the dishes, the adults moved into the living room where Jeanette opened the windows to a warm night breeze and Papa, the patriarch, poured cognac for the men and an orange liqueur for the ladies.

"Thank you," Marnie said. "You didn't need to go to all this trouble for us. It was really a pleasure to help out Grand-mère."

"We cannot possibly thank you enough," Robert said, Jeanette nodding.

They chatted about places they should visit in Paris, about the exciting train trip they had ahead of them as well as the time they would spend in Venice. The Colberts were amazed by the train ride, though Guy got the feeling the whole family was wondering why on earth they would pay an exorbitant sum to ride on a train where they would spend much of the time sleeping. He smiled, imagining them saying to themselves, *These Americans.*

When Grand-mère nodded off in her chair, Guy determined it was time to leave. "Thank you for everything. And now we really must go."

"I have something for you." Jeanette jumped to her feet, rushing into the kitchen.

They could hear the children's voices, cupboards banging, then Jeanette dashed back in with a big basket in her hand. "Here are thank you gifts that you must take with you."

"Oh, Jeanette," Marnie said, "you don't have to do that."

Jeanette patted her hand. "I would like to. We hear such terrible things about Americans, they are ugly like this, they are mean like that, they don't care." She wrinkled her nose.

Guy had to laugh, because that's exactly what American said about the French.

"But you and Guy——" She said his name in the French way, with a long *e*. "You are so very kind." She pushed the basket on Marnie.

"Thank you so much," Marnie said, and Guy added, "Thank you. We really appreciate it." He could see a bottle of wine, cheese, pastries, and more.

Then Grand-mère seemed to rouse, and looking at Guy from her perch on the chair, she held out her arms, murmuring words he didn't understand yet he knew expressed her gratitude. Bending down, he hugged her as tightly as he dared with her fragile bones. Then she held out her hand to Marnie, who took it, squeezing, as she bent to kiss the woman's papery flesh.

Then the whole family, except Grand-mère, trooped downstairs, waving them off into the night with their basket of exquisite French delicacies.

10

"**O**h my God, will you look at all this stuff she gave us." Marnie's mouth was agape as they unloaded the basket Jeanette Colbert had prepared.

There was a quarter round of the delicious cheese that had made Marnie's mouth water, a long narrow baguette, a bottle of the sweet Sauterne wine that complemented the cheese, and a variety of meats to top it with. Plus all the baked treats. "These pastries must come straight from their bakery."

Somewhere along the way, the Colberts had said they got up at three in the morning to start baking. Marnie didn't know how they could eat so late, then get up so early. There were macarons and croissants and madeleines and a spiral pastry covered in chocolate and pistachios that looked like a snail.

"It all makes me feel a bit sick after that huge meal." Guy patted his stomach, which he now worked religiously to keep flat. Then he looked at her, something she couldn't define in his eyes. "Did you have a good time? Was it better than the five-star meal?"

Marnie felt as if it was a test. She'd hesitated in the beginning, but only because she'd wanted to take advantage of every perk they'd been given. But she thought of the hug Grand-mère had given Guy before they left. Somehow they'd communicated without understanding a word between them. The evening had been special to Guy. And he was a very special man for going so far to help the old lady. "I enjoyed the meal and the company very much. They were all so lovely. And I'm going to look up how to make a cassoulet, although I don't believe I'll ever get the crust to cook exactly the way Jeanette did."

Guy snorted. "When are you ever going to take the time to spend all day cooking a chicken casserole?"

His tone irked her. "I can do it on a weekend," she said, her tone haughty.

She anticipated the whole thing degenerating into another fight, and she didn't want that. "Maybe you could help me. We could do it together. I'd really like that." She touched his arm. "That was a wonderful thing you did, the way you helped Grand-mère. You didn't give up, just kept plugging away until her family found her." She'd found his tenacity irritating, but now she saw the happiness he'd brought the Colbert family. "I admire you for that." Then she laughed, wanting to break the tension. "I never did figure out Grand-mère's name. Did you?"

As if something relaxed in him, all the tautness in his face seemed to give way. "No, she was just Grand-mère." He paused a moment, meeting her eyes. "And we helped her together. It wasn't just me."

Marnie smiled. "But she gave you a very big hug while I just got a hardy handclasp."

His smile grew wider than hers. "She just had a soft spot for a handsome guy," he joked. Then he put the cheese and meats in the fridge. "We can take all this stuff for a picnic in the park tomorrow. Maybe the Tuileries."

"That sounds good."

Then her phone buzzed with a text. She'd felt the vibrations in her pocket while they consumed the after-dinner drinks with the Colberts, but if she'd looked then, Guy would have had a fit.

Now, in the quiet of the room, he heard the sound, and he snapped the refrigerator door closed with a thump. "It's probably Wade with a million questions. You'd better get it. I'm taking a shower."

Just like that, he was pissed again. That's how they were these days, up and down, one minute good, the next rotten.

She stepped out onto the balcony, finding the evening still relatively warm. There were several texts from Wade. She probably should have called him, it would have been faster. But she didn't want Guy to catch her on the phone so she answered Wade's questions over text.

There was another from Linda too. *Did you have the confront?*

She'd managed not to think about it for most of the day, but now she sat with the phone in her lap. She was a businesswoman. She had confrontations every day. Why was this confrontation so different? Because it could change her marriage. But she had to ask herself again, if Guy was having an affair, why would he want this trip so badly? And why would he be so angry about her texts and phone calls to Wade if he was the one with a terrible secret?

There were so many unanswered questions. But she didn't want to believe there were hidden sexual meanings in that text from Sharon. She didn't want to believe that a man who was so sweet and caring with an old lady could also be a cheater.

And that was the very thing she texted to Linda.

But of course, Linda shot right back. *I thought my husband was so kind and sweet to old ladies, puppies, and babies. But that doesn't mean he wasn't a cheat. You need to have this out with Guy for your own peace of mind or you'll just keep wondering.*

Marnie looked across the Seine, the twinkling lights of Paris filling the skyline. They'd had a lovely time at the museum. Helping Grand-mère had been good, and dinner with the Colberts was a once-in-a-lifetime event, the food amazing, the company entertaining. Most people never got to experience anything like it on a holiday. She'd only thought again about that text from Sharon when she'd gotten angry with Guy.

She typed her true feelings to Linda. *There has to be another meaning to those words.*

She could almost feel the heat coming off Linda's fingers as she typed furiously, the three little dots wavering on Marnie's screen before the words appeared. *That's my point. You have to know. If you don't, you're going to be suspicious forever, watching every little thing he does, judging, checking up on him. You have to ask.*

Linda seemed to have mulled over every statement, analyzing it, trying to find clues, as if she was reliving her own betrayal. This was more about Linda than Marnie.

People always said you should just talk out your problems, that it was the way to a healthy relationship. But talking about that text might very well start World War Three between them. Guy was so touchy, like he'd been when her phone vibrated with Wade's text. Maybe letting it rest was the best thing.

Did you at least look at his reply to her? Linda typed.

Marnie's stomach suddenly roiled like a witch's cauldron. No, she hadn't looked.

That's invading his privacy, she sent back. But the truth was closer to fear. What if…

Linda typed the "what if" for her. *If he is having an affair, he doesn't deserve any privacy. You have to protect yourself, just like I did.*

Marnie could feel Linda's anger and vehemence even if she hadn't used capital letters.

How should she cut Linda off? If she said she'd do it, she might be lying. If she said she was afraid, she'd never hear the end of it. And if she flat out said she wasn't going to do it, Linda would read her the riot act.

Still, that text message from Sharon was stuck in Marnie's craw. And whenever she and Guy had a fight, it would come up again.

So finally, she answered her friend. *All right, I'll look.* Then she added. *As soon as I get a chance.* She didn't want Linda to come back at her right away to ask what she'd found. And she didn't want to say that Guy was in the shower only to have Linda jump on that as a perfect opportunity to snoop.

Good girl, Linda wrote. The sentiment irritated Marnie. She wasn't a girl.

But wasn't she acting like a girl with her inability to confront?

She typed one last time. *It's late here. I'm off to bed. I'll text you tomorrow.* She added a kissy-face emoticon, signaling she was done with the conversation.

Her phone was losing charge, and she returned inside to plug it in. Guy was already charging his, the phone sitting on the bedside table. The shower was still running.

She'd never spied on him. She didn't think he'd ever spied on her. But that text was eating at her. What did it mean? Would she feel better if she looked? Maybe he'd written back with something that explained everything. Then she could feel better.

Maybe that's why she needed to do it, so her suspicions wouldn't grow and consume her.

She picked up his phone. It felt too heavy in her hand. She knew his passcode. Just like he knew hers. So there would be nothing to hide, because he wouldn't be silly enough to give her his passcode if he was carrying on. Right?

She swiped the phone and the number pad came up. She typed in his code. And her heart literally stopped in her chest when it said the code was wrong. Oh my God. He'd changed his passcode. Why would he do that?

She stared at the virtual keypad, blinking. Until the whole thing went dark again and the date and time popped up on the black screen.

Her heart was pounding. She hit the bottom button again and once more the number pad came up. She tried again, just to be sure.

This time her heart seemed to drop all the way to her toes when it actually worked. God. She'd been so nervous that she must have typed it incorrectly the first time.

She cocked her head, listening for the shower. Still going.

Then she opened his texts.

She didn't see anything immediately. The conversation must be buried, so she scrolled past the date where it should have been. But there was nothing from Sharon at all. She did one final check, typing in Sharon's name. When it came up, there was no text string.

The shower stopped as she deleted what she'd typed. Then she closed the text window, set the phone down, waited until the screen went black.

There were no messages from Sharon.

Guy had deleted everything.

GUY DIDN'T LIKE THE WAY LAST NIGHT HAD ENDED. IT WAS his fault, especially when Marnie was trying to be nice, saying how kind he was with Grand-mère and that she'd loved dinner with the Colberts. But he'd pretty much thrown it all back in her face when Wade texted.

He wasn't going to do that today. Especially since he'd planned a very special trip for Marnie this morning. They asked for a late checkout, and it turned out that the company had already taken care of it. The concierge informed him there would be a car waiting to take them to the station in the afternoon.

"Let's do some sightseeing this morning," he said. "Then we'll have a picnic in the park with all the treats the Colberts gave us." They'd eaten the croissants for breakfast, along with delicious coffee Guy had ordered from room service. Marnie smiled as they headed out to the Metro. "Where are we going?"

He took her hand. They hadn't been hand-holders for years, but this was their anniversary trip, and he was going to make it good.

Back on the sidewalk after the Metro ride, they approached what claimed to be a museum. "It looks like an old palace," Marnie remarked, looking up at the façade.

"That's what they do with a lot of these old palaces, turn them into museums." But he knew she didn't understand exactly what kind of museum this was, even as he led her around to the recently built entrance, a much more modern design. She didn't suspect until he took her into that very special room.

"Oh my God." She held her breath, turning full circle. "These are the Cluny tapestries." She squeezed his hand. "I never even thought about them being in Paris."

A Cluny needlepoint that Marnie had done in the early days of their marriage hung in her home office. She hadn't needlepointed since she'd started climbing the corporate ladder.

But the tapestries were all here in the Cluny Museum, life-size, *The Lady and the Unicorn.*

"They're so beautiful." She put her hand out, fingers in the air as if she could touch the delicate ancient threads. "I've always wanted to see them." Her voice was a reverent whisper.

"I know."

"Why didn't I think of it?" She looked at him in wonder, as if she couldn't figure out where her mind had gone. But he knew why. She hadn't worked her needlepoints in years. A half-done canvas of *The Girl with a Pearl Earring* still sat in a workbasket. She was always on her computer in the evenings, answering emails, reading documents. She never stopped.

Marnie was working even when she wasn't at work. They'd never make that cassoulet, because there would always be something more important to do. Yet he'd always admired that hard-working, dedicated side of her. She had an important job, and she took pride in doing it well. And he took pride in her. But maybe it was his job in this marriage to remind her to set aside time for herself. Time for *them.* That was his goal for this trip, and he needed to stop letting his bad moods get in the way.

"There wasn't time to see it that first day we were here," he said. "But since we've got the extra time, it was the one place I knew we couldn't miss."

She turned and for a moment he thought she'd throw her arms around him. But then, as if she recognized the rarefied atmosphere, she held herself in check.

Guy wished she hadn't.

They examined each tapestry, the intricacy, their massive size, all the work that had gone into creating them. "It would take my whole life to needlepoint just one of these," Marnie laughed.

À Mon Seul Désir, the one she had done, and which was

probably the most famous, had been only eighteen inches by twenty-four as compared to the real tapestry of twelve by fifteen feet.

"You could always try."

She laughed, waved him off. "I'd be an old lady before I finished it, and by then my hands would be too arthritic to put in last few threads."

He didn't get bored watching her fascination. Her wandering didn't annoy him. This was what he wanted, her total concentration. It was far less crowded than the Louvre, not like the Mona Lisa where you had to fight for a spot to see it and other museum patrons growled at you if you stayed too long. They took their time, Marnie immersed in the beauty.

After that, they strolled through the old buildings of the museum, displaying art from the Middle Ages, but before they were done, Marnie had to go back to the tapestries for a last look, turning in a circle to view them all.

They stopped in the gift shop before heading out. There were Cluny books and magnets and notepads and engagement calendars, along with needlepoint canvases and kits.

Then Guy found a completed canvas hanging on the wall. He brought Marnie over to stand in awe of it. It was big, three feet by four feet, the rusty reds, the deep blues, all the varied shades of green, the woman's intricate skirt, the unicorn, the lion.

"That would look great over the fireplace."

She snorted. "I would never in my life be able to finish that."

"Just do one color at a time." That was how Marnie had worked, all one color until it was done.

She gazed at the canvases stacked on a shelf beneath the finished one. "They're way too expensive. And I'd still have to buy all the thread."

"This can be an anniversary present," he urged.

She was still looking at the canvas, her gaze dreamy. "This trip was our anniversary present to each other."

"Then it can be a birthday and Christmas present combined."

But she was afraid. Buying the canvas would make her feel pressured. He could see all those gears turning in her mind, churning out her fears one by one.

"Let's get it. It doesn't matter how long it takes to finish it." He spoke softly, like the little devil on her shoulder. But he could see the longing in her eyes, her need and her desire warring with her fear of not being able to complete a goal. He wanted her to say yes.

But she turned away. "It's too much money."

Screw the money, he wanted to say. He didn't know why he wanted her to have it. Perhaps because it was some sort of symbol. That if she chose to get it, she'd be choosing to sit with him in the evenings and work on her needlepoint instead of shutting herself off behind her computer screen. Or talking to Wade.

He wanted *her* to choose it, but he could feel her already mentally walking away, and he was forced to pick up the canvas. "I'm getting it for you. I want you to have it. You can work on it whenever you're ready. It doesn't have to be right now. I just want you to have this from the Cluny Museum in Paris." He heard himself pleading. "Please. I really want to get this for you." But her reluctance seemed to ruin everything.

He waited for her to say no. He could almost hear the words coming, her lips opening, forming the word. But instead, she said, "I don't know."

Maybe that was enough. She was letting him make the decision. And he bought it.

He could only hope it didn't become this huge thing

between them, where he kept asking when she'd work on the needlepoint and she kept saying she didn't have time.

But he'd think about that later. For now, she would have the Cluny needlepoint she'd always lusted after.

And maybe he could get her to spend the time to work on it.

11

After leaving the Cluny Museum, they'd returned to the hotel for the picnic basket. Guy had uncorked the wine, sliced the baguette, and taken a small knife from the bar for the cheese. Now they were seated in the Tuileries green chairs by the side of a fountain.

He slathered a slice of bread with the soft cheese and handed it to Marnie. The problem was that she barely tasted the delicious cheese, even with a sip of the sweet wine.

Her stomach hadn't settled overnight, and not even the Cluny Museum had truly helped. Although she'd done a good job faking it.

Guy had deleted all his texts from Sharon. Why? And why had he bought her the Cluny canvas? As if he was a man cheating on his wife who had to buy her gifts to ease his guilt.

She knew she should ask him. She hadn't done anything wrong. When that first text came up, it was an accident that she'd seen it. She hadn't been spying. She didn't have to tell him she'd looked at his phone. She could just ask him about the text.

She stared at the scenery, barely taking in the beauty of

the flowering trees or the majestic old buildings lining the Rue de Rivoli with all its exclusive shops. Fashionable ladies in high heels with shopping bags from expensive stores strode purposefully through the park. People wandered the paths, the sidewalks, among the statues, teachers with their charges, tourists snapping pictures, joggers running through, their feet slapping on the concrete, groups of teenagers sitting in clumps, slouching in the green chairs. Those chairs were dotted everywhere, some with sloping backs like loungers where sunbathers raised their faces to the warm sun.

She should have been people watching. She should have turned her face to the sun. She should have enjoyed the cheese and meats and wine the Colberts had so generously provided.

Why had she ever listened to Linda in the first place? Would that text have meant anything at all if she hadn't been listening to Linda's diatribes for months? If she'd cut Linda off early on, maybe that text wouldn't be haunting her now.

"It's pretty freaking fabulous out here, don't you think?" Guy asked.

She answered without a hint of everything roiling inside her. "The day is gorgeous." The sun was warm but not overly hot, and a breeze ruffled her hair and rustled the leaves on the trees. He handed her another slice of baguette, this time topped with cheese and salami.

Marnie forced herself to taste it. It was good. If she could just stop thinking, everything would be perfect, the surprise of the Cluny Museum, Guy's delight in taking her there, the beautiful needlepoint canvas, the picnic in the Tuileries. She should have been kissing him in thanks instead of looking for ulterior motives.

"I love these chairs." She laid her hands on the armrests. They'd chosen two with straight backs because it was easier to eat.

Guy pointed to an empty lounger a quarter way around the fountain. "We could catch a few rays over there after we eat."

There were students studying textbooks on a beautiful day. Businesspeople had kicked off their shoes, propped their feet up, and tipped their faces to the sky, their ties and suit jackets thrown over the backs of chairs.

She looked at him. "But I guess we need to get back to pack."

"Just a little while longer." He turned his wrist to look at his watch. "There's plenty of time."

But the train departure was like a ticking time bomb. As if she had to absolutely say something to Guy before they got on that train. But why did they need to talk about it today? Because he'd bought her that tapestry and it could be a guilt gift?

Holy hell, she'd never tell Linda about that.

Maybe she just needed to find more evidence. But she didn't like that word. That was Linda's word. Maybe she just needed to be more attentive, look more closely at what Guy was doing. But she was the one who worked all the time. How could she know what he did at school? He could be sneaking into Sharon's office where they'd pull the blinds down and lock the door and...

She was getting completely carried away. There had never been a single thing to raise her suspicions. Except for Linda. Sure, Guy had lost weight, not because of Sharon but because of his brother's death. He wanted to get healthy. Wasn't that right?

If he hadn't been sitting next to her, she would have put her fingers to her temples so her head didn't explode. She tried to recall exactly when the weight loss started. Was it before Sharon became principal, before Guy turned the job down? She'd never needed a timeline before.

He handed her another piece of bread. "We need to eat up all the cheese," he said with a deep sigh of pleasure at the taste.

She wanted to enjoy the picnic and the day the way he was. If he was enjoying this vacation so much, could he really be having an affair?

The questions went round and round until she was dizzy. Stop thinking, just stop thinking, that's all she had to do. Whatever was going on with Guy and Sharon—if there was anything at all—she could figure it out when they returned home. Right now, all she had to do was enjoy the time off.

Even if she knew Linda would say she was afraid.

The cheese was gone, the meats gobbled up, the wineglass empty.

"Shall we share a pastry for dessert?" Guy asked, holding up the snail pastry, which he'd found on his phone was actually called *escargot* or *pain russe*.

She patted her stomach. "Full. Let's save it for later. Maybe with a café au lait." She smiled, though it didn't feel real. But it was better than asking him why he'd deleted those texts.

She'd deal with it later.

It wasn't lost on her how much she sounded like Scarlett O'Hara.

The manager, Monsieur Gateau, was on duty when they arrived at the station, and he personally escorted Guy and Marnie to their sleeping compartment.

"We hope you enjoyed your stay in Paris and saw all the lovely sights we have." He patted his white hair as if he was nervous. "We again apologize for the inconvenience and hope that your last two days made up for the trouble."

Guy thought the man had gone above and beyond. He could have sent them to a cheaper bed-and-breakfast instead of a five-star hotel with all the five-star meals. Guy shook the man's hand heartily.

Monsieur Gateau bowed deferentially and left them with the steward.

The compartment was first class, with wood paneling inlaid with a flower design, the furniture and fixtures in an art deco style, probably much as they had looked a hundred years ago. The steward, a young man with a shaved head and pleasant manner, showed them where all the light switches were, the electrical sockets, the complimentary features including his and hers toiletry bags and robes.

Just as the steward left, the maître d' came through to take their dinner reservations, and they chose the earlier seating.

Once the man was gone, Marnie said, "Wow," in an astonished whisper. She'd been quiet since they'd left the Cluny Museum and during their picnic, but he knew that *wow* was real.

Two comfortable seats faced each other by the big window, a table between them decorated with a vase of flowers. Outside passengers bustled back and forth on the platform. The bed was full-size, not just a long couch that would fold out when they were ready to sleep. A washstand with a mirror was enclosed in a polished wood floor-to-ceiling cabinet. The luggage rack was above the closet, which was recessed into the wood paneling with space for hanging clothes, a couple of drawers, and cubbies for shoes. An inside door opened into their own private bathroom with a shower in addition to the toilet.

"Is this what we paid for?" Marnie asked, amazement softening her voice.

Guy slowly shook his head. "Absolutely not. We didn't

even have a private bathroom, just the sink in the corner cabinet."

"I'm so glad we've got a private bathroom." She went up on her tiptoes to kiss his cheek.

He didn't know why, but that kiss set something burning inside him. Though just a peck on the cheek, it changed the atmosphere, as if she'd been ruminating on something all day and suddenly come to a satisfactory conclusion.

"I know it seemed as if I was angry in the beginning when it looked like our reservations were all screwed up," she admitted. "But I didn't really think it was all your fault."

She was apologizing because she'd definitely thought it was his fault. But he appreciated the effort.

"This has turned out spectacularly." She held up her hands. "And you forced the issue. They were just going to say we didn't have a reservation and blow us off. But you insisted."

He'd had the feeling for years that she didn't think he could handle most things, that she saw herself as wearing the proverbial pants in the family, that she was the backbone, the strength. But if he went along that line of thinking now, he would spiral down and screw up this entire vacation. They always seemed to think the worst of each other, always looking for ulterior motives. His issues were about Wade, his jealousy, and hers were about his job, about turning down the principal position.

But maybe he needed to think of things differently. Maybe she was just thanking him for a job well done.

He slipped his hand under her hair, cupping her nape, and pulled her in for a kiss. It was longer than he anticipated. Sweeter.

When was the last time they'd kissed like lovers?

She pulled away. "Let's unpack just what we need for tonight and tomorrow. Then we can have a drink in the bar."

She was excited. It did something to him deep in his gut. It actually turned him on.

THE STEWARD HAD TOLD THEM THERE WERE SEVERAL social cars on the train, three dining cars, a bar car—or club car—and a piano bar, all with comfortable seats and sofas by the windows. The decor of the piano bar was like something out of an old movie, with real wood paneling and old-fashioned light fittings. Marnie wanted a view out the window, and they chose two luxuriously upholstered chairs facing each other, a small round table between them with a pretty, old-style lamp. A white-coated waiter stopped to take their order, a napkin draped over his arm to mop up any spills.

The train pulled out of the station as their drinks arrived. A few small groups of people stood on the platform, waving their family off for this trip of a lifetime, but mostly this train was for tourists.

"I thought it would be more of a rattletrap, loud and knocking us around." Marnie sipped her champagne cocktail. She had *not* asked the price. And she was going to forget about Sharon Bennett. At least for now. Especially after the way Guy had kissed her in their compartment.

Guy chuckled. "It's a modern train under the hood with the old-fashioned trappings the interior."

"Look." She pointed out the window as they got farther out, the iconic Eiffel Tower dominating the Paris skyline.

They were dressed casually, but the car was filling up with people in fancy cocktail attire, already dressed for dinner. "I'm glad I laid out the gold lamé dress," she leaned in to say softly. "Because it looks like people dress for dinner."

Guy relaxed deeper into his chair. "We've got plenty of time. Even their early seating is late for us."

The servers were international, and Marnie heard a mix of languages. Everything was top-notch fare, from the expensive champagne she was enjoying to the fresh orchids sitting on the tables and the sumptuous carpet beneath her feet. When the pianist started playing, she was glad they'd chosen seats on the other end. Not that the music was loud, in fact, the conversations were beginning to drown it out.

It wasn't a bullet train; it wasn't meant to be. This was a leisurely luxury trip, more about the journey than the destination. Soon enough they left the city limits behind and entered the countryside with rolling hills, long green grasses, acres of vineyards, and small quaint towns.

"Oh my God. That must be some old château or even a castle." She pointed to a sprawling manor house with turrets on all four corners.

Guy leaned his chin on his hand to gaze at the massive structure, its gardens unkempt, its tall stately trees untrimmed. "I've heard some of these old homes are white elephants. Nobody wants them. The upkeep too expensive."

She smiled, feeling dreamy. "What would it be like to own a French château that we could go to for the summer?"

Guy smiled with her. "It would eat you out of house and home."

She slapped his hand playfully. "Hey, I'm always the one saying we can't do this and we can't do that. You're supposed to be the one who says yeah, let's do it."

He winked. "I have to keep your spendthrift tendencies under control."

She gave him a cross-eyed look punctuated with a growl.

Sipping her champagne, she watched the scenery as they trundled by, admiring the picturesque town centers where time almost seemed to stand still. The banter with Guy felt good. It seemed that so often they were at each other's throats. She was glad she hadn't brought up the text, or the fact that he'd deleted everything. She didn't want to fight.

Guy flipped his wrist to glance at his watch. "Let's get dressed for dinner now, while we're not rushed. I want to take a shower." He grinned. "I've never taken a shower on a train."

It was almost suggestive, as if he wanted her to join him. But she'd showered at the hotel and he hadn't joined her then.

Back in their stateroom, and it was stately, far more than just a compartment, she did her makeup and stepped into the gold lamé dress that fit snugly in all the right places. It flared just below her hips and the hem swirled around her thighs when she moved. It was sexy, with a plunging back that made it impossible to wear a bra, and the silky material slid enticingly against her breasts.

Before leaving for work the morning of their departure, she'd laid out three evening dresses, the gold lamé, the black cocktail dress she'd worn for their anniversary dinner, and a blue dress for elegant dining.

Her phone pinged with a text. It was Wade. Though the shower was running, she didn't dare call him and risk ruining the evening if Guy surprised her. Although it rankled that Guy was allowed to communicate with *his* principal, while she wasn't allowed a strictly business conversation with a colleague.

She breathed in and out, deeply, did it twice, then whispered aloud, "Don't ruin your dinner, Marnie."

She sat in the chair by the window, resting her elbows on the table and scanned Wade's text. It contained a few minor things, and at the bottom, Wade asked if she could call him when she got a chance.

In truth, she wanted to call him. It was so much easier to deal with things on the phone, without all the back and forth of texting. He probably wanted to ask how the trip was going, and she'd end up doing something stupid like blurting out that she thought Guy was having an affair. Wade would be supportive and sympathetic. He'd talk her off the ledge. But Guy would undoubtedly walk out of the bathroom in the middle of her conversation.

She answered by text, told him they were going to dinner and that she'd call later if she could. His words winged back almost immediately. *Okay, good, we'll talk later. Hope you're having a good time. You deserve to enjoy yourself.*

She'd just hit Send when Guy stepped out of the bathroom, a towel wrapped around his waist.

She set her phone down on the table with a guilty snap.

"Wade? With more questions?" There was a harsh edge in his voice.

It pissed her off that he always questioned her. While she never questioned his texting with Sharon.

Then, as if he regretted his tone or didn't want to start a fight, Guy suddenly grinned. "You look amazing."

She rose, smiled, fluffing out the hem of her dress. Neither of them wanted to ruin this expensive trip. "Why don't I get a table and another round of drinks while you finish up?" Guy would be dressed in no time, but with the number of people in the club car, the dining car was bound to be busy. She wanted to make sure they got a good seat.

"Sounds good." He nodded. "A Campari and soda for me."

She made a face, and Guy laughed. And she thought how sexy he looked with a grin and a bare chest.

All she had to do was stop thinking about Sharon's text and ignore Guy's jealousy over Wade.

If she could do that, they'd have a very good time.

12

Though Marnie wasn't late for dinner, the tables for two, which were along one side of the dining car, were already filled. There were, however, several openings on the other side at the four-seater tables. It was possible they might be joined by other passengers to fill up the table, but for now, the maître d' led her to an empty table, and she took a window seat.

The seats were luxuriously upholstered in green, a flowery pattern in the wood panels, gold luggage racks around the edges of the ceiling, maybe to remind you that you were on a train. The table setting was of the best quality with a vase of flowers in the center, an antique-styled lamp by the window, and the curtains pulled back for the view.

It was still light outside—the sun wouldn't set until after nine—and she gazed out the window at the scenery as the train rolled through the countryside, far beyond any big cities now. A shepherd herded his flock away from the train tracks, a dog nipping at their heels. A line of cars flew down a motorway in the distance, and they passed château after château, some of them crumbling, though their vineyards were certainly thriving.

After a waiter took her drink orders, she turned back to the window, immersing herself in the scenery until a deep voice interrupted.

"I asked the maître d' if I might join you. Is that all right?" It was an American voice, without any accent to identify his region.

"Of course." She waved a hand in invitation. She'd anticipated that they could be joined by someone.

As he sat opposite her, he took her breath away. He was so good-looking, it was almost unsettling. Probably around her age, his dark hair was shot through with gray, his strong jaw slightly darkened with a barely there beard. His eyes were the bluest she'd ever seen, and his teeth were so white they sparkled like a toothpaste commercial.

He stuck out his hand. "My name's Boyd."

She shook, his hand big and warm, his grip strong. "Marnie," she said.

He smiled. And that smile was enough to kickstart her heart. "Marnie like the old Hitchcock movie with Sean Connery and Tippi Hedren?"

Marnie couldn't help grinning at him. "My mother loved Alfred Hitchcock, and especially Sean Connery in that movie."

"An unbeatable combination." He kept smiling.

The more he did, the more she felt like she knew that smile. Had she met him during one of her business dealings? She dealt with suppliers, customers, equipment contractors, and venture capitalists, as well as lawyers and accountants. But him, she would have remembered. The man was unforgettable.

Her drinks arrived, and the waiter automatically set the Campari and soda in front of Boyd, saying, "Your Campari, monsieur, and for madame, the champagne cocktail." Then he was gone.

Boyd picked up the glass, holding it to the light as if he'd see a prize at the bottom. "How did you know my favorite drink?"

This was her opportunity to say the drink was actually for her husband. But Marnie merely smiled. She couldn't say why she didn't tell him. Maybe she was flummoxed by this man's over-the-top good looks. He was so attractive that he made her tongue-tied.

He took a sip before she could stop him. Not that it mattered, she would simply order another for Guy.

He raised his glass as she picked up her cocktail. "Cheers." Then he drank, not just a sip, but a long swallow. "Tell me about yourself, Marnie. Where are you from?"

"San Francisco."

"And what do you do in San Francisco, Marnie?" He repeated her name as if he liked saying it. "Are you a socialite? A politician? A scion of San Francisco aristocracy?"

She laughed outright, full-throated. Maybe it was the gold lamé dress or the teardrop diamond earrings, but there was something about the way his gaze followed the line of her throat, as if he wanted to lick her. She felt a tremor inside, a breathless quiver in her chest, and she wished Guy would hurry up.

"I'm CEO of a manufacturing company." She picked up her champagne with her left hand, so he could see the wedding ring.

"A CEO." He raised a brow, but whether in admiration or disbelief, she couldn't tell. "And therefore a very smart, savvy woman."

As she set her glass down, he took her hand. "And where is your dutiful husband while you're on this trip?"

"He's getting dressed for dinner. He'll be here soon." Why

wasn't she pulling her hand away? "In fact, that was his drink." She jutted her chin at the Campari.

Boyd guffawed, loudly, turning heads, and she was struck by that sense of familiarity again. "I am so sorry." He knocked his temple with a fist. "I should have known a beautiful lady wouldn't be alone. I'll order your husband another drink when he gets here."

She was aware of people looking at them now, his laugh having drawn scrutiny, and she pulled her hand away. "I feel like we've met before. You seem very familiar."

"I absolutely wouldn't forget meeting you, Marnie. So no, we haven't been introduced."

He was good with the flattery, but she was sure they'd met. "What you do? I travel quite a bit with my job, and maybe we've come across each other in a business capacity."

Before he could answer, a twentysomething girl rushed the table, her eyes manically bright. Her black dress was the shortest it could be without actually showing off her rearview assets, and there were several speculative glances from other tables. She was quite young for this venue. Marnie guessed the average age of the occupants of the dining car was at least fifty.

The girl pursed her lips around her words as if she were singing. "Oh, Mr. Hannigan, I'm so sorry to bother you, but could I have your autograph? I'm your biggest fan."

"Of course," he said graciously. "What's your name, sweetheart?"

"Amalie." She handed him a trip journal already open to a blank page, and he wielded the pen in an illegible scrawl.

As he handed it back, Marnie felt stupid.

The girl dashed to her table, filled with a gaggle of twentysomething girls, and Marnie wondered how they could afford to be on this train. Parental support, of course.

Then she turned back to Boyd Hannigan.

No wonder he'd seemed familiar. He'd graced movie screens and the covers of magazines she saw in the grocery store. The man's sex appeal was off the charts, sizzling right off the page. But in person, he was devastating. No wonder he was a megastar. She should have known. "I'm sorry. I'm such a ditz I didn't recognize you."

"But you did. You just didn't know where you knew me from."

She snorted a laugh and felt even more ridiculous. "Everyday people don't expect to see a famous movie star sitting across their dining table." Her face heated with mortification. Why did it feel bad that she was just an everyday person?

She expected them to be mobbed by passengers, the girl having started the ball rolling, but no one else approached. They looked, trying to be furtive, but she sensed their gazes, all of them probably wondering who the hell that unknown woman was with Boyd Hannigan.

"So why aren't you accompanied by a huge entourage keeping all of us everyday people at bay?" Acknowledging what she was seemed better than ignoring it.

"I don't bring my entourage on a romantic holiday with my wife."

Marnie's stomach bottomed out. They were going to have dinner with Boyd Hannigan and his famous actress wife Selena Rodriguez? It was unbelievable. The stories she could tell the boys when she got home. The story she could tell her friends and everyone at work. *Wow.*

Then Boyd Hannigan dashed all her hopes. "Unfortunately, she was delayed. She was supposed to have finished shooting a week ago. But the director is so demanding, and she's still on location." He smiled at Marnie, and she thought she detected something odd, something a little sexual. But he was talking about his wife, so it had to be her imagination.

"She'll meet me in Venice." He laughed. "At least that's what she's promised. And we've already rented a villa."

"Aren't you worried about being mobbed by all these passengers, especially since you're on your own?"

He raised one eyebrow. "But I'm not on my own." Honestly, she couldn't mistake that look. His extraordinary blue eyes spoke volumes. Attraction. Desire. He was coming on to her. Even though he knew she was married. And *he* was married.

Then he shrugged. "I specifically asked the maître d' to seat me with you so I wouldn't be mobbed." He jutted his chin at the gentleman by the door, welcoming guests. "I can count on him to keep them all at bay."

"Wouldn't it be easier just to dine in your stateroom?"

There it was again, that look. She felt it all the way to her belly. And lower. Maybe it was only because he was famous. It was amazing to catch the eye of such a huge celebrity. That was why it did things to her insides, not because she'd actually *do* anything about it. Guy would be here any moment. But she would have this for the rest of her life, as she grew older by the day, when her skin turned to crepe and her jowls began to droop, she would always have this evening on a train with a sexy, gorgeous, very famous man who actually seemed to desire her even though she was fifty-five years old.

"I like the company of other people." He reached over, trailing a finger along the back of her hand. "Especially a beautiful woman."

She thought she might go up in flames. She should have moved her hands to her lap, away from his touch. But she didn't.

God help her. She liked the attention. It wasn't as if she would sleep with him, but wow, the things she could tell her friends.

"Even though I do have an extremely luxurious suite," he

smiled. Like a predator. "With a king-size bed, if you can believe it. It takes up practically the whole carriage."

She recognized the suggestion. *Would you like to see it?*

Then, from the doorway, the maître d' was pointing out their table to Guy. She wasn't sure if the feeling in her stomach was relief or disappointment.

She was a slut. Even if it was only in her own thoughts.

That made her think about Wade and all the intimate conversations they had after the offices emptied out. It made her think about the things she sometimes felt. Could those have been lusty thoughts about Wade? Maybe she just never wanted to admitted that to herself.

But no, it wasn't lust. It was just that Wade was a good listener. And Guy had stopped listening to her.

Maybe Guy was right, though, that she was too attached to Wade. Maybe she told Wade too much.

She felt the tiniest bit sick to her stomach. It was probably the wrong thing to do, but she gulped her champagne to cover it.

"Hello." Guy slid into the seat beside her.

"I'm sorry," Boyd said with a smile and not even a hint of everything that had been sizzling in his gaze. "I stole your drink, not realizing your wife had ordered it for you." He raised his hand and signaled the maître d', who left guests at the doorway to rush to their table.

"*Oui*, monsieur?" His teeth gleamed as white as Boyd's.

"I'm afraid I stole this gentleman's drink. Please get—" He looked at Guy expressively. "We haven't introduced ourselves. My name is Boyd. And you are?" He held out his hand.

They shook. "Guy Slade."

Boyd turned back to the maître d'. "A Campari and soda for my guest Guy Slade." Then he looked at Marnie. "And another champagne cocktail for his beautiful wife Marnie."

Then he leaned close to the man, lowered his voice, "Everything is on my tab, of course, all night, whatever my friends want."

The maître d' almost winked. "Of course, monsieur." Then he rushed to their waiter who was just coming down the aisle, gesticulating, pointing, before going back to attend his station at the door to allow the line of guests to enter.

"Thank you," Guy said. "That's extremely generous."

Boyd Hannigan smiled, the predatory gleam returning. "It's my pleasure. Your wife allowed me to join your table, and she's been very entertaining."

Afraid he was about to touch her, Marnie put her hands in her lap.

She wondered if Guy would recognize Boyd. It wasn't as if either of them scoured the internet or read celebrity magazines. But they did watch movies.

Guy leaned back in his chair, nonchalantly, hooking one arm over the back so he was slightly turned toward Marnie. "Aren't you..." He let the sentence hang a moment, as if he was still trying to figure it out. But Marnie realized he knew. "Boyd Hannigan, right?"

Boyd smirked. "Do you know how long it took your wife to recognize me?"

Guy laughed with him. "She's buried in meetings and ledger books all day at work."

"Yes, she told me she's the CEO of a manufacturing firm. You must be very proud of her."

Guy shifted imperceptibly then looked at Marnie. "Yes, I'm very proud. Did she tell you that she's actually the family breadwinner?"

There was silence a moment. Marnie didn't know whether to be embarrassed or pleased. But she thought she understood Guy. He was a proud man. He didn't want to hide anything. He wanted it out in the open in case Boyd asked him later.

"She hasn't said anything about what you do."

Marnie wondered if it was a challenge. And Guy stepped up to it. "I'm a physical education director—" She noted that he didn't say *teacher*. "—at a private school near San Francisco."

Boyd sat forward as if he were truly interested. "You coach football?"

"I'm head coach."

This time, Boyd's smile was real, not that she actually knew this man. "That's how I first got noticed," he explained. "I was on the football team in high school, and my coach always had scouts there for the big universities. He said he wanted me to go places. Unbeknownst to me, there was a talent scout as well."

Guy cleared his throat. "Unfortunately, I don't read a lot of magazines so I don't know the whole story."

Boyd seemed eager to tell. "My coach was a great guy. He loved his players." He smirked. "And not in the way the news is always talking about these days. He was just a plain old good guy who looked out for us. He said I might be a good player but I wasn't great, but that I could do something with my looks." Boyd Hannigan guffawed again. And again, all eyes turned to them. "And lest you think the only thing he cared about was celebrity, he also told me I wasn't smart enough to get into any of the good universities. So on the one hand, he builds me up, and on the other, he doesn't let it go to my head. But it was the truth."

For the first time, Marnie thought she was seeing the real Boyd Hannigan, the sudden lightening of his blue eyes and the cast of his mouth, slightly down, but not a frown.

"Anyway—" He swirled the ice cubes in his glass. "I have a

soft spot for great coaches." He looked at Marnie. "And if she chose you, I know you must be a great guy as well."

Guy's drink arrived along with Marnie's second cocktail. When the young waiter was about to reach for her first glass, Guy stopped him. "She's not done with that yet."

Guy knew her so well. "I don't like to waste it," she explained softly, especially at these prices, even if Boyd was paying.

Before the waiter left, Boyd said, "I'd like another Campari and soda, thanks."

Then he clinked glasses with Guy. "To a kindred spirit in the alcohol choice." He smiled. "And to a thrifty couple.

It was the strangest compliment, and Marnie couldn't help laughing. She lifted her glass too. "To a very nice celebrity. And you get the highest marks for not being a total dickhead. You even thanked the waiter."

Then she drained her first champagne cocktail and picked up the second.

GUY DIDN'T EVEN TRY TO STIFLE THE GASP. MARNIE HAD just called Boyd Hannigan a dickhead. Although actually she'd said he wasn't one.

Hannigan laughed again, loud, uproarious, causing eyes to look in their direction. But the man was completely unembarrassed. He obviously didn't mind drawing attention to himself. Or to Marnie.

"I'm not sure whether I should be insulted." He wiped his eye as if she'd made him laugh so hard he'd cried.

Marnie bantered back. "It absolutely was a compliment. We everyday people read about all these misbehaving celebrities, getting married at the drop of a hat, getting divorced just as quickly, drugs, orgies, cheating."

Guy felt a hitch in his chest. Jesus. They surely had been talking. *Really* talking. He felt like an onlooker, as if something was smoldering between them. Then Marnie put her elbows on the table and clasped her hands under her chin.

She was challenging the man. It was crazy. He was a huge celebrity. He could... well, what could he do? Nothing, really.

Guy decided to get in on the act. "Not to mention sexual harassment." At least with that comment he might be able to figure out the man's intentions.

"I'm happy to say that neither I nor Selena have ever experienced anything like that. Or perpetrated it."

"His wife is Selena Rodriguez," Marnie supplied.

Guy said, holding the man's gaze, "I know who she is." He left it at that, the slightest challenge.

Hannigan picked it up. "And there's nothing in my past that's going to suddenly jump out of the woodwork to bite my ass."

"Glad to hear it," Guy acknowledged.

It was the strangest conversation, the strangest meeting ever. And he wondered what the rest of the evening would bring.

🙋 1 ? 🙋

Their waiter arrived then, a tall man with a thin mustache and a foreign accent, perhaps German. The menus were already on their place settings, but Guy hadn't even looked, and, it seemed, neither had Marnie and the great celebrity Boyd Hannigan.

"I'll have the pistachio-encrusted swordfish," Hannigan said, surprising Guy with the quick decision.

Marnie said, "I'll have the duck a l'orange."

Guy looked at the short menu, only four choices, fish, foul, meat, or vegetarian. "I'll have the roast beef and Yorkshire pudding."

"A good choice, monsieur. We always have that on our menu for our British passengers coming from London."

The busboy arrived a moment later with a relish plate of lentil salad surrounded by carrot sticks, celery stalks, and white sticks he didn't recognize.

Hannigan, unashamed of his ignorance, pointed. "What's the white stuff?"

Guy would have thought he was a man of the world,

knowing everything. Or at least wanting everyone to think he did.

"It is jicama, monsieur. Slightly—" The busboy paused a beat, perhaps searching for the right word. "I would call it a nutty flavor. It is delicious with the lentil relish."

When they were alone again, Hannigan picked up the jicama stick. "I've never heard of it."

"It's good," Marnie said. "You'll like it."

The celebrity tried to scoop up the lentil relish, but it fell off the stick. Then he spooned lentils onto his plate and pushed them onto the jicama with his fork. Taking a bite, he rolled it around in his mouth as if he were mingling the flavors.

"That's pretty damn good." He smiled broadly, then pointed at Marnie. "Now let me see you pick up that relish with a carrot stick."

But she chose a celery stalk, scooped the relish into the groove, and bit into it. After swallowing, she held her hand over her mouth as if there might be something stuck in her teeth. "That relish is amazing."

"I certainly can't pick that up with a carrot stick." Guy spooned it the way Hannigan had. He actually liked the man for admitting he didn't know how to manage the relish plate.

Hannigan waved at the busboy who rushed over. "The lady here," he said with a flourish at Marnie, "absolutely loves that relish. Could you ask the chef for the recipe?"

When the busboy left, Marnie stifled a laugh. "I can't believe you did that."

He held her eyes a moment, then switched to Guy. "If you want something, you have to ask for it. The worst anyone can do is say no."

With Hannigan's laser-pointed gaze on him, Guy felt as if they were talking about something completely different.

The salads arrived first, the vinaigrette tart with hints of citrus. "I'll ask for the recipe for the vinaigrette," Guy said with a smile.

Hannigan shook his head, smiling as well. "We wouldn't want to embarrass them by having them come back to tell us it's out of a bottle."

"I can't imagine bottle dressing on a luxury train to Venice," Marnie added.

Hannigan reached over to stroke the back of her hand. "Oh, you'd be surprised what they'll get away with if they can."

Guy hackles rose at the touch. It wasn't proprietary, but it was intimate. And he was compelled to touch Marnie's arm in a possessive gesture, his message clear. *Keep your hands the hell off my wife.*

"Marnie makes a delicious lime dressing that we both prefer," he said, and wanted to laugh. They were dueling with dressing recipes.

The busboy rushed to their table after the waiter had delivered their meals, handwriting scrawled across what looked like a paper towel. He shoved it at Hannigan. "From the chef," he said, his voice cracking.

Then the man himself appeared, a chef's hat perched on his head and one single stain on his otherwise pristine white jacket. "Monsieur, I am delighted you have asked for a recipe. I am Chef Badeaux and the relish is of my own creation. It is just a dash of that and a pinch of this, but I have tried as best I could to write down the ingredients and measurements. I hope you enjoy, and perhaps you will remember the name of Chef Badeaux." He turned on his heel and marched back through the dining car to what was probably a galley kitchen from which waiters and busboys constantly emerged like insects out of their hole.

Guy was sure they were the center of every conversation as heads huddled together and hushed whispers abounded.

Hannigan looked briefly at the recipe, then handed it to Marnie. "I hope you can decipher it."

This time, as if he'd understood Guy's warning, he didn't touch her.

The Yorkshire pudding was smothered in a rich brown gravy, the roast beef was just this side of rare, the potatoes were perfectly crunchy on the outside, and the broccoli was the brightest green and seasoned with lemon pepper. Guy almost groaned. If it had been just Marnie and him, he probably would have.

Hannigan cut into his pistachio-crusted fish with a fork, lifting a flaky morsel to his mouth, closing his eyes as he tasted it. "Jesus H. Christ, that is a freaking amazing." Then he cut off a piece, shoveled it onto his fork, and dumped it on Marnie's plate. "You should really try this." He loaded another slice onto his fork with his knife and was heading toward Guy's plate.

Guy fended him off. "Thanks, but I'm absolutely fine with my roast beef."

Hannigan grinned widely. "Come on. Don't be afraid of a little fish. I'm telling you it's so amazing you have to try it." He dropped it on Guy's plate despite his protests.

Guy couldn't say why that changed the course of the evening, but it did, as if they'd broken down a barrier. The conversation flowed. Marnie insisted they both try her duck, while Guy put his hands around his meat protectively. "I can't give up a single bite of this. It's too good. And you're certainly not getting any Yorkshire pudding."

Hannigan guffawed. He did that a lot, seemingly oblivious to the stares of strangers around him. And really, why should he care? He was a celebrity. He was used to being the center of attention. But Guy was glad the man didn't have a booming voice that carried across the entire dining car.

Hannigan raised his voice to a falsetto. "It's only polite to share, Guy."

Guy cut a tiny piece of meat and, in defiance, shaved off only a sliver of Yorkshire pudding, then leaned over to scoop it onto Hannigan's plate.

The man snorted. "You miser."

Guy did exactly the same thing for Marnie, which prompted another round of laughter.

They talked about everything, from his best students to Marnie's new product line to Hannigan's latest movie.

"Okay, cone of silence," Hannigan said, with a dramatic hand gesture. "If this gets out to the press, I'll know it came from you and I'll be sending someone to get you." He pointed his finger as if it were a gun, his voice dropping menacingly just the way he'd sounded in that mob movie he'd made last year when he'd hobbled a man.

Marnie made a circle around her head. "Cone of silence."

Hannigan looked at Guy. And Guy raised one eyebrow. "Cone of silence, I guess."

Then Hannigan smiled like it was all a joke. Everything was a joke to this man. Guy didn't think he'd ever met anyone quite like him.

"I hated that last movie. The director was a bear. I couldn't do anything right. The writer hated my guts every time I made a suggestion. And the casting director kept trying to get me on her couch."

For a moment Guy and Marnie said nothing. Guy couldn't even smile and had no idea what he was supposed to say.

Until Hannigan let out another guffaw that echoed across the dining car. He pointed a finger. "You should see your faces. Priceless."

Marnie exchanged a brief look with Guy as Hannigan said, "It's actually a great film. I'm really proud of it. I think it's some of the best stuff I've done." He tapped his chest modestly. "If I do say so myself. But you know it's all about the synergy of cast and director, the screenwriter, and all the people we work with. Have you ever had that feeling, where you finish something and you just know it's better than you'd ever dreamed it could be?"

Marnie nodded. "Yes. It's not a movie, but sometimes when I've been working on a project or a deal or a new product, and suddenly it all comes together, I get that feeling. And I know the result is going to be fantastic."

Hannigan looked to Guy.

He had to say something. "There was a kid I worked with. His parents were getting divorced, his girlfriend had dumped him, and the in crowd had kicked him out. I saw him going off the rails, but I just couldn't seem to reach him anymore. He was slipping away day by day. When he tried out for the football team, he wasn't the best choice, and we probably wouldn't win the championship if I chose him instead of another kid who had what I was looking for. But my gut said that boy needed something, and I got this idea that I was the only one who could save him. So I picked him." He lifted his shoulders, not quite a shrug. "By the end of the season, he'd turned his grades around, gotten a new girlfriend, and found his friends again." He slapped his hand lightly on the table. "And the team was winning every game. I'd never felt more proud."

Marnie looked at him a long questioning moment. "You never told me. Which kid was that?"

"Jordan Mills."

She blinked. The name didn't mean a thing to her. He could have sworn he'd told her. It was on the tip of his tongue to say he had. It was last fall, after Chris died, and then he'd been consumed with whether or not to take the principal's job. Now he couldn't say for sure that he'd told Marnie. He just shrugged his shoulders. Maybe he'd left her out of that, too, just as he'd left her out of the decision about taking the job.

The busboys were clearing the tables for the next seating, calmly asking lingerers to move on. But no one approached their table. Obviously, Boyd Hannigan, celebrity and megastar, was a guest of honor. No one cared if he overstayed his welcome.

But it was Hannigan who finally said. "They look like they want to clean all the tables. Why don't we head to the bar car and have another drink?" He raised one eyebrow. "Sound good to you?"

Guy wondered why the man was so interested in them. But as they stood and Hannigan looked at Marnie, Guy knew exactly why the man was hanging around. She was stunning in the gold lamé, the dress highlighting her delicious curves and trim, athletic build. She'd never let herself go, working out at the gym in the company's headquarters.

And Boyd Hannigan was appreciating every curve.

"That sounds great," Marnie said after a brief glance at Guy. "I'll just use the powder room and meet you both in the bar." She smiled, revealing once again what a knockout she was.

Before Guy could even open his mouth, Hannigan said, "We'll save you a seat by the window," as if she belonged to him and not Guy.

Then they headed in different directions.

The maître d' in the club car led them to a reserved table for three by the window. Of course Hannigan had a reserved table. No wonder the man hadn't felt rushed. The seating was primarily sofas or two seats facing, and there were only a couple of arrangements for parties of more than two, unless you wanted to sit on the sofas and talk across the aisle, which some groups were doing.

Moments later, the maître d' brought the drinks they

hadn't finished in the dining car. And Hannigan said, "Would Marnie like coffee, do you think?"

Guy nodded. "That would be great. Thank you."

Hannigan ordered her a Grand Marnier French coffee.

"The French usually finish dinner with cognac," Hannigan said after the maître d' left.

Guy waved him off, tapping his Campari and soda which was still half full. "This is enough for me.

Hannigan slouched back in the comfortable chair. "Your wife is an extremely beautiful woman. You're a very lucky man."

"You don't have to tell me."

"It's hard to believe she has two grown kids in college. They must have skipped grades to get there. Or you two were high school sweethearts and had your kids at graduation."

Guy chuckled, even though he felt Hannigan was laying it on thick. "She takes good care of herself."

Hannigan waved a hand up and down, encompassing Guy's body. "You both take good care of yourselves. So many people let themselves go after fifty."

Guy laughed. "You're no slouch either."

Hannigan smiled that movie star smile. "I have to pay people to keep me away from the cookies and pastries and éclairs and anything else I want badly." They laughed together before he went on. "Seriously, I have a personal trainer, a nutritionist, a gourmet chef, and someone who actually serves me all of it." He chuckled. "But when I'm on vacation, it's no holds barred." He pointed at his Campari. "Sometimes I just want to chow down on two Big Macs and supersized fries, even if they don't call them supersize anymore."

They had a laugh about that, then Guy decided to admit the truth. "I was getting pretty beefy. But my brother died of a heart attack."

Hannigan immediately jumped in. "I'm sorry to hear

that." He reached over to slap Guy's arm. "That's really tough."

"Yeah. But it made me take a good hard look at myself in the mirror. And I knew I was heading toward a coronary. So I made some life changes. One of them was losing weight."

"But you're a phys ed teacher. What's up with that?"

Guy snorted a laugh. "Have you seen some physical educational teachers and coaches?"

Hannigan nodded. "As a matter of fact, I have. When I made that movie three years ago playing a head coach of some podunk high school basketball team, they made me gain fifteen pounds for the role."

"Brutal," Guy empathized.

"So, about your wife."

There was something about his brilliant gaze and nonchalant tone that made Guy's hackles rise like before. "What about my wife?"

Hannigan gave him a long look. "Like I said, she's extremely attractive." He paused as if he was reading a script. "You probably already figured out that I'm very attracted to her." He left the comment hanging, as if he expected Guy to say something.

Guy just let him hang himself.

The man didn't even look embarrassed. "I'm just wondering how you'd feel about letting her spend the night with me."

Okay. He'd known it was coming. Yet it was still galling. And a hell of a lot more than his hackles were rising. "I've wondered if all that stuff you read in those celebrity magazines might actually be crap, that there's a lot of you in Hollywood who are just normal people, that you're aren't all a bunch of whack jobs." Then he added, "But I was sure as hell wrong."

He wondered what was taking Marnie so long. But she

was a woman, and she probably wanted to freshen her makeup as well as her hair, especially since they were sitting with a famous movie star and the focus of everyone in the carriage.

His words didn't even phase Boyd Hannigan. "Here's the thing you learn when you're in the public eye." He held up a hand. "No, wait, even before you're in the public eye, when you're struggling to get there, you learn that you ask. That it's up to someone else to tell you no. Because if you don't ask, you never get anywhere. And the people who do ask usually get what they want. Besides, you're absolutely free to say no."

There was probably something to what Hannigan was saying. The people who got ahead were the ones who went for it, the ones who knew what they wanted and who didn't let anything get in their way. There was certainly something to admire about that. He liked to think he was a man who asked for what he wanted, a man who went for it, but sometimes he wasn't so sure. The last time he'd told someone what he wanted, it was Marnie and it was this trip.

But asking for a man's wife was in a whole different realm.

Marnie's coffee drink arrived, and he could smell the alcohol in it. The interruption gave him a moment to think about what he really wanted to say. And he made a decision. Maybe it was the wrong one. Maybe it was just a stupid test. But he said, "I don't own her. Marnie is allowed to do whatever she wants. So you'll have to ask her." He wondered if Hannigan would have the balls.

Yet in the moment after he said it, he felt a prick of fear.

What if she said yes?

SHE FOUND THE MEN SEATED AT A TABLE BY THE WINDOW IN the club car. She'd returned to their stateroom to freshen up.

Her lipstick was almost gone, and her hair needed fluffing. And, as crazy as it sounded, she'd stripped out of her dress and slid into the lacy tap pants she'd bought to entice Guy. She couldn't say why she hadn't put it on at the beginning of the evening or why she'd decided to dress in it now. It certainly wasn't because of Boyd Hannigan. There was something about being with two handsome men that made her feel sexy lingerie was appropriate.

As she approached, she saw something written on Guy's face. He was angry, the line of his jaw rigid, his eyes narrowed. While Boyd Hannigan was relaxed and slouching in his chair, the hint of a smirk on his lips.

They'd ordered her a coffee drink in a stemmed glass, probably something alcoholic. Guy stood so she could take the seat by the window.

She didn't apologize for taking so long. They would both note her fresh lipstick and know what she'd been doing, even if they didn't know about the lingerie. That was her naughty little secret.

"Thank you for the coffee. It will be perfect." She lifted the glass, tasting the coffee and rich liqueur, and hoped she didn't end up with whipped cream on her lip. She felt the alcohol's kick in her bloodstream, sweet, hot, and delicious.

"Hannigan here has a question for you," Guy said without preamble.

She was surprised there wasn't an edge to his voice, especially with that narrow-eyed glare. But he smiled, looking at Boyd as if they had some man secret between them.

Boyd wrapped his big, strong hand around his half-empty Campari glass and slugged down a quarter of it as if he didn't feel the burn of the alcohol.

"I've just been telling your husband what an attractive woman you are."

"Thank you," she said automatically, and tried to tamp

down the thrill zipping through her hearing that a sexy, handsome movie star thought she was attractive. Her body reacted beneath the gold lamé and lacy lingerie.

Boyd went on. "And I asked your husband's permission." He looked at Guy.

"I told you it wasn't up to me. It's up to Marnie." There wasn't a single inflection in Guy's voice, nothing betraying what he was thinking or even what the hell was going on.

Boyd finished his thought. "And I asked him if I could borrow you for one night."

She was dumbfounded, so much so that she didn't really get what he was talking about. You mean like—" She made a very unladylike face. "—spend the night with you?"

Boyd grinned and nodded, his face boyishly handsome.

She still didn't think she got it. Because what she thought he was implying just couldn't be right. "You mean, like, spend the night with you in your bed?"

Boyd nodded again.

Even that wasn't enough. She wasn't the kind of woman this happened to. "You mean, like, have sex with you?"

That was when Guy finally spoke. "Yes, he means exactly like that."

❧ 14 ❧

Guy's offhand tone sounded as if he didn't care that Boyd Hannigan was asking her to have sex with him. He hadn't even punched the man.

But she had to admit she felt the offer on the inside. Her skin tingled. The lacy tap pants suddenly felt soft and silky and sensuous against her body.

As if she was tempted.

"What? Is this like that old movie with Demi Moore and Robert Redford. *The Proposal?*" Her face heated. Because Demi Moore had been young.

"Except Hannigan here isn't offering us a million dollars," Guy said, still using that same flat tone.

She was surprised he even remembered the movie, but she felt his words like a slam.

"I would offer the million dollars." Boyd tried to smooth everything over. "But I have the feeling you neither need nor want the money. And Demi Moore certainly wouldn't be my type."

The way he looked at her made her body heat, and with nothing even resembling embarrassment. It was as if his eyes on her curves were saying, *This is all about you, baby, and no one else will do.*

It was crazy. But there was a terrible person inside her jumping up and down with glee. *Yes, yes, yes.*

Yet she looked at Guy, wanting to screech at him. *Didn't you tell him absolutely not?* It was as if she could turn all her awful feelings back on Guy, as if he hadn't defended her honor and she could make him the bad guy, pun intended.

When actually it seemed that she was the one who had no honor at all.

Guy looked at her as if he saw right through her. "I told him you're the CEO in the family and you'll make up your own mind."

It was as if he was testing her.

Yes, she might be a little tingly—what woman wouldn't be when Boyd Hannigan, of all people, propositioned her. It was only natural. But she'd never *do* it. And she didn't like the look in Guy's eyes, as if he suspected she might *want* to do it.

She deliberately put a hand on Boyd's arm, telling herself she didn't feel the heat of his skin beneath the shirt, and said sweetly, "Thank you very much for the wonderful offer."

Boyd grinned. "I hear a 'but' coming."

She gave him what he expected. "*But...* Guy and I don't have an open marriage."

She could almost feel the triumph oozing out of Guy's pores and even wondered if he'd had a bet going with Boyd. So she didn't give the automatic response about how terribly in love she was with her husband and would never consider such a thing.

Because how did she know Guy wasn't already having an affair with his school principal?

Guy followed Marnie down the aisleway to their compartment, watching the enticing sway of her hips, the play of muscle along her toned calves. Her rear view so damn sexy.

They'd left Hannigan smiling on his own in the bar car.

Guy should have felt triumph when she'd turned the man down.

But there was something about the way she did it, as if it had nothing to do with Guy.

And what had he wanted anyway? A declaration that would suddenly fix all the problems in their marriage?

The worst was that he was almost sure she wanted to do it. The thought gnawed at him like a dog who wouldn't give up his bone. There was a sexy flush to her skin and a scent filling the air, something sweet and hot and primal. He knew it well, the delectable aroma of Marnie's arousal. And he'd detected the peak of her nipples beneath the gold lamé dress.

She'd wanted it, he was absolutely sure.

And the thought made him crazy inside.

Only the light over the bed was on. While they were out, the steward had entered for turndown service, and the bed was ready and waiting for them.

Marnie went immediately to the washstand, opening the cabinet. The inside light switched on, and she looked at herself in the mirror above the sink, making sure every hair was in place, as if she was checking the picture she'd made for Boyd Hannigan.

Her eyes met his in the mirror, and his nostrils flared as if he needed to drag in two extra breaths. She turned, backed up against the washbasin. "Well, that was rather amazing, having dinner with a movie star."

So she wanted to pretend it hadn't happened. He called her on it. "What made you say no?"

Her eyes narrowed. "Because I'm married," she said with a

hard edge, keeping her voice low as if she was afraid the occupants of the next cabin would overhear.

"What would you have said if I hadn't been there?"

The real question was whether she'd stopped herself with Wade on all those business trips or during the evenings they'd worked late?

Her color heightened. "Are you accusing me of something? Because as I recall you were sitting right there, and you didn't tell him absolutely no way." She was suddenly magnificently furious, her hands jammed on her hips, her face close to his. "Why didn't you punch him in the nose and tell him to keep his hands off your wife?"

He shrugged nonchalantly, but his fists bunched as if that was exactly what he'd wanted to do. "Because you're a liberated woman, and you can do your own punching."

"Oh, give me a break. You were testing me."

He didn't bother to deny it. "You wanted to do it."

She closed the cabinet, stomped past him to the chairs and table by the window, moonlight making the gold dress shimmer. Then she whirled. "You're such an asshole."

He smiled snidely. "I don't hear you denying anything."

Something started boiling inside him, something that had been simmering for months, maybe years. "I was sitting right there, Marnie. I could smell how badly you wanted him." He took a step closer. "You have this hot, sexy scent when you want it and you want it badly." He took another step. "And your skin is all pink and warm, like it is right before I slide inside you."

With one more step, he made out the widening of her pupils and smelled the pheromones. He could feel the heat of her skin without even touching her. And he raised his hand to her breast, cupped her in his palm and flicked a thumb over her nipple. "You're hard for him, Marnie."

She raised her hand as if she might actually slap him, and he caught her wrist, her bones delicate in his grasp.

"Go ahead and deny it," he muttered. "Deny how hard you're breathing just thinking about it."

They were both breathing hard.

And he wanted her, even now, as crazy as it was.

"Maybe I just wanted sex." She spat the words at him, ending with a hiss. "Since you haven't been able to do anything in our bedroom for weeks."

The disgust in her tone made it sound as if he hadn't touched her for eons. But it had only been a couple of weeks, maybe three. Or four. Or... He couldn't quite remember.

"So I don't make love to you for a couple of weeks and that gives you carte blanche to follow some slick movie star back to his suite because I'm supposedly not up to the task?"

She was caged against the table, and he pressed closer, harder, bent her slightly backward. She had to feel him. She had to know he wanted her right now. And he had to wonder why he was so goddamn turned on.

Her eyes were defiant, blazing, and she whispered, "Then prove you are."

He was on her then, his hand at her nape as he plundered her mouth like a Viking plundering treasure.

HE TOOK HER MOUTH RAVENOUSLY, LIKE HE WAS STARVING for the taste of her, his tongue deep, his taste sweet.

They hadn't kissed like this in forever.

He held her head in both hands and consumed her with his whole being. He was rigid against her belly. She didn't care if it was because another man wanted her. She didn't care that he was angry. She just wanted this, any way she could get it.

He put his hands on her bottom, hauling her up on the table. She was the one who pulled her skirt to her hips, wrapping her legs around him as if she were pulling him deep inside her.

He rubbed against her, rotating his hips, setting her on fire. Leaning back on her hands, she let him do whatever he wanted. Because she wanted it.

Thank God the table was bolted to the floor.

He reached under the dress, pulled her tap pants down her thighs, the delicate lace dangling on her high heel for just a moment.

Guy stared at the confection. "Did you come back to the room to put on your sexy lingerie for him?" He didn't look at her, simply watched the dainty bit of cloth as it tipped off her shoe and floated to the carpet.

He obviously remembered what she'd been wearing before he stepped into the shower. Her normal everyday fare.

She wondered if she should lie. She wondered what would make him harder.

And what would make her hotter.

She held his gaze, her voice low, seductive. "Yes. I did. Why do you think it took me so long?"

He watched her like a predator about to pounce. Then he hauled her up against him, pivoted, and fell on top of her on the bed. She lost her breath, and it was far more than just his weight on her. Hooking her legs around him, she was spread wide and ready for him.

"If it was sex you wanted tonight, why didn't you just say so?" His voice was harsh, angry, and oh so sexy.

He reached beneath her for the fastening of her dress, and she heard a thread pop as he pulled it off her shoulders. She didn't care, not one bit.

He stopped a moment, stared at her nipples, tight and dark and begging for his kiss. Then he bent to suckle her. It was too exquisite for words. She could only moan and writhe and toss her head on the bed. When he pinched the other nipple, she cried out because the pain was so good it made her wet.

He moved between her legs, mimicking the act she wanted so badly. He reared back then, shoving down his pants, toeing off his shoes, while she lay there with her dress wrapped around her waist.

He was gorgeously naked, and there was some something dark and feral about him as he fell on her. Hands on her bottom, he pulled her to him, her legs falling wide as he buried his face against her.

Oh God oh God oh God.

She wasn't sure whether she said the words aloud or if they were only in her head. Rearing up against him, her fingers tangled in his hair, she held him close, tight, rocking with the rhythm of his tongue.

God, it was good, so good. All the tension of days and weeks and maybe even months built inside her, screaming to get out.

He thrust two fingers inside her, played her exactly the way she needed. And she cried out as she came. The climax was like no other, ever. She writhed beneath him, relishing every drop of sensation.

Even before she was done, he was over her, plunging deep. She didn't know if it was the same climax, or another bursting out.

When she felt him throb inside her, his pulse urging her on, his climax took her with him once again. Her last coherent thought was that nothing could be like this, not ever.

Not even sex with a hot, hunky movie star.

HE WAS SATED. LIKE A MAN STARVING FOR YEARS ON A desert island who'd suddenly been given a feast.

They hadn't made love with that kind of intensity in months. It might actually have been years. They were older, they'd been married for thirty years, sex had become routine. One of them felt an itch, rolled over, and they scratched it together.

But nothing had felt like that in a long, long time. It was partly the emotions. They'd both been pissed, daring each other, pushing each other.

It felt like a scene from *Gone with the Wind*, the terrible argument ending with Rhett carrying Scarlett up the stairs. Fade out.

Now he knew what it felt like. Powerful. Intense. Then the sweet lethargy of holding her in his arms.

He reached up and turned out the lights.

Marnie gasped. "Look at all the stars out there."

It was completely dark now. And outside, billions of stars seemed to float past the window. Though he could feel the rocking of the train beneath them, looking out at the stars, it was almost as if they weren't moving at all.

"It's so beautiful," she whispered.

His pulse raced with the sexy timbre of her voice, as if she were talking about the way he'd made her feel. And suddenly he wasn't sated. He wanted to do it all over again, wanted to take her all night long.

He thought about telling her how good it felt, how he wanted it to be like that every time. But it would spoil the mood.

Talking always seemed to spoil the mood between them. No matter what they said, they always seemed to end up fighting. About the principal job. About how much she worked. About Wade. About the things he didn't do right around the house, even though he'd been doing all the same stuff for years because she was the workaholic.

No. He didn't want to talk. He just wanted to lay here with her in his arms, feeling the pop and crackle of his climax before it died down, smelling her sweet perfume, feeling her smooth, soft skin against him.

In a minute, he would turn to her again. In a minute, he would tear her dress all the way off. Then he'd kiss his way down her body, spread her legs, taste her again. Make her scream again.

He heard her soft sigh in the dark cabin, felt it thrum through him as if it signaled her satisfaction.

Then she asked, "Are you having an affair with Sharon Bennett?"

15

Marnie felt Guy stiffen against her. And not in a good way. It was the worst time to ask, but she'd been feeling so good, so in tune with him, as if their hearts were beating as one, as if their minds were melded.

As if they could actually talk without arguing.

His voice went rough, shooting out of him like gravel from beneath tires. "What the hell are you talking about?"

She'd started it, and there was no way to back out. She'd said what was burning in her belly, and if she didn't get an answer, she might scream.

"Sharon. The principal." Should she tell him she'd seen Sharon's text? It was right there on his phone, on the lock screen. She hadn't even pried to get into it. She only did that later. "The other day, when we were in Paris, your phone pinged while you were in the shower. And part of her text popped up."

She could hear him breathing hard and heavy, practically vibrating against her.

"That was three goddamn days ago."

Which meant he knew exactly what text she was talking about.

Her heart started to pound. *Oh God oh God oh God. Don't let it be true.* What the hell would she do it if it was true?

"And you're just now asking me about it? Is that what you've been stewing about for the past three days?"

She jumped into defense mode. "I haven't been stewing. I've been trying to enjoy myself."

"Right." He snorted. "And that's why you thought about sleeping with Boyd Hannigan."

"I did not," she denied, more vehemently than she needed to.

She rolled out of the bed and wrestled her dress off. As if she were suddenly self-conscious being naked, even in the dark, she grabbed the fluffy robe off the hook, wrapped it tightly around her, and only then turned on the light. "You were the one who didn't tell him it was out of the question. I was taken totally by surprise. I didn't even understand what he was talking about at first."

"I could smell how turned on you were." His voice was almost a snarl.

She stopped, stood still a moment, collected herself, then started in on him. "I know exactly what you're doing. You're trying to turn this around on me. Well, we've already had that argument, and I'm not going to let you make this about me. Tell me about Sharon and what happened. She said she didn't like the way you two left things. What is that supposed to mean?" She was spitting mad, like a cat the moment it saw a raccoon dash across the deck, hissing, growling, and ready for battle. But she didn't shout. The neighbors had probably gotten an earful already.

How had they gone from lying gloriously sated in each other's arms to this? It was her fault too, but she couldn't turn back. "Go ahead. Explain it, Guy."

He was still on the bed, still naked, and even now, her heart was racing. He propped himself up on his elbows. "It didn't mean a goddamn thing."

"It sounded like you two had a lovers' spat."

"You have to be lovers to have a lovers' spat."

She backed up against the table, leaned on the edge, crossed her arms over her chest. "Tell me what that text meant." Then the words spilled out, though she'd never meant to say them. "And tell me why you deleted the entire string."

He sat up, glared at her. Then he grabbed his slacks, stepped into them, not even bothering with his boxers. When he stood, he towered over her. She didn't move, didn't let him intimidate her. She had the moral high ground here.

"So now you've taken to snooping through my texts?"

"The phone was charging. It was right there. So, yes—" She tilted her chin up. "—I looked. I wanted to see what you two said. But everything was gone."

"You—" He managed to stop himself, but she knew the name he'd been about to call her.

He stood above her, bare-chested, moonlight streaming down on him through the window. The only thing marring his beauty was the shadow she cast across him.

"All right, I'll tell you. But you won't believe me. You always think the worst. Especially after Linda's divorce. She'd been spewing vitriol in your ears ever since. And now she's even got you checking my texts. Tell me, do you go through my pockets looking for receipts? Do you call the credit card company just in case I charged a motel room?"

She willed her face not to heat. She had gone through his pockets, but only once, and only after a particularly grueling dinner with Linda. She couldn't help herself. No woman would be able to help herself. But she was never going to admit it.

She raised her chin. "I thought you were going to tell me about the texts, but all I hear is you blaming me for everything."

He advanced one step. She held her ground on the edge of the table. She couldn't move, that would be giving him the advantage. "Go on, tell me, Guy."

He was close enough for her to see his flared nostrils and the rigid lines of his beautiful face. "We had a fight. It was about a school matter. Nothing personal at all. She disagreed with how I handled a situation."

She wasn't letting him off the hook so easily. "What school matter? And what exactly did you do that she didn't like?"

The train suddenly lurched, and she almost lost her balance. Standing up, her arms folded, she planted her feet. It wouldn't do to fall ignominiously to the floor.

He glared at her a long moment, as if he shouldn't have to explain. "I suspended one of the boys. Then she got a call from the father who's a very big donor, and she wanted me to reconsider. I refused."

Wasn't that usually the way? The teacher wanted to take action, and the principal was thinking about the money.

"What did the boy do?"

"I caught him bullying another student, and I suspended him. We don't accept bullying on any terms. And I don't care how much money the kid's father donates."

"Are you talking about Randall?" She remembered the boy, and when Guy nodded, she asked, "And how did she expect you to resolve it?"

"She wanted me to change the suspension to detention. She thought that would pacify his father. But I got her to see that went against our zero-tolerance policy on bullying. So we talked to the parents together, and they finally understood the gravity of what Randall and his minions had done. I told them the suspension would stand, and Sharon backed me up."

If all that was true, why had he deleted all those texts? It didn't make sense. "So why would she text you days later to say she didn't like the way you two left things?"

He shrugged, looked away, his bare chest still gleaming in moonlight. "Probably because I won the argument. And she didn't like it."

"Probably?" She continued to push. "You didn't answer the text?"

He hesitated then, a telltale moment, and she didn't know whether to believe his explanation. "I told her we'd forget about the whole thing, never talk about it again, and that everything would be back to normal when I returned from this holiday."

She waited for more, staring him down. But he failed to meet her eye.

"Then I deleted her texts because I'm freaking sick of talking about it and thinking about it. It's no different than you and Wade and all your texts and all your phone calls. I just wanted to come on this vacation and put school and all that crap behind us. I wanted you to put all your work behind us. And all we're doing is fighting about the same old shit."

She wanted to spew on him, scream that none of it made sense, pound on his chest to get the truth out of him.

But she took one long moment to think about it. Maybe it did make sense. Maybe she'd been looking at every little thing he did and comparing it to Linda and her marriage.

And she did text Wade at the drop of a hat when she had an important thought. Yes, she texted and talked to him too much, but at least it was all out in the open, not like the texts Guy had deleted.

Except that Marnie had deleted texts from Wade that might be misconstrued if anyone saw them. They were harmless, but taken out of context, Guy might not have thought so. And she'd pushed the Delete button.

Guy grabbed a shirt, stuffed his arms into the sleeves and buttoned haphazardly, stopping once to rebutton before shoving the tails into his slacks.

"What are you doing?"

He looked at her, a scathing glance that raked her from head to toe. "I need a drink." He sat on the edge of the bed to put on his shoes.

What he meant was that he needed to get away from her.

He didn't slam the door. He closed it very quietly. Maybe that was worse.

Why the hell had she said anything at all?

Everything had been so perfect, so good. Even now, her body tingled, and she wanted him all over again.

She picked up her dress and was glad to see it hadn't torn. After hanging it up, she picked up his boxers and threw them in the bag for dirty clothes.

Then she sat in the chair by the window and watched the stars race by.

Maybe she shouldn't have brought it up at that moment. But really, when was the right time? When they were fighting? Or once they got home? Or on the plane? When on earth was the right time? Then again, maybe it was the way she'd phrased it, so bluntly, so out of the blue. She should have been less confrontational.

Then she went back to the real question. Had the fight with Sharon been about a bully?

Or had Guy been lying?

HIS BLOOD WAS RAGING AS HE STALKED TO THE CLUB CAR.

She thought he was having an affair. The goddamn nerve

she had when she spent hours texting and talking with Wade the asshole. And he'd had one measly text that could be misinterpreted.

Marnie had really gone off the rails this time.

At well after ten, the club car was jumping, and the sofas and chairs were full.

All except the table where Hannigan sat alone, staring out the window. Guy was about to march through. Maybe he could find a spot in the other bar, even if he had to stand. All he wanted was a place by himself where he could get drunk.

But Hannigan turned at that moment and waved him over. He wasn't in the mood for the man's crap. He wasn't in the mood for all the attention the movie star garnered. He wasn't in the mood to listen to Hannigan's laugh. He might actually put a fist in the man's face.

Everything would have been amazing if Marnie hadn't started asking him stupid questions. She always had to ruin anything good.

And maybe he'd feel a lot better if he took out some of his rage verbally on Boyd Hannigan. Yeah, it sounded like a great idea.

He marched over, practically threw himself into the seat. And prepared to tear the man a new asshole.

Except that Hannigan said, "I'm glad you came back for a drink. I wanted to apologize. I totally misjudged the situation."

The apology threw him off. How was he supposed to rage after an apology? Instead, he picked on the thing that bothered him. "Exactly how did you misjudge? She was married. She had a ring on her finger. Did you think she was coming onto you before I arrived?"

Hannigan waved his hand. "Nothing of the kind. It's just that your wife is a very beautiful woman, and her beauty overruled my better judgment."

Guy snorted. "Do you do this a lot? Just sit down next to a beautiful woman and ask if she wants to go to bed with you even though her husband's right beside her?"

Boyd Hannigan allowed himself a small smile, not his usual trademark grin. "I have occasionally done that. I can usually read the waters. In fact, this was the first time," he said, adding a shrug, "that I failed to judge things correctly."

Guy scoffed from deep in his throat. "So how can you tell?"

Hannigan drummed his middle finger on the table. "It's hard to describe. It's in the way a man looks at me and then at his wife. Or the way she looks at me and then her husband. It's all silent communication. Then I throw out a few soft-balls, like sharing food, and I see what kind of reaction I get. Sometimes it's just the way they look at each other."

Now Hannigan had him hooked. "How did Marnie and I look at each other?"

"There was intention there." Hannigan cut himself off. "No, *intention* isn't the right word. There was a sensation of you testing each other. How you felt about her being an attractive woman. And about other men finding her attractive. She wanted you to notice that I was attracted to her. And when you did notice, she seemed to like it."

Guy admitted he had liked it, as crazy as that sounded. The way Hannigan looked at Marnie was part of what had turned him on. Yes, there was anger, but it was also a huge turn-on.

Not that *his* desire was the point. "It doesn't mean I wanted to share," he said with an edge sharp enough to slice.

Hannigan shook his finger as if he was actually getting it. "That's exactly where I misjudged. And I apologize. I'm afraid it looks like you two had a fight when you got back to the cabin. And I'm really sorry for that too."

Guy wanted to say they'd had the best sex of the last two

years. But he didn't want to give Hannigan ammunition. "Apology accepted."

"But I may need to grovel a little more to Marnie," Hannigan added.

Against his will, Guy burst out with a laugh. "You are the craziest man I've ever met." He pointed his index finger, his elbow resting on the table. "Is that what it means to be a celebrity, that you're a crazy person?"

Hannigan laughed, not the guffaw that filled the bar car, but a soft laugh of camaraderie. "Yeah, you totally need to be at least a little crazy."

"What does your wife think about all this, you picking up strange women on trains?"

He sighed, shrugged, shook his head. "She has her own peccadilloes, as they say."

In other words, they had an open marriage.

"So tell me what all those smoldering looks were between the two of you?" Hannigan asked, leaning back, crossing his legs, relaxing into the conversation.

Guy felt himself laugh even though he hadn't meant to. How could you not like this crazy celebrity? Boyd Hannigan said whatever he thought. And maybe that wasn't such a bad thing.

"How the hell should I know?" Guy shrugged, shaking his head. "Only you can say what you thought you saw." Yet there had been some hugely smoldering looks between him and Marnie, looks that had exploded back in their stateroom.

Hannigan gave him a knowing smile.

How had the man read the tension seething between them? Boyd Hannigan should have been too self-involved to notice anyone but himself. But maybe that's why actors were so convincing, because they watched people, observed their reactions, and built them into a character they could play.

What the hell, why not tell him? Isn't that what men did,

unburdened themselves to their bartender, while women unburdened themselves to their hairstylist. Although Marnie would have slapped him for that misogynistic thought.

And he admitted, "We might be going through a rough patch."

"Are you too much of a workaholic?"

Guy guffawed almost as loudly as Hannigan. "It's not me. She's the CEO."

"I get it," Hannigan crowed. "You're the physical education director, and she's the big breadwinner. And you're jealous as hell."

He should have been offended, but for some reason Guy wasn't. It was probably what a lot of people thought but never had the guts to say to him. And for once it gave him an excuse to answer the accusation. "I'm not jealous. It's what she wanted to do. She thinks signing a huge deal is satisfying, but I want to work with kids. I want to help them make changes in their lives, to find direction when they don't have any." He leaned over the table, really getting into his feelings. "I work at a private school, and a while ago, our principal retired. The board wanted me to apply for the job. It was a great opportunity. But you know, it's all administration, dealing with the board, placating parents and donors. It's not working with the kids unless there's a problem the teachers or directors can't handle." He leaned back like Hannigan, dropped his voice lower. "So I turned it down."

Drinks came, another Campari for Hannigan and a whiskey sour for Guy. Hannigan settled deeper into his chair. "And I take it Marnie was pissed you didn't take the job."

"I think she was mostly pissed that I didn't tell her about the job until after I'd already turned it down."

Hannigan chuckled softly. "You really screwed the pooch on that one."

"Yeah. But I knew she'd want me to take it. And there

would have been endless fights. I figured if it was done deal, she'd just get over it eventually."

"But she hasn't." Hannigan nodded.

"We just don't talk about it."

"Which means it's simmering below the surface." Hannigan was spot on. "But most men would have taken the path of least resistance. You know she's going to be pissed so you take the job just to shut her up."

Guy shook his head, sniffing his disdain for that. "I might have done that a couple years ago. It would have been worth the extra pension." Then he told Hannigan the whole thing. "Remember I told you my brother died a few months ago?"

Hannigan nodded. "And you lost a few pounds because you were afraid you'd go the same way."

"Yeah. But it was more than that too. He was a couple of years younger than me, and he was an educator just like I am, principal at a very prestigious school. And even though he never said it in so many words, the job was grueling. I told him he needed to slow down, take a break, that he was going to work himself into an early grave. Then he had a heart attack, and he was dead." Guy snapped his fingers. "Gone, just like that."

"That's really hard, man."

"And if I became principal at my school, I thought what the hell good would the extra pension do if I'm dead?"

"Marnie didn't understand?"

He realized he was complaining about his wife. And that was something he never did. Not to an outsider. Not even to his good friends. He'd never even badmouthed Marnie to Chris. He tried to backpedal. "She knew where I was coming from. But she didn't think I had to deal with it the same way my brother did. First of all, my brother always went at things full bore. He hated delegating. He had to do everything himself. He was a good guy and all, but he didn't know how to stop sometimes." He paused, wondering why he was spilling his guts to this man. And realizing that the answer was because he didn't have anybody else to spill his guts to. Hannigan was a complete stranger. He was the proverbial bartender. "I didn't tell Marnie about the job because I knew she'd be so reasonable that she'd talk me around to seeing there was a way I could do it. That I didn't have to be like Chris."

"But you never really wanted to do it."

Guy shook his head. "I want to work with the kids. That's my life. I don't want to travel all the time. I don't want to suck up to customers and vendors and lawyers and venture capitalists or go to boring dinners and parties."

Hannigan was nodding, leaning on the table, chin in his hand. "So do you think she's having an affair?"

T he question floored Guy. "What the hell makes you ask that?"

Hannigan shrugged. "She travels. She goes to dinners and parties without you. She's got plenty of opportunity, and she's with a lot of men who would find her deliciously attractive."

"Marnie would never do that." But his gut rumbled. *Deliciously attractive*. Guy knew just how delicious Marnie was. But it was only one man he was truly worried about.

Hannigan shrugged again. "If you say so."

But Guy was thinking about Wade, about all those damn texts and phone calls. He was thinking about the trips they took together. Did they really get two hotel rooms? Or did they just put that on expense reports for appearances?

"No, she wouldn't do that," he said again. It was the repetition that made Hannigan raise an eyebrow.

Guy was busted.

He turned it around on Hannigan. "You believe that only because it's what you and your wife do. You're on different movie shoots, and so you take advantage. Women are probably falling all over you. And men are surely falling all over your wife."

Hannigan snorted softly, smiled, but there was something off about it. "Yeah, I guess that's part of it. It's such easy sex when you're apart so often and for so long. It's almost like you aren't married at all for long periods of time."

"But what do you do when you're together again?" Guy was truly curious, not just trying to divert the conversation away from Marnie.

Hannigan was silent a long moment. "We don't talk about it. We act like we've never been apart, like there's never been anybody else."

"But then, if you don't talk about it, how do you know she does it? Maybe it's just you."

Hannigan didn't even flinch. "She told me from the beginning that she didn't think she could be monogamous when we'd be apart for so long. We instituted the old "don't ask, don't tell" policy. And that's how it's been ever since."

"What *do* you talk about?"

He tapped his fingers on the table. "We talk about the shoot, about the projects we're considering. We talk about everyday stuff just like you do, the toilet that needs fixing, and how the new pool guy is working out. And we do our best to stay out of the gossip magazines."

Guy put his drink on the table and crossed his arms. "Aren't you afraid Marnie and I will call up a magazine and tell everybody about our evening together?"

Hannigan smiled, laugh lines crinkling his eyes. "I've got a whole team who will smear you and destroy your credibility." He lightly punched Guy's arm. "But I don't think either of you will say a thing. You're not like that, seeking notoriety or the money you'd get for a story." Then he asked, "Are you going to tell her you're afraid she's having an affair?"

Guy shot back, "I'm not afraid. In fact, she's the one who's suspicious of me."

Hannigan bellowed a laugh, turning every head in his direction. "No way."

Guy nodded his head. "Oh yeah. She thinks I'm having an affair with the woman who took over the principal's position."

Hannigan slapped his forehead. "I had you pegged as a straight arrow."

"I am a straight arrow." He sipped his whiskey sour. "That's what we're really fighting about." He didn't say the fight about Sharon had started only after they'd had the most amazing sex since the weeks after Jay left for university. "Marnie saw a text on my phone."

"You're shitting me." Hannigan leaned in avidly. "What did it say, Mr. Straight Arrow?"

"Something about how Sharon—she's the principal," he explained, "was upset about the way we left things."

"That sounds bad."

Worse, Guy hadn't admitted everything. "I told Marnie it was about an argument over a kid I caught bullying another student. I suspended him. And when the dad, a big donor to the school squawked, Sharon wanted to reduce the punishment to detention."

Hannigan winked. "But that wasn't all."

"No. We had several talks about it, then a meeting with the kid's parents. It eventually got resolved. But we had a discussion in Sharon's office." He forced himself to add, "After hours. Alone."

"Holy shit, do tell. You made a pass at her."

Guy scraped his hand down his face. "The other way round. She made a pass at me."

Hannigan widened his eyes and mouthed, "You're joking."

"I didn't tell Marnie that part. I don't think she needs to know because I turned Sharon down flat."

"So you kept the juicy details to yourself, and she didn't believe the part you told her."

Guy shook his head. "No, I think she believed me."

"You *think*?"

He breathed in deeply, wondering why he was telling Hannigan all the stuff he couldn't tell Marnie. Stuff he hadn't discussed with anyone. The only person he might have told was his brother. Another fallout of losing Chris, he'd also lost his best friend.

But Hannigan was a complete stranger who didn't seem judgmental. Like a bartender. And Guy told him the rest.

"I finally answered Sharon's texts and said I didn't hold anything against her, and it wouldn't change our relationship as long as it didn't happen again. She texted back that it was all good and she was sorry. But then I deleted everything. It was over. I didn't need to rehash it. Except that Marnie looked at my phone and saw the texts were gone."

"And she was not happy," Hannigan guessed accurately.

He saw then exactly what he'd done. He hadn't lied, but he was still hiding things from her. The other big mistake he'd made was not asking her about Wade. The opportunity had been perfect. He could have asked if she was having an affair and cleared the air of all his suspicions.

But he and Marnie didn't talk. That worked for Hannigan and his wife who actually were cheating on each other, and a lack of discussion was the only way for their marriage to survive.

But not getting all their issues out in the open was just driving a deeper wedge between him and Marnie.

He shrugged, having never thought how suspicious his actions were until Marnie called him out. "You're right, she wasn't happy. In her mind, there was no reason to delete those texts, unless there was something I didn't want her to see."

"It seems you've got yourself in quite a pickle."

Guy chuckled despite his roiling emotions. It wasn't an expression he thought a big celebrity would use.

Hannigan went on. "You're afraid to ask her if she's having an affair with one of her business associates because then you'd actually have to deal with it if she said yes. And you're afraid to tell her your principal made a pass at you because then she might want you to do something about it."

He went back to where the discussion had begun, maybe because he didn't want to answer. "Isn't it a bit like you and your wife? You don't talk about it because if you did, you'd have to decide whether you really wanted it that way or not?"

Hannigan tapped his glass, his fingernails clicking. "You're probably right. I might actually have to tell her that I'd prefer it if she didn't screw every director she worked with. The truth is it makes me jealous as hell."

Wow. Who'd have thought a big movie star would be jealous when he could have any woman he wanted? "So why don't you tell her?"

"Because if she didn't do that, she wouldn't be the sexual, sensual woman she is. I'm not sure I'd love her any other way. So I tell myself it's easier to pretend that we're not married when we aren't together. And then we can both live with it." He slugged back the remains of his Campari and soda. "But you're not a man who can live with it. And I'm pretty sure your marriage can't either."

Guy leaned on the table, staring at the stars as the train trundled on. And oddly enough, Hannigan stared with him. "It's pretty damn amazing out there."

Guy nodded.

Then Hannigan said, "I've got a great idea. Get your wife,

and I'll have them turn out all the lights in this car, and we'll do some stargazing."

"They'll never turn out the lights," Guy said.

Hannigan just smiled. "All we need to do is ask."

That was Boyd Hannigan's motto. If you want it, just ask for it.

It was something he and Marnie had never figured out how to do, at least not in their marriage.

GUY HAD WALKED OUT, JUST LIKE THAT.

Marnie thought he'd be back in a few minutes, but she'd waited. And waited.

She needed to talk, to get everything out. She'd tried calling Linda but there was no answer.

Then Wade sent an innocuous question she could easily answer with a text. But she *needed* to talk. *Of course* she wouldn't talk about tonight's explosive sex with Guy. But just talking about anything would make her feel better.

She called him. Even to herself, she didn't want to admit how good it felt to hear his voice.

"Hey," he answered. "It must be really late there. Aren't you supposed to be sleeping on a train right now?"

Oh yes, it felt good, too good. Scary good. "We're on the train. You wouldn't believe how luxurious it is, plush chairs, a real bed instead of a pullout. And the food is amazing. Guy just went out for a drink in the club car and to do some stargazing because the stars are so bright." She was rambling.

"Why didn't you go with him?"

She stared out the window at the stars, billions and billions, sparkling in the night sky.

She could have told Wade she was tired, that it had been a long day. She could have told him she didn't feel like mingling

16

with people anymore. She could even have told him they'd met a famous movie star who'd propositioned them.

But she confessed. "We had a fight."

She could hear him breathing, and she turned out the light, dropping them into an intimate darkness, the stream of stars and the thrum of the train their backdrop.

Wade's answer came as softly as the night. "I'm sorry. Do you need to talk about it?"

Yes, she needed to talk. She needed to ask herself why she'd been driven to destroy that perfect moment when she lay in Guy's arms after they'd made love. But she couldn't talk with Wade about lovemaking. She couldn't talk to him about sex as if he were Linda or a girlfriend. None of their conversations had ever involved sex. Not while he was married, not when his marriage had fallen apart, not when he was finally divorced, and not now.

"I'm not sure whether Guy is having an affair with his principal or not."

It was out there. She was talking about Guy's affair, even though he'd denied it. Was that the same as talking about sex? No. But it was something terrible and intimate. Maybe she shouldn't have said it at all, especially with the silence that fell between them.

Until Wade asked, "Did you talk to him about it?"

She nodded, then she told him, "I saw a text on his phone."

Again, he was silent for too long, finally saying, "What did it say?"

"Just that she didn't like the way they'd left things. That she felt bad. Something like that." She couldn't remember the exact words anymore. "And then he deleted all the texts. I never saw his answer."

The silence was killing her.

Then, so softly she strained to hear, he said, "Don't do it,

Marnie. Don't sneak into his phone and look at his texts. Don't search his pockets for receipts or look into the charges on his credit card."

It was the exact opposite of what Linda told her to do. She wanted badly, so badly, to ask if that's what his wife had done. Or maybe he'd done it to his wife. Either way, the suspicion had destroyed their marriage.

She lowered her voice to a whisper. "I already did it, Wade. And now I've asked him about it, and he's denied it, and I don't know what to do."

In that moment, she wasn't a CEO, and he wasn't her CFO. He was her confidant.

"But you still don't believe him."

"Why would he delete all the texts if it was as innocuous as he said."

He didn't even ask what Guy's excuse was. There was just that crushing silence again, longer this time, so long it frightened her.

Finally, *finally*, when she was ready to tear her hair out or burst into tears, he said, "I really don't think you should talk to me about this, Marnie. You should talk to one of your girlfriends or someone who doesn't—" He cut himself off then.

A part of her wanted to scream. *Someone who doesn't what?*

But she knew deep, deep inside that the answer would be the end of their friendship. Maybe even the end of their teamwork. She didn't press.

"You're right. I'm sorry for laying that on you. It's just late here. I'm overtired. I really apologize. Please forgive me."

"No problem." His voice was back to normal. "Did you see my text?"

"Yes," and she was just about to answer his question when the stateroom door opened and the light fell across the carpet, falling just short of her feet.

SHE WAS ON THE PHONE WITH WADE.

All Guy's rage welled up in him again.

He heard her say, "Hey, I'm onboard with that. Go ahead. Guy just got back. If you've got any other questions, text me." After a brief pause, she added, "Okay, thanks, bye."

He and Marnie didn't talk. They just let things bubble and boil until everything turned to rage inside him.

He wasn't so far gone, however, that he didn't realize anything he said now would come out all wrong. And they might not even have a marriage left when it was all over.

She gently laid the phone on the table, stood, the stars flashing by the window outlining her in the white robe.

He took one deep breath before saying, "I met up with Hannigan. He wants to do some stargazing. He's going to have them turn off all the lights in the bar car. Why don't you join us?"

"I need to get dressed."

That was obvious. He tried not to dwell on the fact that she'd been sitting there in the dark talking to Wade with nothing on but a robe.

He'd actually believed that everything between them would be over if he ever asked her about Wade. Now he knew it would be over if he didn't. But if he asked about Wade, he'd have to tell her everything about Sharon.

He closed the door and turned on the light. "I'd like you to come with me."

"Okay." She moved to the bed for the sexy panties she'd been wearing. "No," he almost shouted out the word. "Don't put them on."

They gazed at each other a long moment, and he saw the question in her eyes. Then he felt the shift in the air, recognized the moment she thought of what they'd done in the cabin only an hour before. Her scent filled the compartment, the arousal. He felt it rising in him, despite her accusation, despite his guilt, despite his fear, despite the awful dark intimacy of the stateroom when she was talking to Wade.

She crossed to the dress where she'd hung it up on the door and with her back to him, she dropped the robe, revealing her shapely bottom and the curves of her hips as she stepped into the dress.

He wanted her right then. Wanted to push her against the wall, drop to his knees, taste her, then drag her to the floor and take her. To show her that she was his.

But they needed to talk first. And before he could do that, he needed the calming effect of the stars.

She reached behind, waggling her fingers. "Could you zip me up?"

Was she teasing him, knowing the thoughts running through his mind and his body? Probably. Yet he lost himself in the sight of her bare skin disappearing into the gold lamé as he zipped.

He saw exactly what Boyd Hannigan saw, a beautiful, sexy, sensual, *delicious* woman.

She didn't turn around. "I need to fix my lipstick." She groaned as she stepped close to the mirror. "And my hair."

"Don't touch it. It's perfect."

Messy wasn't the right word. Tousled. Sex-tousled. He wanted to take her back to the club car just like that.

She gaped at him in the mirror's reflection. "I can't go out with my hair like this." She ran her hands through it.

"It's sexy. Just like that. Don't touch it."

Did he want to show off to Hannigan?

He watched her smooth on our lipstick and add a little blush to her cheeks.

No. It wasn't about Hannigan. He wanted to hold the memory of those glorious minutes close to him. He wanted to look at her and remember the feel of her skin, the taste of her on his tongue, the feel of his body inside her. A visceral memory that tore at his guts.

Then he said, "You're perfect."

She turned to him, tipped her head, "Are you sure?"

He was close enough to wrap his hand around her nape, pulling her in, opening his mouth. Tasting her. Savoring her.

When he backed off, her lids were at a sexy half-mast as she murmured, "You've ruined my lipstick again."

"Your lipstick is perfect." It was barely smudged, didn't even escape the confines of her lip liner. But she looked well and truly kissed.

"It's all over you." She swiped her thumb across his lips. "There. Better."

He held out his arm. "Then let's go."

Later, he would put his hands up that gold lamé and find her bare flesh.

But right now, he wouldn't think how different everything would be if her answer was yes when he finally asked her if she was having an affair with Wade.

BOYD HANNIGAN SLOUCHED DEEPER INTO HIS CHAIR AS Marnie and Guy Slade entered the club car.

She was an extraordinarily beautiful and sexy woman, with her breasts pebbled against the gold lamé and her just-fucked hair.

Oh yeah. Guy had been holding out on him, never mentioning what they'd been doing in their cabin after they left him. He wondered if his admiration had spurred them on. He liked the idea that it did. He rose, ushered Marnie into the window seat, and leaned close to breathe in the scent of her arousal.

It reminded him of Selena. Then he got hard, because every time he thought about Selena he got hard.

Boyd raised his hand, waved. He didn't snap his fingers. He never snapped his fingers at waitstaff or anyone else who helped him. Because that was a dickhead thing to do. Years ago, when he'd been a summertime caddie at the country club, he'd had fingers snapped at him. It was demeaning. Besides, a wave and a smile accomplished the same thing and better.

The lights went out, and the car was filled with oohs and aahs at the star-studded sky. Guy took Marnie's hand.

They hadn't talked yet, Boyd could tell. There hadn't been time. He wondered if they actually would. Or if Guy Slade would blow off everything Boyd had said.

But then he hadn't told Guy everything.

He hadn't told him that there'd been no other women. That he'd never expected Marnie Slade or her husband to take him up on his proposition. But he'd enjoyed making her feel desirable. He enjoyed knowing he'd sent them back to their cabin to fuck like bunnies.

But Selena was the only woman for him. When she was away on location, the thought of her with another man made him absolutely insane. But she was what she was. If he tried to change her, tried to put chains on her, tried to mold her into a one-man woman, he'd lose her.

And truly, that was the only thing he wanted to change about her. The other men.

Marnie gasped as a star shot across the sky, and Guy leaned close, raising her hand to place a kiss on her knuckles, while she turned to smile at him, an intimate smile she probably thought Boyd wouldn't recognize in the darkness.

A surge of jealousy rose up from deep within.

They weren't perfect. They were each afraid. They each thought the other was having an affair. But they didn't go their separate ways for half the year and pretend they weren't married. Marnie didn't sleep in another man's bed. At least he thought she didn't.

Boyd desperately wanted what they had, even the petty squabbles.

He wanted a wife who didn't need other men.

He wanted to be normal.

❦ 17 ❧

arnie was entranced by the bright canopy of stars as they trundled past the silhouettes of rolling hills. She'd never seen so many falling stars, never noticed so much beauty in a dark night. Holding hands with Guy, she didn't have to think about lies or half-truths or reality. All she had to do was gaze at the starlit night.

A waiter arrived with a round of coffees. Marnie had asked for regular, without the alcohol this time. It was late, and she didn't want the night to end. She wasn't ready to sleep. Sleeping seemed like such a waste. When she turned to accept her cup, she saw that Boyd had also ordered a plate of chocolate-covered strawberries steaming on a bed of dry ice.

"They look scrumptious. Thank you."

Boyd pushed the plate at her, pointing. "Try that one. It looks the juiciest."

She couldn't say why every word out of his mouth seemed like a come on. Maybe it was his bedroom eyes. Maybe it was the super sexy characters he played, men who always got the woman in the end, and sometimes more than one. Like James Bond.

Then she thought of Guy's reaction, how a little jealousy had turned him on.

A teeny-tiny thought of his principal tried to wedge its way into her thoughts, but she shut it down. She'd think about the woman later.

As she bit into the juicy chocolate-covered strawberry, her moan was entirely sexual. Even in the darkness, she saw Guy's nostrils flare, like a stallion scenting his mate.

She scooped up a trickle of juice from her chin and gave it a carnal lick off her finger. "This is the best. You have to try it."

Juice dribbled onto the table as she held the other half out to Guy, her fingers sunk into the stem. When he opened his mouth, she fed him, his lips kissing her fingertips. A tingle shimmied through her belly as her dress slid sensuously across her nipples.

She pretended Guy had told her the truth, that Sharon wasn't a threat, that tonight it was all about her and the starlight and the gold lamé dress under which she wore nothing else.

Guy held out a strawberry, let her bite close to his fingertips, then wiped away the juice on her lip with his thumb, licking it off as if he was tasting her.

She gave another low moan, and it had nothing to do with the taste of strawberries and chocolate on her lips.

"It certainly looks like I need to have one of those," Boyd said, surprising her. She'd almost forgotten he was there.

"Strawberries and chocolate are an aphrodisiac," he added as if he were a teacher reciting a dry math principle.

Guy laughed, a boyish sound she hadn't heard in a long time. The laugh he'd used with his brother.

It made her wonder what he and Boyd had been talking about when she gone.

"Come on, Guy, feed me a strawberry." Boyd's grin was filled with fun.

Guy laughed at him. "Screw you. Get your own strawberry."

Oh yeah, something had happened while they were alone. They were like old frat buddies getting together. "Then let Marnie feed me," Boyd said, the glitter of challenge in his eyes.

She waited for Guy to tell him to screw off.

But he said, "Aren't you afraid some zealous fan will take a photo, and it'll get back to the media?"

Boyd guffawed. "The headline would be something about Boyd Hannigan feeds chocolate-covered strawberries to mystery woman while husband watches. What happens next?" He spread his hands in the air as if they could read along with him.

She wondered if he relished the idea of being outed. She looked at Guy, then at Boyd again. There was definitely something between them. Challenge? Jealousy? She wasn't sure.

Plucking a strawberry from the dry ice, she held it out to Boyd. He bit into it almost to her fingers, his lips not quite grazing hers. She felt his warm breath on her skin and the heat of his gaze as he pulled away without a single drop of juice dripping down his chin.

Tossing the stem onto the plate of discards, she turned to Guy, holding out her hand. "I'm all chocolatey."

Guy licked every morsel from her fingers.

More than desire welled up inside her. The sensation filling her was almost like a mini orgasm, made all the more potent because she wasn't wearing a stitch beneath the dress, no bra, no panties. She had to squeeze her thighs together as heat blazed in Guy's eyes, a silent message that said he could take her right there on the table in front of Boyd Hannigan and everyone else in the club car.

It had been like this when the boys had first gone off to college and the house was empty. She remembered one of those nights so clearly, a Sunday. She'd insisted on Sunday dinner, even when the boys were gone. She didn't work, there was no phone on the table, and she always made something special. That night it had been chicken cacciatore, and Guy had come to stand behind her, his body pressed to her backside. He'd sniffed the air, telling her how good it smelled. She'd given him a taste from a spoon, right over her shoulder, and she felt the vibration of his groan against her back. "How much longer?" he'd asked in a husky voice that went straight to her center. "Twenty more minutes," she'd told him, and the moment she'd put the lid back on the Dutch oven, he'd grabbed her around the waist, hauling her up on the island, the cool marble against her warm bottom. It had been hard and fast and more delicious than the cacciatore. She'd come not once but three times.

When had those luscious interludes ended? When had she let work take over every waking moment?

She wondered if that night was the last time she'd seen that look in Guy's eyes. Until now.

Maybe he hadn't been screwing the principal. Could he look at his wife like that if he'd been getting it on with his boss?

"You two are missing the stargazing," Boyd said.

Guy, his gaze on her lips then rising to meet hers, said, "I'm looking at stars right now."

She heard Boyd's deep chuckle. "Those strawberries are definitely an aphrodisiac. Maybe you should take the rest of them back to your stateroom."

"Trying to get rid of us, Hannigan?" Guy asked the fun-loving man.

Boyd held up his hands. "I'm just a facilitator."

When Guy looked at her again, his eyes were as dark

chocolate as the strawberries. "Maybe he's right. We can put these strawberries to good use back in our room."

He stood, holding out his hand, and Marnie rose, too, looking at a grinning Boyd with no idea why he looked so happy with himself.

His hand linked with hers, Guy picked up the still steaming plate. "Thanks for the strawberries," he called over his shoulder as they left.

"I'll save a seat for you in the morning," Boyd's voice floated back.

Since Guy was holding the strawberries, she used her key card on the door.

He didn't drop her hand, walking with her to the table by the window and set down the plate.

Turning on only the single light by the window, he cupped her face in his hands and kissed her, long and sweet, sweeter even than the kisses they'd shared earlier tonight. He kept kissing her as he walked her backward. She sat when her calves hit the bed.

But instead of coming down with her, he stepped back, his face in shadow.

"I didn't tell you everything about Sharon."

Her heart curled up inside her and died.

"I'M GOING TO MAKE LOVE TO YOU TONIGHT," HE TOLD her. "Not sex like we had earlier. But making love. And that can only happen after we talk."

The smile faded from her lips, the glitter in her eyes turned to ice, and she crossed her arms militantly as she looked at him.

He held up a hand. "I'm not having an affair with her. I didn't lie about Randall or his parents or the discussions." He paused. He hadn't rehearsed the words, and he was afraid they'd come out all wrong. "But I didn't tell you everything."

"Are you trying to make this more palatable by telling me you're going to make love to me?" Disdain dripped from her voice.

"She made a pass at me," he said bluntly.

"Right, *she* made a pass at *you*." She said it with such sarcasm, her words hit like a punch.

But he'd started, and he had to finish. "It happened after the meeting with the parents. It was late, because they couldn't get there earlier. And Sharon was happy with the final resolution."

"Oh," she drawled. "She was just so happy with your resolution that she threw her arms around you and kissed you."

He had to hand it to Marnie. When she got sarcastic, her tone could cut off his balls.

"That's exactly what went down. I was shocked at first, but I stepped back."

She smiled, and that smile always made him feel as if he'd committed some catastrophic sin. Even if he hadn't.

"Tell me, how long did it take for you to push her away?"

He told himself to be honest, told himself the only way to get through this was to tell her everything. Because she would sniff out a lie if he didn't.

"A moment."

"How long is a moment?" Her eyes narrowed as if she were calculating.

"Seconds."

"Two seconds or fifty-nine seconds?"

She was pissed. He didn't blame her. He should have told her the truth when she asked him earlier. No, he should have told her when it first happened. But he honestly didn't know how many seconds. A couple of seconds of shock. A couple of seconds of asking himself what the hell he was supposed to do. Then the seconds to peal her off him. "Five seconds." That was probably right.

She looked at him. Just looked. And he couldn't help shifting nervously.

"Did you like it?" Her teeth clicked on each word.

He didn't have to think. "It was just uncomfortable."

She stood then, walked around him, as if she couldn't bear to touch him. At the table, she brought a strawberry to her kissable lips.

"Just uncomfortable?" she asked, her smile sweetly vicious. She stepped closer, leaned in until he could smell the heat of her skin, the leftover scent of her arousal in the club car. "How uncomfortable?"

He didn't swallow. He knew it would look bad. "Very."

"So you didn't like it even one teensy bit?" She bit once more into the strawberry, her red lips around it, enticing, mind-altering.

"No." He felt the word strangle him.

Another step, until he could see his reflection in her eyes. "Not even one teeny-tiny second before you pushed her away?" she whispered. "Tell me the truth."

He couldn't help himself. He closed his eyes. He remembered. He felt that one infinitesimal moment when his lower half told him to go for it. A moment even less than the beat of his heart when he'd wondered how she would taste, if she'd taste as good as Marnie. The moment before he knew no one would ever taste as good as Marnie.

"There's no one like you," he whispered. "Not for me."

He wondered how long it would to take her to get over that infinitesimal moment he wasn't actually admitting to? How long she would punish him?

But they were done talking about him. Now it was time for Wade.

"ALL RIGHT, NOW YOU KNOW ABOUT SHARON, WHETHER you believe me or not."

Marnie let her stony expression declare that she wasn't willing to give up her anger yet. That was the problem with lies, once you started telling them, no one believed it when you finally got around to the truth.

But now she had her own lies to handle as Guy asked, "So tell me about Wade."

She took the seat by the window, reached for one of the strawberries. The fruit and chocolate melted on her tongue. She ate lingeringly, as if Guy's question wasn't worth answering.

But inside, her heart was beating fast and hard against her ribs.

"What about Wade?" The question was a stall as she licked chocolate from her lips. In the silence before he answered, the train swayed slightly back and forth, clacking along the tracks in an incessant rhythm.

"Are you having an affair with him?"

She didn't give an inch, holding tight to her self-righteous anger. "So now, because *you*—" She raised a finger to point at him. "—have some suspicious texts on your phone, you want to turn the tables on me?"

He sat on the edge of the bed, leaned forward, elbows on his knees. "Yeah, I'm putting the question back on you."

Her hands were clammy. She picked up another straw-berry, ate it, slowly, giving herself time to think. There was the truth. And then there was the whole truth. Which should she tell? Laying her phone carefully on the table, she said, "You can read any of my texts. I don't delete them. And you can listen in on any of my phone calls. There's nothing there."

Then why did the rush of her pulse whoosh across her eardrums?

He stood, paced the room, stopped in front of her. "Why don't you just say no, Marnie? Why don't you tell me that what I'm thinking isn't true?"

She breathed, letting her nostrils flare with annoyance. "I'm not having sex with Wade." And that was true.

"Then what *are* you doing with him?"

"I work with him." Yet, if that's all it was, why did she feel guilty? And she felt forced to add, "He's never made a pass at me. I've never made a pass at him. I've never even touched him." The words were laced with sarcasm aimed at Guy and his tête-à-tête in Sharon's office.

"But have you wanted to, Marnie?"

She didn't answer. Because that same tête-à-tête had meant very little. Sharon had kissed him, and he'd been thinking of his wife. While all her tête-à-têtes with Wade were... She couldn't put words to what they were, to the intimacy she sometimes felt, especially when she talked to Wade at night. And if she let go of her anger, she'd be faced with their own guilt.

"Tell me if you ever think about having sex with him during all those old late-night conversations when your voice gets low and soft."

"It's work," she hissed.

"If it's just work, why do you sound so intimate? And why does it drive me so goddamn crazy listening to you?"

She stared him down. It was the only weapon she had against the very same word that had come to her mind. *Intimate*. "So you spy on my conversations too?"

"I'm not spying. But I have eyes and ears. I see how your body changes when you're talking to Wade. You have a bedroom voice."

The thrum of her pulse in her ears was getting louder. She

had no clue Guy had seen all that. Her body was like a mirror to her soul, her thoughts written all over it.

"Why did Wade's wife divorce him?"

She didn't like this, not at all. She hadn't done anything wrong. She would never have an affair with Wade. Yet she couldn't take that one extra step for Guy and say that she'd never had a thought. And if she said that aloud, she wasn't sure they could ever recover.

"I have no idea why they got divorced."

"He never confided in you?"

"He was very tight-lipped about his divorce." And that was truth.

"Why? Because his wife thought you two were having an affair?"

"Absolutely not." God help her, yes, she'd suspected that. Especially after what Wade had said about not checking Guy's pockets or emails, as if his wife had done that to him. "He never told me anything personal about his divorce."

And she'd kept telling herself they'd done nothing wrong, that his wife was a jealous woman, that of course they had to work closely. Wade was her righthand man. And even if she'd sent him late-night texts, they were just putting her thoughts down so she didn't forget. She didn't mean that he had to get up and answer them. She'd never expected him to call.

But he had. And she'd always answered, because it was work.

At least that's what she'd always told herself.

She stood then, held out her hand, closing the distance between them. "Look, I'm sorry if the texts and phone calls bother you. I'll stop doing that. If I've got a thought I need to tell Wade, I'll record it on my phone and talk to him about it the next day."

From his spot on the bed, Guy looked up at her, his gaze

impenetrable. Had she said the right thing? Or had she just pissed him off more?

"I've never had an affair with Wade," she added. "I've never even been tempted."

It wasn't a lie. She'd never lain awake at night having sex fantasies about Wade. But she'd gotten too personal with him. She'd taken their work relationship to a different level when she confided her personal business, especially the way she had tonight. And that hadn't been the first time she'd confided personal things.

But it had to be the last. "I can understand how all the phone calls would bother you." She cupped Guy's cheek. "I really mean it. I'll stop all that. Because it isn't even necessary."

Then finally, after all the words she'd said when he'd said nothing at all, he finally spoke. "I appreciate that." He sighed heavily. "Let's tell ourselves we're going to talk about this stuff. If I'd come to you with my feelings about Wade and you'd come to me when you saw that text from Sharon, maybe this fight never would have happened." He curled his hand around hers. "Shall we promise?"

"I promise." Squeezing his hand, she felt lighter. Like she'd dodged a bullet.

Because it felt way too easy.

18

Guy kissed her gently, sweetly, pulling her between his legs, their bodies nestled close. "It's late," he whispered. "We should go to bed now."

She rubbed herself against him. "You don't feel like you're ready to go to sleep," she said in the sexiest voice she could manage.

"Oh, I'm not ready to sleep."

His eyes gleamed in the starlight through the window as he stood and backed her up against the table, reached behind her, and held out a chocolate strawberry. She opened her mouth, devouring half of it, then he sucked the juice and the chocolate from the other half.

"We're going to leave this little light on right here." He took two steps back, taking her hand in his, walking her to the bed. "That way I can see every sweet hot bit of your gorgeous body as I undress you." He was already unzipping the gold lamé.

"Aren't you afraid somebody's going to see?"

"First of all." He reeled her in until she was only a hair's breadth away, close enough to feel his body heat. "We might not be moving at the speed of a bullet train, but no one's going to have the binoculars trained our window." He leaned in to nuzzle her neck, licking her throat, taking her earlobe between his teeth, and blowing warm breath against her ear. "And second of all, I'd like to think that they are. And that you're making them so damn hot. Just the way you make me."

"You're such a voyeur."

"I do believe that's an exhibitionist."

There was no real danger of being seen. But she liked what the thought did to him.

And it did one more thing for her. It relieved her guilt. Guy liked the idea of another man lusting after her. It had turned him on when Boyd had propositioned her, and she told herself it would do the same if he thought Wade lusted after her too.

Not that she lusted after Wade, of course.

Guy wrapped his hand around her nape, kissing her while he slowly slid down the zipper of her dress.

"Do you know how much you turned me on out there in the bar car, knowing you didn't have a single thing on underneath that dress?"

She shook her head. It had turned her on, yes, but to know how it affected Guy stole her breath.

The frenzy with which they'd gone at each other earlier had been explosive. She'd been wet in two seconds flat. But this was even better as he slid the dress off her shoulders, down her arms, until her breasts were free. Then he placed her hand across her midriff. "Hold the dress right there."

When had a night between them ever been so sexy? Certainly not since his brother died.

He sat on the bed and pulled her in, plumping her breast in his hand, then sucking her into his mouth. It was so delicious she moaned.

When he tweaked her nipple, she gasped. If she'd been

wearing panties, they would have been drenched, and even now, she felt the moisture on her thighs.

Fisting her hand in his hair, she pulled his head back. "I need it now. Right now."

He was fast, grabbing her hips and pulling her hand away to let the dress pool around her shoes. Then she was flat on her back on the bed, and he leaned down for a long swipe of his tongue from the edge of her pubic hair all the way to her breasts.

He stood, towering over her, while she lay completely naked on the bed.

"Touch yourself," he muttered, his voice hoarse.

She spread her legs slightly, put her hand between them, and arched into her own touch, moaning as she did it.

He toed off his shoes, tore off his shirt, dropped his pants, stepped out of them.

And he was gloriously hard.

She didn't think she'd ever been wetter.

One knee between her legs, he put his hand over hers, the two of them stroking her. It was almost too much. She could almost come.

Her words came out on a gasp. "I need your mouth on me."

He was there, taking her with his lips, his tongue, his fingers inside her. It was only a moment, not even a second, and she caved completely, squirming beneath him on the bed, bracing her hands on the wall behind her and bearing down on his mouth, coming so hard she cried out.

She thought he'd stop then, but he tormented her until tears streamed down her temples.

She didn't feel him move until he slammed deep inside her, and she was coming again. She'd been coming all along, couldn't stop, dragging her fingernails down his back until she clutched his butt and ground against him. That's what she wanted, the hard slam, the grind of his body against her, the climax going on and on, her body racked with pleasure.

Until she was boneless and breathless beneath him.

He pulled out slowly, knelt over her. "I want your mouth on me."

He leaned over and wrapped his hand behind her neck, lifting her until he breached the inner recesses of her mouth. She licked him, took him deep, swirling her tongue around him even as her neck muscles began to quiver. Then she pushed him to his back, climbed between his legs, and licked just the tip until he groaned, until he trembled, until he begged.

She had always loved his taste, his scent. She'd always loved his masculine grunts and growls of pleasure. She loved the way he tangled his fingers in her hair and guided her, not because she'd done something wrong, but because he needed his hands on her. He arched and groaned. She knew him so well, and he was close, almost there. But when he came, she wanted him inside her.

Rearing up, she straddled his hips and drove down on him, seating him so deeply that she reveled in the way he filled her, to her womb, to her heart, to her soul.

Bracing herself against the wall and with his hands on her hips, they took each ferociously, like animals coming together. Like they had in their younger days when there were no kids and they had the freedom to do it anytime and anywhere in the house.

Then Guy put his thumb on her at just the right moment. She came all over him, squeezing him tight, and that was all it took for him. They cried out together, not caring about anyone next door.

She collapsed against him, breathing hard for long moments. Until finally Guy shifted, pulling the covers over them.

For the first time in years, they fell asleep tangled in each other's arms.

❀

HE HELD HER WHILE SHE SLEPT. THE LOVEMAKING HAD been out of this world. Better even than the earlier explosive session.

But now, with her breaths soft and rhythmic, he couldn't stop his mind from working overtime.

He wanted to believe her. She'd sounded as sincere as he'd been. But had she given in too easily, spouted the answers she knew he wanted to hear?

He closed his eyes, breathed in deeply, let it out in a long sigh.

He would have to believe her. Because if he didn't, they'd never survive. And he wanted the nights like this to go on and on.

❀

THE SHOWER WAS TOO SMALL FOR TWO PEOPLE. THAT'S what made it fun, like they were young again. They couldn't get enough of each other and the impracticality didn't matter.

Even while she dressed, Guy couldn't seem to stop touching her. And Marnie loved it, the gentle squeeze of her breast, a quick hand cupped between her legs, a kiss on her shoulder, his hand in her hair pulling her head back for a fast, deep kiss.

It was like a honeymoon. No, it was like those weeks of fascination when they'd first met, when all she could think about was him, when all she'd wanted was to make love.

It was as if they'd rediscovered each other, rediscovered how amazing good sex could be.

When she saw a text on her phone from Wade, guilt was like a stab straight to her heart. She quickly swiped it away so Guy wouldn't see.

She'd never done anything wrong, she told herself. She'd never touched Wade, never kissed him, never fantasized about him.

Then Guy grabbed her, and she felt her heart all the way in her throat.

"You look so damn hot in those tight short pants." He pulled her close, rubbed himself against her.

"They're called capri pants," she told him with a drawl.

He kissed her so deeply, she thought he'd tear her clothes off again.

"Now you've gone and done it," she said, laughing. "You've ruined my lipstick. I have to fix it before we have breakfast with Mr. Boyd Hannigan."

He ran his finger under her lip, a sexy glint in his eye. "There, all fixed."

She ran her finger over his lips. "You've got it all over you too." She rubbed the color away.

"That's not where I want your lipstick." He tugged her hand down to his erection.

"Oh," she said from deep in her throat. And squeezed him. "You need to save that for later."

They left the stateroom with the sheets rumpled and smelling of sex.

And Marnie stopped thinking about the texts on her phone.

BOYD PULLED OUT THE CHAIR FOR MARNIE.

They looked like they just had sex, a lot of it, all night long.

Her cheeks glowed pink, and her lipstick was smudged as if Guy had to steal one more kiss before they left the room.

Guy was all puffed up like a cock that had just crowed.

Boyd was jealous. He admitted that. He'd talked to Selena in Colorado where she was filming. She'd seemed distracted, and he wondered if she had a man in her bed.

The thought was killing him.

But he pasted on his famous movie-star smile, the one that made all the ladies swoon. "You both looked chipper this morning. I trust you slept well."

They glanced at each other, and the seductive smile on Marnie's lips twisted the knife in Boyd's guts.

Selena smiled like that when they were together, and Boyd was sure he wore the same besotted expression Guy did.

"We did some more stargazing," Guy said with a grin of pure male satisfaction. "It was an amazing sight."

The stars he'd seen were in Marnie's eyes.

He wondered if Selena had stars in her eyes for another man these days.

What was the saying? Hoisted by your own petard. That was him, snared by his own scheme.

He'd signed on for this. He'd thought he'd get the most beautiful woman in the world, and he could have anyone else he wanted too.

The problem was he didn't want anyone else. Not even the beautiful Marnie Slade.

There was no one for him but Selena. There hadn't been since the first day he'd seen her up close.

"I've heard the eggs Benedict are amazing," he said.

Guy's hand moved beneath the table. Maybe he was stroking Marnie's thigh. "Eggs Benedict is Marnie's favorite," he said with sly smile that said Marnie had another favorite first thing in the morning. And she'd probably gotten it today.

His guts felt all jumbled as he looked at them. They were the quintessential normal American couple on holiday. They were everything he wanted to be.

He wished he could turn back the clock fifteen years, when he would have said to Selena, *No, I don't want anyone else in our marriage. I just want you.* And she would have opened her arms, saying sweetly, lovingly that he was all she wanted too.

But he and Selena would never be a normal couple. They would always be followed by paparazzi. They would always live by different rules.

And he was damn tired of those different rules that said he would never have what Marnie and Guy Slade had.

THE FOOD WAS EXCELLENT, EGGS BENEDICT PREPARED JUST the way Guy liked them, the yolks still runny.

He'd never felt better in his life. Last night had been beyond all his expectations. He'd cleansed his soul, told her everything, learned everything from her. They'd talked, finally cleared the air, and it was as if they were starting over.

At least that's what he'd been telling himself since he woke with Marnie in his arms. And he would make himself believe it, live it.

She looked so damn beautiful this morning, the slight blush on her cheeks, the slow dip of her eyelids, as if she was remembering the taste of him in her mouth. As if she wanted more.

Hannigan was his usual amusing self. Guy wondered which of the many faces he'd displayed was the real Boyd Hannigan. Maybe he didn't even exist. Maybe he'd been acting so long, he was nothing more than a conglomeration of all the characters he'd played.

The coffee was the best Guy had ever tasted. He smiled to himself, thinking that this morning, everything was the best. They should have been tired. It had been well past one o'clock, probably closer to two when they'd fallen asleep.

And yet, he was energized.

They were rolling out of Innsbruck, famous for its winter sports, and heading through the Alps as they finished breakfast. The waiter brought them fresh coffee in the club car. They could have gone back to their own stateroom, sat in their comfortable private chairs, watched the scenery as they cruised through the mountains, but Hannigan wanted them to join him.

What was up with the man? He was a celebrity. Why did he want to hang around with the masses? Unless he still had his eye on Marnie.

It was good to see she hadn't put her phone on the table, waiting for a text from Wade. But then it was too early. And besides, after the last night, he shouldn't be jealous.

He absolutely wasn't going to let himself be jealous.

"So tell me about your kids, Marnie," Hannigan said.

Marnie could go on for hours about the boys. Come to think of it, so could Guy.

His phone buzzed in his pocket. Marnie jerked, as if, for a moment, she thought it was her phone.

Guy looked at his screen. "Speak of the devil," he said. "It's Ethan."

Marnie gasped. "It's four o'clock in the morning on the East Coast. What on earth is he doing up?"

Guy shrugged. He remembered all those late nights in college, many of them spent with Marnie. "Probably pulling an all-nighter."

"Doesn't he know that's bad for his health?" But she was smiling, perhaps remembering their late nights.

"He's a college student. If he's not doing that, then he's not having fun."

He swiped his phone, opened the text, and a photo popped up, along with Ethan's message. *Is that you and mom?????*

"Holy shit," he said on a mere breath.

"What?" Worry crept into Marnie's voice.

He looked at her, then Hannigan. "I think we've been outed."

He held out the phone, and they leaned together to look at the picture.

Hannigan guffawed, while Marnie touched Guy's phone, enlarging the photo, then wrinkled her nose. "It's grainy, you can't really tell who anybody is."

"But your son certainly knew his dad." Hannigan pulled out his own phone. Then he chuckled. "I found it." And he read aloud. "Is that Boyd Hannigan on an exotic European train ride? Who's the mystery couple? And where is Selena Rodriguez?" The man actually grinned.

Guy took his phone back from Marnie. "Aren't you worried your wife will see it? You said you two like to keep this kind of thing on the down low."

Hannigan was still grinning, as if he was totally pleased with himself. "This is just tabloid fodder. We deal with it all the time. Everyone knows it means nothing." Then he looked at Marnie, his grin fading. "Do you mind being tabloid fodder for a little while? Though no one can even tell that's you."

"Except my son recognized me." Guy wasn't sure how he felt about this. Was there a way it could be bad?

Hannigan's grin vanished altogether. "It's really not a big deal. I promise. No one's going to know who you are. Your son only recognized you because he knew you were on this train." Then he shrugged easily. "Go ahead and tell him you guys are with me. Let's see what he says."

Marnie waved her hand at Guy. "Ethan will love it."

It would totally wow the kid, Guy was sure, and he typed an answer. *Yeah, we're with the famous Boyd Hannigan. We had dinner with him last night, breakfast this morning. And now we're just hanging in the club car.*

No more than two seconds could have passed before another text flashed on his screen. *Holy crap man that's insane so are you giving mom a hall pass??????*

He laughed. "He says that's insane. And then he asks if I'm giving Marnie a hall pass, whatever the hell that means."

Hannigan snorted his coffee and almost choked himself. Still spluttering, he said, "He wants to know if you're giving your wife a hall pass to sleep with a celebrity."

Marnie put her hand over her mouth, laughing.

Guy held the phone away like it was a snake. "I can't believe my kid just said that to me." Then he pointed at Hannigan. "We already went over that last night. This answer is no hall pass."

"Come on, man," Hannigan whined, giving them a woebegone teenager face.

Then they were all laughing. It didn't twist his guts the way it had last night. Today, everything was different. He and Marnie were different. At least he told himself they were.

He handed her his phone. "Here, you text *your* son."

She reared back haughtily. "Since when is he just *my* son?"

"Since he said I was supposed to give you a hall pass."

She shook her head, her thumbs flicking quickly over the screen. She was always faster at texting than he was.

She smiled, widely. "I told him you're disowning him. And then I sent him a kissy-face emoji straight from his mother."

He pointed his finger. "You'll pay for that later."

She leaned in and dropped her voice to a sexy note that tightened everything in him. "Oh yeah. I know you'll make me pay. That's why I did it."

If they'd been alone, he'd have whispered in her ear exactly how good her payback would be.

But he took his phone and typed to his son. *This is your father again. Get to bed. It's late.*

The only thing he received was a devil emoji.

He looked at Marnie. "That kid certainly doesn't get it from me."

"The hell he doesn't. He's a dirty young man. And you're a dirty old man." She leaned in to kiss him.

"And you like it that way." So did he. The banter felt good, freaking fantastic, in fact.

Hannigan slapped a hand on the table. "Get a room, you two. It's embarrassing."

That made them all laugh again.

19

Marnie had turned off the notifications on her phone, and yet the device was still burning a hole in her purse. The text from Wade was probably the last question from the night before. She swore not to read it in front of Guy. She swore not to feel a little jump in her heart, but she did. Only this time the heart tremor was guilt.

She loved the flirty banter with Guy in front of Boyd. She even loved Ethan's question about the hall pass. It was utterly cute. And she was crossing her fingers for Guy's payback.

Still, she couldn't help feeling guilty. She'd promised Guy she would talk things through. But how on earth was she supposed to tell him that sometimes she felt that little kick-start around her heart when she saw a text from Wade or his name popped up on her caller ID. Honestly, what purpose would it serve to tell Guy?

She excused herself to use the restroom. She could text Wade while she was gone, give him whatever answer he needed, then she didn't have to think about him anymore today, at least not until the late afternoon.

She didn't look at her phone until she was in the bathroom. The text was just a note about how much he was reserving for returns and allowances on the new product.

Another wave of guilt washed over her.

She remembered the way her heart would beat faster, anticipating what Wade was going to say. Yes, she could admit it, as bad as it was. She'd waited for a personal note. She'd waited for that kickstart to her heart. It wasn't about sex. It was about… something else.

But she saw it all with new eyes now. It was an affair without having an affair. It was needing to get that kick from someone other than Guy. If Guy had been feeling that kind of thing about Sharon, she'd have scratched his eyes out. And then she would have gone for Sharon.

She kept her answer to one word. *Great.* No long ramblings designed to get him to engage with her.

She wondered about Wade's divorce. Maybe his wife thought he felt the same kick. It seemed like the only reason Wade wouldn't have told her why his wife was divorcing him. Because Marnie was to blame. Especially with that comment about not checking up on Guy.

She fixed her face, her lipstick, her hair, and headed back to the club car. She took the seat by the window, next to Guy. He was a beautiful man. Why had she ever needed a kick from someone else?

Then she gasped. "Oh my goodness. Will you look at that view?" She'd been so busy with the text from Ethan and getting rid of Wade's text that she hadn't even looked out the window.

"It's pretty amazing," Guy agreed.

They'd pulled out of the adorable town of Innsbruck with its colorful buildings framed by the mountains and were now climbing through the Alps. Snow glistened on the peaks, but the slopes were green after the snowmelt and the spring rainstorms.

"Hannigan wants to play cards." He jutted his chin at Boyd. "For money."

Boyd laughed. "Or a hall pass."

She shook her finger at them. "No hall passes. Especially now that my son has actually mentioned them."

"Spoilsport," Boyd grumbled.

It struck her again what an amazing experience this was. To meet a famous movie star, like *totally* world-famous, a man's whose name everyone in the world knew, even her son. And that man wanted *her* to get a hall pass.

What would Linda think?

But she said, "How can you play cards with all this gorgeous scenery?"

Boyd just smiled. "We're men. We multitask."

A waiter delivered playing cards, and Boyd dealt for gin rummy.

But Marnie kept losing, more engrossed in the views outside as the train cut through a natural mountain pass toward Italy. It rattled over huge bridges built high above the valley below. They flew by farms and small towns dotted through the pass, the grass a brilliant emerald bursting with wildflowers, steeples of churches rising to the sky, the colors of the houses bright, cows and sheep dotting the fields, creeks flowing through, and the evergreens and aspens—at least that's what she thought they were—climbing up the slopes of the mountains. The peaks were breathtaking. Roads snaked through the valleys, and in the distance, she could see an elevated roadway on huge pilings, probably the major highway between Austria and Italy.

"You lose again," Boyd said, laughing and pointing at her.

She jutted her chin. "And you're losing out on all these sights."

"I'm watching," Guy said, leaning across, breathing deeply as if he were taking in not only the scenery but her as well.

Clouds drifted across the blue sky, touching down on snow-capped peaks. A castle with turrets perched on the edge of a steep cliff. "Look at that," she pointed, feeling breathless with the beauty, the majesty.

"Extremely defensible," Boyd said. "The knights who built these things could fight off invaders, charge tolls to pass, and make sure they kept order in their villages."

Guy leaned back to look at him, his eyebrows pulled together. "How do you know stuff like that?"

Boyd grinned. "I made that movie back in the early days, the one about the crusades."

Now Marnie could see the buildings behind the castle, higher on the slope. It was no longer a village, but a thriving town, farms spreading out from it on both sides. She wondered how they could farm on those slopes.

As the train trundled on, she spotted more castles, some all by themselves on high plateaus surrounded by steeps sides, some with trees, some where even the greenery couldn't thrive. "How did the people even get up there?"

"They had to build roads or even steps. Sometimes they brought supplies up by pulley." Boyd fanned his cards, changed their order. "But even worse, what about water? They needed really strong pumps if there wasn't a nearby well."

"Plus it's probably windy as hell," Guy observed.

"Well, it's not for me," she said. "I like my hot and cold running water."

She played haphazardly, taking in all the beauty. This was what she needed, time to enjoy, to be in the moment without worrying about the next big project or product release or the daily grind. She needed to enjoy the sun falling on her face or the sound of birds or a squirrel chattering in a tree. Her mind was always so busy that she didn't pay attention to everything around her, didn't relax, didn't stop thinking, thinking, thinking. Until her mind felt over-whelmed.

In the middle of a gin hand, she touched Guy's arm. "Thank you for making sure I didn't find an excuse to get out of this trip."

He leaned over, kissed her cheek. "Thank you for coming with me." His gaze was a sincere deep chocolate. And they shared the moment.

Until Boyd said, "He's checking out your cards, you know."

Marnie slapped her cards to her chest.

"I was not," Guy denied.

"Were too," Boyd insisted. They laughed at the childishness of the argument.

And Marnie felt it was one of the perfect moments of the trip.

They played—and gazed out the window—until it was time for lunch. They were in Italy now, the Alps behind them as they moved to the dining car.

She ate a salad with shrimp so plump that the juice ran down her chin. Guy ordered salmon and Boyd had coq au vin.

"Thank God we're getting off this train before dinner," she said. "I can't keep eating like this." She patted her stomach.

Boyd's gaze roamed over her appreciatively. "You don't need to worry about how much you eat, Marnie. Besides, you're on vacation. You have to try every luscious delight they have to offer." He waggled his eyebrows lecherously, and all she could do was laugh. Boy, could the man make her laugh.

She and Guy would have to watch every single one of his movies once they were home, and reminisce. Remember when Boyd Hannigan said this and when he did that.

She let herself go, enjoying another fabulous French dessert, opera cake with almond sponge soaked in coffee liqueur, layered with ganache and vanilla cream, all topped with a chocolate glaze. It was to die for. She finished with another liqueur-laced coffee.

When she sipped the last of her drink, Boyd snapped his fingers. "Since I didn't get a hall pass, and I'm not propositioning you, you guys really have to come and see my stateroom. There's a bigger table there and some comfortable chairs where we can play cards and order more coffee." He waited a beat, then, almost as if he was afraid they'd refuse, he added, "What do you say?"

She looked at him straight-faced. "Do you have your own plane too?"

He shook his head, sprawling in his chair. "It's easier to charter when I need to fly. Planes are a drain of resources." And Boyd talked them into it. "Prepare to be amazed."

He was like a little boy with a new toy. She would have thought a movie star would no longer care about things like the opulence of his grand suite. Luxury should be old hat to him.

Yet Boyd Hannigan didn't seem like a movie star at all. He wasn't full of himself. He didn't think he was better than them. He was just fun-loving. The fact that he had affairs while his wife was on location—even asking men if he could sleep with their wives—seemed to be the only difference between them.

He opened the door of his suite. And it was the entire train car, with only a narrow aisleway down the side which was probably used only by staff.

He stepped aside, waving his hand with a flourish. "What do you think?"

Marnie lost her breath.

It was a palace. The canopied king-size bed at the far end sat on a raised dais, curtained by maroon velvet, gold tassels hanging from the canopy. The bedspread was a matching maroon, with a complicated pattern of flowers and leaves and woodland animals.

The plush carpet was a lighter shade in the same tone as the bed curtains, and the sitting room was large enough for a velvet-covered sofa in yet another matching red tone, along with armchairs by the windows for anyone who wanted to watch the view. Just as Boyd had said, an oval dining table with four chairs took up the middle of the spacious compartment between sitting room and bedroom.

"Wow," Guy said, running a hand over the soft velvet of the sofa, his eyes slightly wider as he took in the lavish appointments.

A crystal chandelier hung over the table, and antique light fixtures framed each window. When Boyd saw Marnie looking, he moved to a long wall panel, flipping different switches.

"Each light has its own circuit. If there's only two people, they could sit by the window and have only that light on."

"These are some pretty rich digs," Guy said, awe lacing his voice.

Once again, Boyd smiled like an excited kid. "Actually, it looks like a freaking bordello with all this red."

Guy laughed with him. "Yeah, it's kind of bordelloish."

"That's why I love it," Marnie said "It makes me think of the Old West." She tapped her bottom lip. "In fact, it reminds me of that old TV show *The Wild Wild West*." Marnie couldn't remember if the decor of James West's train car was all done in red, but it had been plush, at least as far as she remembered.

Boyd shot her with a finger pistol. "I loved that show. And his sidekick Artemus Gordon had such cool gadgets. He was like Q in all the Bond movies. Q demonstrated all the cool things he had, and we all knew Bond was going to mistreat them."

"Especially the cars," Guy said, his eyes crinkling attractively.

"I wonder how many Aston Martins he wrecked." Boyd stroked his chin.

Marnie hadn't been much of a Bond fan except for Sean Connery. And she asked the practical question. "Where's the bathroom?"

Boyd blew on his fingers and said, "The pièce de résistance."

He led them to a door next to the bedside table. Covered in red and gold velvet wallpaper like the walls, she hadn't noticed it. Boyd ushered Marnie in.

She gasped as the sheer immensity of it. A jetted tub sat beneath the window where one could watch the clouds roll by during the day and stargaze at night. Candles sat on every corner and along the back rim. In addition, there was a large stall shower, along with two pedestal sinks, each with its own mirrored cabinet. The toilet and bidet were secreted behind another door.

"The towel racks are heated," Boyd said in a whisper. He should have been used to the luxury, but maybe it impressed him because he'd found all this on a train.

"You were right. This is fabulous." Then she couldn't help herself. "How much did it cost?" She knew the question was rude, but she absolutely had to know.

He quoted a number that almost made her faint. "For one night?" she repeated incredulously.

"Yeah. But if you think I was splashing out extra when I said I'd cover all the drinks, it's included in my package." As if that made all the difference to the ginormous price.

How would it be to live like this, plunking down tens of thousands of dollars for one night on a train? And Boyd hadn't even used his stateroom that much. He'd spent so much more time with them in the dining and bar cars.

Out in the parlor—because really, you had to call the ornate sitting room a parlor—Boyd ordered lattes and Cointreau. "If you've never had it, it's a delicious orange liqueur. With the coffee, it'll be like a sweet orange latte. Sound good?"

He worked his magic on them with that little kid's smile. Even if she hadn't been eager to try it, she would just to make him happy.

Then he winked at her. "If you want to try out that Jacuzzi tub, feel free."

She wondered if he'd want to join her, but she laughed the question away. "Not today. But thanks for the offer."

The bottle of Cointreau and the lattes arrived, and they took their seats.

"Your turn to shuffle," Boyd said, shoving the deck at Guy. They played for three hours, rolling through vineyards and farmland, the Alps falling far behind them. They played through the stop in Verona. If they'd had longer, Marnie would have liked to tour the town, but there wasn't enough time to see much more than the train station.

Boyd started off the games by winning back the euro coins he'd lost to Guy in the dining room. But the tide changed, and Guy began to win again. Then it was Marnie's turn to have luck. She was actually paying attention now, not that the scenery wasn't fascinating.

Boyd jumped up and down and slapped the table when he lost. He did that when he won too. It was all amazing fun. Marnie couldn't seem to stop laughing.

"Take some pictures," Boyd told her. "You can use my phone."

She snapped pictures of their winning cards, of Boyd and Guy hamming it up. Then Boyd took the phone back and added pictures of her and Guy. When the waiter returned with fresh lattes, Boyd made him take pictures of all three of them, like they were tourists.

Finally, he handed the phone back to Marnie. "Look them over, delete anything you don't like."

They were all fun and flirty, and she noted that the big bed was prominent in the background.

"Go ahead and send yourself whatever you like," he added graciously.

She stared at him. "Aren't you worried about gossip magazines?"

He let out a half laugh, half snort, shaking his head. "What for? It's all three of us. And we're all fully clothed. And the photos are on my phone."

"You're pretty trusting," she said.

Guy added, "What if we send them to our kids, and they're plastered all over the internet like that other photo?"

Boyd flopped back in his chair. "I don't care. It's not like your kids can give salacious pictures to the tabloids."

"But what will your wife think?" Guy pushed.

"She's going to think I was having fun on my trip when she ditched me for her—" he stopped, and Marnie thought at first he was going to say a lover. But then he quickly added, "her movie shoot. She knows I like to have fun. And you two —" He pointed at them. "—are very fun. And have we done anything wrong?" He lifted his shoulders and held up his hands. "No. We stargazed, we played cards, and we ate really good food."

"But don't you care about your privacy?" Marnie asked.

He was silent a long moment before he said, "There are very private moments that I would never share. But all we've done is have fun, and I don't care who sees it. And Selena isn't going to think a thing about it." Then he added, "Use both your phone numbers, yours and Guy's, and send yourself the photos. And if you want to send them to your kids, have at it. In fact, put some on your Instagram." He grinned widely. "And I hope it gives them a thrill. That's all I want. Just a thrill."

BOYD WAS AMAZED HOW EASILY IT HAD WORKED.

He'd seen the man snapping pictures last night in the club car. He wasn't a tabloid reporter, but he had the look of a man who couldn't wait to put them on social media with a sensational comment.

They had good Wi-Fi on the train, and it had gone down just the way Boyd wanted, probably even faster. When he'd talked to Selena last night, she hadn't seen the photo yet. But she would today. Once Marnie sent those photos to her sons and posted them on Instagram, they would go viral. And Selena's publicity people would be ringing her phone off the hook.

He looked at his watch. He figured it would come to a head around five o'clock, or even before that because Selena would be up excessively early to get ready for the day's shoot.

Boyd didn't know what reaction he'd get, only that he'd get one. If she was mad, so much the better. Maybe it would open a dialogue. Maybe he could say something about their "open" relationship being speculated upon in the tabloids, and how they should cool it with their individual lovers, make a big show of coming together and declaring that the photos were really nothing.

Then maybe he could tell her that's what he wanted for real, a purely monogamous relationship. Maybe he could make her see it was good for both their careers, good for the relationship. Good for them. He'd make love to her, the best she'd ever had.

He let Guy win again, then Marnie, then he won a round.

They were playing with what amounted to nickels and dimes, but it was fun.

He wondered what Selena would think of the Slades. He wondered if she'd like them.

He wondered if she'd ever come around to his way of thinking.

20

With the train arriving in Venice in an hour, they returned to their compartment to pack.

Guy wrapped his arms around her waist, pulling Marnie against him. "How about a quickie before we pull into the station?" He nuzzled her hair and kissed her earlobe, sending shivers through her.

But she elbowed him, laughing. "We have to get ready."

He didn't let her go. Nibbling her neck, he slipped his fingers inside her blouse and beneath her bra, stroking her nipple.

She loved this. It was as if they were brand new. Sex hadn't been like this since his brother died. Playful and flirty. Suddenly she was desperate to go for it. And the quickie was so delicious, so satisfying, her climax explosive. She did up her pants and buttoned her blouse while Guy zipped up and buckled his belt. They hadn't even taken off their clothes, which made it even sexier.

"You wrinkled my blouse," she groused teasingly.

He wrapped his hand around her neck and pulled her in for a deep kiss. "I ruined your lipstick too."

She felt sweetly languorous. She could have crawled into bed with him, spent another luxurious hour.

But they had to pack. And smiling to herself, she remembered exactly why she had to fix her lipstick.

Guy was in the bathroom when her phone pinged. She didn't have to look. It was Wade. She could tell by the stab of guilt in her midriff.

How long would it take for that immediate reaction to go away? How long would it take for her to feel like she wasn't lying to Guy but protecting him from something he wouldn't want to hear.

Her lipstick and makeup were freshened, her hair back in place, and their bags packed, when the door rattled with a knock. It was probably the porter.

But when Guy opened it, Boyd Hannigan stood on the other side.

"We'll be arriving at the station in five minutes. Let's watch the train pull in."

Marnie was once again struck by his boyish enthusiasm. She would never have thought a big movie star could be like this, excited about each new adventure.

Guy moved to grab their bags.

Boyd waved a hand. "The porters will bring them."

Marnie felt giddy. They were in Venice, the city of canals, the trip of a lifetime. Why had she fought so hard against it? But she knew the answer. She'd been obsessed with work, feeling she had to do it all. Yet while she was gone, Wade and the company had been fine without her.

Did that mean she wasn't needed? Or did it mean she had more freedom than she'd ever imagined? Just as she'd thought on the ride through the Alps, she wanted the freedom to stop and smell the flowers.

The platform was far more crowded than she anticipated, as if the people of Venice were here to greet the new arrivals.

But when she saw the photographers, she quickly realized all these people were here for Boyd Hannigan. Everyone had seen the photo Ethan had sent them.

And the paparazzi was here *en masse* to greet him.

❀

EVERYTHING WAS GOING BETTER THAN PLAN.

Boyd could see her on the platform, surrounded by her adoring fans. Selena must have seen the photo and jumped on a plane immediately. It was more than he'd ever hoped for.

As he stepped off the train, he was sure to put his hand on Marnie's back, ostensibly to guide her. But Selena would see the touch. Unaware, Guy took her hand and tried to propel her away from the crowd around Selena.

Until Boyd reeled him in with a hand on his arm. "You have to meet my wife."

The two of them looked at him with eyes that were so deer-in-the-headlights he wanted to laugh.

Marnie gaped. Then she said, her words almost a gasp, "You want us to meet Selena Rodriguez?" With terror widening her eyes, she glanced at the crowd.

There were mostly paparazzi, but some fans were clamoring for an autograph as well. Selena loved autographs, and for at least five minutes, she signed and smiled while the paparazzi snapped pictures. She knew how to work a crowd.

Then she saw him, and he wanted to think her eyes lit up.

He wasn't stupid. She was here because she was afraid of the rumors based on that photo. She'd always said they needed to be discreet. And he'd always been the soul of discretion, since he'd never done anything he needed to be discreet about. Until now.

Maybe she thought this was a change in his behavior.

And it scared her.

He held his arms wide as he approached her. "Selena, darling. I didn't expect you so soon. I thought it would be a few days."

He pulled her close for an insatiable kiss that made her fans swoon and the paparazzi click their cameras so quickly they produced smoke. She tasted of surprise, then delight, and finally she melted against him. Her taste was exactly what he craved.

When they parted, he gazed down into her eyes, silently telling her how much he missed her and everything he was going to do to her the moment he got her into their bed.

But that was several hours away.

He held out an arm to Marnie and Guy, his smile wide, because really, the expressions on their faces were a sight to behold. *Freaked out* was probably the best description.

In a voice loud enough for the paparazzi to make note, he said, "I want you to meet some friends I picked up on the train."

He waggled his fingers, pulling them over as if they were puppets on a string.

"Marnie and Guy Slade, this is my wife, Selena." He didn't need to say her last name. But there was also a part of him that didn't want to point out that she'd never taken his name. Because of course she never would. She was already a super-star before they got married.

He was jealous that Marnie was a Slade just like Guy.

Selena gave him one glance, just one, a question in it that asked so much. Had he slept with Marnie Slade? Did they have a threesome on the train? Was he bringing them along because he wanted a foursome?

The avaricious cameras surrounding them wanted to know every dirty detail as well.

For the first time he felt a tingle of guilt. He hadn't meant to expose Marnie and Guy to scandalous gossip. He only wanted Selena to wonder. He never imagined she'd show up on the platform to greet him.

He wondered what this media attention would do to the Slades. But then he knew how it worked. All the paparazzi would see was a glorious vacation in Venice with an American couple who appeared to be in love and were celebrating their thirtieth wedding anniversary. And that was the story their publicists would feed the media. Then the fans would ooh and aah and say how wonderful Boyd Hannigan and Selena Rodriguez were for making this the holiday of a lifetime for the Slades.

He put an arm around Guy, slapped his shoulder, and started the spin. "It's their thirtieth wedding anniversary. I thought we could show them the town."

It was a moment, a long moment, in which so many emotions flashed through Selena's expressive eyes that he couldn't pinpoint any one thing.

Then, suddenly, like the moment the sun pops over the horizon and turns everything brilliant, she smiled her gorgeous movie star smile that had captured the hearts of billions. "Of course, my darling, we must. We absolutely must."

SELENA RODRIGUEZ HAD A MOTOR-LAUNCH OUTSIDE THE station, waiting for them to board.

"Of course we're not going to make you take a *vaporetto*," Hannigan said as he practically pushed them into the boat.

Guy was shell-shocked. He'd gotten used to Hannigan while they were on the train, but they'd been relatively alone, no one accosting them. The mob at the station, however, had been crazy. And it was disappearing as they pulled away from the steps and further into the canal.

Motor-launches waited for passengers, and gondolas were docked between wooden posts all along the canal's edges, most of them with the famous heart-shaped seats just waiting for tourists.

Okay, could he just say it was freaking amazing? Selena Rodriguez saw him staring and said, "That's the Ponte degli Scalzi," as they passed under a spectacular marble bridge. "And that's Chiesa dei Santi Geremia e Lucia-Santuario di Lucia." She pronounced it like a native.

There was so much to see, the amazing buildings perched right on the edge of the canal, restaurants with their café tables right next to the water. And everywhere the boats, big boats, small boats, gondolas, *vaporetti*, which were like ferries.

Okay, he was a guy. He should maintain. But this was freaking incredible. Selena Rodriguez, megastar, was giving him a tour of Venice!

"What hotel are you staying at?" Hannigan wanted to know. "I'll tell our pilot." He was already pouring the chilled champagne waiting for them when Guy gave him the name.

Hannigan made a face like he wanted to puke. "You can't stay at that dump." He handed the two champagnes he'd skillfully poured to Marnie and Selena.

"I'm pretty sure it's not a dump," Guy said. Surely not at those prices.

Hannigan wasn't listening, already pouring two more glasses and handing one to Guy. "We've got a villa with two master suites. It's way too big for just us."

Selena Rodriguez didn't move a muscle, not even the flutter of an eyelash. Until she said, "Darling," and took Hannigan's hand. "Maybe they want to stay at the hotel they've chosen. After all, it's their anniversary."

Hannigan was waving his hand imperiously when Marnie said, "We really can't impose like that."

Guy added, "That's expecting too much of you guys."

Next to him, Marnie twitched, as if calling two mega-celebrities "you guys" was beyond the pale.

"Come on, you guys," Hannigan repeated the phrase. "It'll be fun." His wife looked at him.

Guy sensed a storm brewing in the deep brown depths of her eyes. A major explosion was about to ensue.

Then somehow her gaze morphed. She smiled, and he saw the trademark twinkle in her eye as she asked politely, "Have you ever been to Venice before?"

Marnie shook her head, and Guy said, "No."

She smiled full on, almost blinding him with the whiteness of her teeth. Selena Rodriguez was the most beautiful woman in the world, at least that's what the celebrity magazines touted. Her silky black hair fell almost to her waist, thick and glossy. Her nose had the perfect tilt, her cheekbones were high, her lips lush. There wasn't a wrinkle on her forehead or between her brows or at the corners of her eyes, even though she had to be at least forty-five. The tabloids hadn't lied. She was beautiful, even more so face to face.

But she was too perfect, too sculpted, too... untouchable. And Guy took Marnie's hand.

"I would enjoy showing you all our favorite places around the city." Selena smiled sweetly, somehow innocently. "Please, we would love having you stay at the villa with us." She squeezed Hannigan's hand. "Boyd is right, it's far too big for just the two of us."

Guy exchanged a look with Marnie. And she gave his hand a squeeze of approval.

"That's very generous of you. Thank you. We'd love to."

And Marnie added, "Thank you so much."

No one was going to believe this back home.

No one was going to believe this.

"Pinch me," Marnie told Guy.

He reached out and pinched her nipple." She laughed, backing away. "You filthy man."

The butler—yes, there was a butler—had ushered them to a magnificent suite. It wasn't just a bedroom and bathroom, but had its own sitting room as well, including a fully stocked bar, plus all the sundries she could possibly use in the bathroom.

"I can't believe Hannigan talked our hotel out of charging a cancellation fee at this late date." Guy set her suitcase on the plush bench at the end of the bed. "He certainly knows how to turn on the charm and get whatever he wants."

"That's why he's a movie star," she said, holding her hands up in surrender. She stood for a moment, head slightly cocked, looking at him. "But why did he invite us to stay with them? It's kind of crazy."

In the armoire, she hung the three fancy dresses Guy had packed for her, and laid her lingerie in the bureau.

The furniture was old, dainty, the room decorated ornately like something from the French Revolution era. Or maybe even the Renaissance. There were small statues and Venetian glass vases on the tables and an elaborate marble mantelpiece surrounding the fireplace, along with thick carpets over terrazzo tile floors.

Guy snapped his suitcase closed after stowing his clothing. "Maybe they want to talk us into a foursome."

She swiped at him playfully. "Oh, you'd like that."

"And you're saying you haven't had a single fantasy about Boyd Hannigan?" He bumped her hip.

She gave him a very prim smile. "Of course not."

Then she suddenly felt sick. Boyd was fascinating because he was a huge celebrity and he'd been interested in *her*.

The feelings about Wade had been completely different.

And those feelings were traitorous. She changed the subject, masked her guilt. "Should we dress for dinner?"

She unbuttoned her blouse, stepped out of her capris and stood before the closet in panties and bra.

Guy grabbed her from behind, rubbed himself against her, and he was shockingly hard. "Did you wear that sexy ensemble for him?" he whispered in her ear, his warm breath sending little shockwaves of desire through her, even as she was thinking that God, no, she'd never worn sexy lingerie for Wade.

Relief flooded her when she gauged the humor in Guy's voice and realized he was teasing her about Boyd Hannigan.

"No, dear," she said primly, then added with a husky undertone, "I wore it just for you."

"You make me crazy, woman."

Then he hoisted her onto an ornate round table she thought would crack beneath her, and in the next moment, her panties dangled from her foot as Guy unzipped his pants. She could feel him right there, stroking her with his crown.

"Does it turn you on to think of me with Boyd?" She leaned back on her hands.

"No." He grinned, easing just inside until she thought she'd die of the pleasure. "It's the influence of this decadent Venetian palace and you standing there in your incredibly sexy panties and bra, tempting me, damn near begging me to take you."

She didn't point out that the ensemble was her usual comfortable cotton fare.

"Then," she dropped her voice to a whisper. "Take me."

He did, right there on the table, taking her with a slow tantalizing glide that made her crazy.

They hadn't made love so much in years. It was glorious. It was amazing. It was like thirty years ago, their honeymoon, when they'd gone to Hawaii and spent almost every moment in the hotel room, or hiked to a secluded beach and made love on the sand.

She grabbed his buttocks, on the edge of mindlessness, murmuring, "My God, baby, harder, faster, baby, baby, my God."

He brought her over the edge with a hard thrust, and the moment she clenched around him, her body contracting, she felt the throb of his climax deep inside and the low rumble of a growl in his throat.

THEY STAYED LIKE THAT, PERCHED ON THE TABLE, FOR long moments, his body prone on top of her as the aftershocks rippled through him.

Her arms wrapped tight around him, she whispered, "You make me crazy."

"You make me wild."

It was as if they'd turned the clock back, and they were in his dorm room, doing it fast and hard before his roommate returned, then the long languorous moments when they should have been getting up, putting their clothes to rights, yet neither of them able to move, the fusion of their bodies too good to let go.

God, he'd missed this. He'd missed *her*. He didn't know how they'd managed to grow so far apart.

Eventually his body told him he wasn't twenty anymore but fifty-five, and his back started to ache.

"Jesus, I'm getting old," he muttered.

She cupped his cheek, her eyes almost teary. "Older maybe, but so much better."

He wasn't letting this intimacy disappear. When they got home, he wouldn't let her work herself to death. He wouldn't let the principal get in his way. He wouldn't let Wade get into her head. They were good at this, good, hot, crazy lovemaking. He would plan weekend getaways, seduce her at night in the hot tub they barely used anymore.

It was all clear in his mind, exactly what they were going to create.

He hauled himself up before his back spasmed. She lay there a long moment, looking at him, their bodies still fused, her legs around his waist, the front clasp of her bra undone, one breast bared. He couldn't even remember doing that. Maybe she had.

"You're the most beautiful thing I've ever seen." His voice cracked with emotion.

She blushed, the pink spreading up her skin, its heat warming his hand on her belly.

As if she was embarrassed, she said with a cheeky grin, "Better than Selena Rodriguez?"

He remained sober, intent. "Not even a comparison. She's so far out of your league, she'll could never catch up."

"Flatterer." But she was smiling.

He meant every word. He helped her up until their bodies were flush, her panties pooled at their feet, her bra falling down her arm. Holding her chin in his hand, their lips close, he told her, "There's no one like you. There never has been. There never will be."

Then he kissed her with all the pent-up emotion that had haunted him since his brother died, all the anger, all the fear, everything draining out of him. And there was just this kiss, just Marnie, just the taste of her and the feel of her skin beneath his fingertips.

When their lips parted, she laid her hand over his heart. "Do you know what I absolutely love?" She waited for him to tip his chin in question. And he absolutely needed to hear. "That I'm completely naked and you have all your clothes on. It's so divinely sexy."

He felt something stir deep inside, his sex flexing itself, tightening, getting ready.

Then the house phone rang.

HER BIG SEXY HUSBAND PICKED HER UP, ONE ARM ACROSS her back, his hand under her bottom as she wrapped her legs around him, their bodies fitting together like puzzle pieces falling into place. He walked her to the house phone and rested her against the wall.

She picked up the receiver. "Hello," she said brightly as if Guy wasn't seated deeply inside her. And getting harder.

"It's Selena, darling. Boyd and I talked about it. We think a delicious meal of home-cooked Venetian delicacies right here in our own villa would be perfect. I've hired the most amazing chef for our stay. He's promised a smorgasbord of everything Venetian."

Marnie looked at Guy, eyebrows raised. She'd been holding the phone so he could hear everything. When he nodded, she said, "We'd love that, Selena. Thank you." And after a moment, added, "Should we dress for dinner?"

She amused herself. After all, she was naked and dressing for dinner could mean throwing on any old thing.

Yes," Selena said excitedly. "Let's pull out all the stops."

Guy groaned, and it vibrated through her, turning the heat inside her from simmer to boil.

"Shall we say an hour and a half in the dining room?"

"Perfect," she purred as Guy started to move inside her.

"We'll see you both then." And Selena was gone.

Guy was so very there, making her crazy as he growled in her ear. "Plenty of time for another quickie before we get ready for dinner."

Only it wasn't quick, it was deliciously slow.

And Marnie didn't give a thought to what she'd wear to dinner.

"SHE SOUNDED BREATHLESS. AS IF I CAUGHT THEM IN THE middle of sex," Selena said.

Boyd nuzzled her neck under the covers on the big bed that had probably belonged to a Venetian king. "Does the idea make you hot?" he murmured against her fragrant skin.

She stretched languorously against him. "*You* make me hot, my love."

He'd been on her the moment they were alone. He'd never been able to get enough of Selena. He never would. She was just as insatiable.

But he needed to know. "I wasn't expecting you to get here for a few days. What happened to the shooting schedule?"

She squeezed him tight. "I thought it was a shame to waste the villa. So I told that nasty old director he needed to take the break we'd planned on instead of pushing through." She tangled her fingers in his hair. "Then I jumped on a plane."

The nasty old director was probably her lover, which was why she didn't say his name. Boyd didn't let his jealousy get the better of him, not now when it was obvious that she'd chartered a plane the moment that photo went viral.

Perhaps she was jealous too. And he liked it.

She dropped her voice to a sexy note. "So, darling, tell me, have you enjoyed the lovely Marnie?"

The question was a bright spot. Because they never asked, never told. And if Selena was asking, it meant she didn't like it.

He didn't answer the question, saying instead. "Have you seen the way Guy looks at her?"

She laughed softly. "As if he could eat her up." She put her hands on his shoulders. "And now, darling, I think *you*—" She pushed him down her delectable body. "—should eat *me* up."

Everything was going according to plan. Selena was here, in his bed, in his arms. And if he hadn't missed the mark, she was jealous.

The side benefit of all his machinations was that Guy and Marnie seemed besotted with each other in a way he was sure they hadn't been for years.

Just call him matchmaker. Or fairy godfather. Or Howard Hughes leaving a tow-truck driver all his money.

Selena Rodriguez was exquisite in a shimmering gold caftan with burnt orange overtones that draped her luscious curves. With her thick, glossy black hair falling to her waist and her lush ruby-red lips, she was every man's wet dream.

Most certainly she was the wet dream of the two men seated at this table.

Marnie wasn't jealous. She wasn't making comparisons. Guy had made love to her again, starting up against the wall after she hung up the phone, then carrying her to the bed. Their delicious lovemaking had lasted so long they'd had to rush through a quick shower, then practically throw on their clothes. She'd barely had time to rub lotion in or redo her face before she'd slipped into the blue dress, hoping it was fancy enough.

But when they left their suite, Guy had leaned in close, whispering, "You look totally fuckable."

She thrilled at his words, the naughtiness of them.

And she kept saying them to herself as she looked at Selena Rodriguez.

No, she wasn't jealous. She had Guy. And he most definitely wanted her. Desperately.

There'd been four texts from Wade when she got out of the shower, but she didn't have time to look at them, let alone answer them. And she didn't have time for that niggle of guilt at the sight of them.

More importantly, she'd left her phone in the room.

"We must try a little bit of everything," Selena proclaimed from the head of the table.

The dining room was the size of a grand hall, the table large enough to seat twelve. Two glittering chandeliers hung over its length, and solid silver candlesticks added flickering candlelight to the ambience. The walls were dark paneling, with wooden seats built in every few paces, where, presumably, the servants had sat, waiting to attend their nobles. At the far end, floor-to-ceiling French doors opened onto a balcony overlooking the canal.

"And I won't tell you what it is until after we're done," Selena continued, raking them all with her earthy gaze. "Otherwise, you'll all just say it's too gross."

"Now you've got me really scared." Guy shuddered dramatically.

"I assure you, you'll love it." She was breathless, as if she were offering herself instead of a Venetian delicacy.

She was truly spellbinding. Her husky voice was as mesmerizing as a hypnotist's. She wasn't just beautiful, she wasn't just sexy, she was otherworldly. A goddess. It was no wonder she captivated worldwide audiences when she was up on the big screen. She oozed charisma and sensuality.

Their waiter, the butler who had attended them earlier, brought in two starters. The first was a delicately fried fish in a vinegary marinade covered with onions, raisins, pomegranates, and pine nuts. The other platter held grilled pieces of cornbread, or something like it, and a flaky fish spread. The wine was a mellow red that delighted Marnie's pallet with every new bite of food. And she was not a red wine drinker.

Once they'd tasted from each platter, Selena said, "This starter is *sarde in saor*." She pointed to the marinated fish. "Do you like it?" Clapping her hands when both Marnie and Guy nodded their approval, she laughed. "It's sardines. Yes, those horrible little fishy things we used to get in a can."

"They're certainly not like anything we have at home," Guy said, enjoying another forkful.

"And that—" Selena waved a hand over the spread. "—is *baccala mantecato*. It's a mousse made of cod blended with olive oil and garlic and a bit of parsley. And the bread is grilled polenta. But you can serve it with fresh bread too."

The unobtrusive waitstaff, which included the butler, were constantly arriving with new delicacies for them to try. The wines changed as well with each course. Only after tasting did Selena describe what was in each dish.

They dined on *bigoli in salsa*, a pasta covered in a sauce of onions and salted fish. Then *risi e bisi*, a rice dish with peas, a little soupier than Marnie was used to. The *lasagnette al nero di sepia* didn't appear appetizing, but the seafood-based lasagna, black with squid ink, was tasty despite its color. *Moleche* was a seasonal delicacy, tiny deep-fried crabs. *Fegato alla Veneziana* came on a bed of creamy polenta, and Marnie was glad Selena didn't tell them it was liver and caramelized onions until after she'd eaten it. For a couple of bites, she'd thought it was veal pounded very thin. But then she hadn't eaten much veal either.

Marnie tried everything, enjoying it all without stuffing herself, but still, the wine was going to her head. She couldn't quite follow every detail of the conversation and turned to water to clear her foggy brain.

It was the most surreal sensation to be sitting here with two superstars in a fabulous villa that probably cost fifteen thousand dollars a day, and yet it was almost as if Selena and Boyd were trying to please *them*.

"I've planned our itinerary for tomorrow," Selena said, that seductive movie smile on her lips and her face. She was younger than Marnie, though at least forty-five, and she was in darn good shape, probably because she had a personal trainer, a masseuse, an esthetician, a nutritionist, and a chef all on permanent staff.

Marnie's thoughts sounded catty and mean, when Selena and Boyd had been nothing but good to them.

"What are we going to do?" She didn't have to force enthusiasm into her voice. The idea of touring Venice with Selena Rodriguez and Boyd Hannigan was the most exciting thing anyone could imagine.

She had no idea what Guy had booked for the Venice portion of their trip, if anything at all. She hadn't paid attention, being too busy with work. Now, the thought made her stomach heave with how little she'd been involved in the planning. And how that had made Guy feel.

Thankfully she hadn't brought her phone to the table. Her inbox was probably imploding with texts, and later tonight she'd have to handle anything important. But she dreaded looking at the phone. What if there was something personal? Not that they'd ever gotten sexy on the phone or in texts. But sometimes he was playful. Or he asked her how she was doing, as if he could sense her mood. Wade knew if something was bothering her, and he could always get her to talk about it. She'd told him far too much about her marriage, capping it off by telling him she was afraid Guy was having an affair. But Wade had told her it was best not to talk about *that*.

She must have lost her mind.

She tuned in to Selena again. It was safer than wallowing in her own thoughts.

"We'll hit two of my favorite spots that just happen to be right next to each other, the Doge's Palace and Basilica di San Marco." She waved an expressive hand in the air. "I also took the liberty of booking us for the Piombi, where Casanova was imprisoned. And we'll go down into the Pozzi, known as the Wells, a terrible place." She shivered dramatically. "It's a private tour so there will be only the four of us." She gave a melodious laugh. "And we won't have to listen to any American tourists talking too loudly."

"Aren't you American?" Guy asked, a half-smile curving his mouth.

Marnie thought Selena might turn on them then, but instead she smiled. "I'm from a very middle-class family. I was born in Hayward, California."

Naturally both Guy and Marnie knew that Hayward was in the East Bay, across the Bay Bridge from San Francisco.

Boyd went on with Selena's story. "She never hides her humble upbringing." He put his hand against his chest. "I'm a Riverside brat. My father was a professor at the UC there."

"But," Selena went on. "I still think that sometimes Americans can be too loud." She looked at Marnie. "Don't you agree?"

She felt as if it were a test and was unsure of the right answer. "We definitely have the ugly Americans, but then there's the overly reserved British and the snooty French. We all have our stereotypes. But in our two days in Paris, we met the most marvelous family who were so kind and the furthest thing from snooty. So you never know."

Selena clapped her hands. "Well said. But you two." She waved a finger between Marnie and Guy. "You don't fit the stereotype. You don't run around tooting your horns and raising your voices to get attention." Selena gave them a closed-mouth killer smile. "But I did see those pictures on your Facebook page." Her gaze seemed to drill right through

Marnie. "A little stargazing?" she asked, one eyebrow raised, her lip slightly curled like Cruella de Vil.

It was Boyd who came to Marnie's rescue. "I told her to post them. She wasn't going to." He grinned at Marnie. "In fact, I distinctly remember her saying she wanted to respect our privacy." He bit into crunchy toast slathered with creamy pâté

"Why?" his wife asked with that same silky tone.

Marnie exchanged a look with Guy. It was suddenly uncomfortable, and they were both rethinking their decision to stay at the villa.

Then Boyd laughed. "What's the point in a coincidental meeting on a train with a famous celebrity if you don't get to tell people about it?" He grinned at Guy. "And their sons were absolutely delighted. They're the talk of their dorms." He touched Selena's hand, patting her as if she were a sleek panther he was to trying to keep from slashing his throat.

Then suddenly Selena Rodriguez smiled. It was dazzling, a nuclear explosion that could blast you right off your seat. "You're so right, darling." She put her hand over Boyd's. Something passed silently between them that Marnie couldn't interpret. Then Selena said, "Of course Marnie would never post anything we didn't want her to."

She felt another uncomfortable tingle.

But Selena Rodriguez and Boyd Hannigan were smiling, laughing, and twinkling like the stars they were.

It was only a few days. Marnie wanted to enjoy them. Because this was a once-in-a-lifetime opportunity. A multi-million-dollar villa in Venice with two mega-celebrities, private tours of the Doge's Palace, then the Basilica di San Marco. They would never experience anything like it again.

Then their desserts arrived.

IT WAS A SMORGASBORD OF DELICATE TREATS. THERE WERE fritters rolled into balls and deep-fried then dusted with sugar.

"They're called *fritole alla veneziana*," Selena explained. "At one time you could only get them at Carnival. But now they're a staple."

They were damn good. Along with the *buranelli*, buttery cookies shaped like an S, and a tasty cross between a cake and bread called *fugassa*.

Guy was surprised to see how much Selena Rodriguez ate. She wasn't one of those skinny women who wore a size zero and needed cosmetic surgery to get rid of the wrinkles because they didn't have enough adipose tissue beneath the skin. She was full-bodied, not fat, but toned. Men had salivated over her breasts. Her cheeks were beautifully round, her lips plump. She might have had Botox on her forehead and a few injections around her mouth, but her skin wasn't stretched into the caricature of a monkey or any of the hatchet jobs he'd seen done on celebrities' faces. Selena had done none of that. She was a flawlessly beautiful woman.

Guy took Marnie's hand beneath the table, sensing her inferior thoughts. She was probably mulling over cosmetic surgery or someone sticking needles in her face. But she was gorgeous exactly as she was. She had amazingly few wrinkles, and the tiny crinkles at her eyes were from laughter and having enjoyed life. He leaned close to kiss her sexy earlobe.

After enjoying the last bite of *baicoli*, a biscuit he dipped in his brandy-infused coffee, he said to Selena and Hannigan, "Your hospitality is amazing, the way you've opened your villa to us. And the tour tomorrow sounds spectacular." Holding Marnie's hand, he added, "We don't know how to repay you. But I can at least pay for tomorrow's tour."

Hannigan burst out with a laugh. "Like hell you will."

And Selena said, "That's very sweet of you, but there's no

need to pay. Honestly, we would go anyway. And our guide doesn't charge by the person."

Guy wondered if they were offended by the talk of money. They didn't have to worry about a single dollar they spent.

He and Marnie, on the other hand, always had tuition on their minds. It was one of the reasons he had chosen that particular private school to apply to. With the boys going to Harvard and Columbia, the tuition worries hadn't ended.

He wasn't about to boo-hoo and claim they were poor because of all the payments they had to make. They were doing very well, solidly upper middle-class, but unlike public perception, not all CEOs made millions of dollars a year in stock options and bonuses. Which was why Marnie had wanted him to become the principal. The extra income would have made her more at ease. He could admit now that he'd been selfish.

And they certainly didn't have a net worth like this couple.

He didn't accept their offer because he didn't have the money to pay; he simply decided it was gracious. "Thank you. This whole thing is really nice of you guys."

Marnie added her thanks. "Just so nice. Thank you."

Hannigan smiled. "You probably thought all celebrities were stuck-up assholes." Then he cajoled. "Come on, admit it."

Marnie answered. "Well, the press does make a big deal when a celebrity goes awry. And that's really all we see, celebrities gone amok. We don't hear much about nice down-to-earth people like you."

Selena gave a tinkling laugh. "Oh my God, down to earth?" She punched Hannigan's arm. "What line of bull has he been feeding you?"

"Hey," Hannigan said, reeling back from her as if she'd hurt him. "We played gin rummy."

Selena dissolved into giggles. "Don't tell me he swindled you out of thousands."

Guy laughed too. "I did lose a few euros."

"He's a crazy man." She stood, picking up her steaming mug of liqueur-laced coffee. "But that means I'm totally going to thrash you both. Because I am way better than he is."

And that's what they did. Guy could already hear the explanation he'd have to give his sons. *Honest to God, we played gin rummy in teams and Selena Rodriguez was my partner.*

He and Selena won, playing for points and not money.

No one would ever believe. They'd be much more likely to believe that Boyd Hannigan had tried to get Marnie into his bed, that he'd even had the chutzpah to ask Guy. He would almost rather say that to his friends, his family, and his work acquaintances than admit that all they did was play rummy. It did sound a bit pathetic.

Selena rose gracefully, stretched her arms over her head and let her body fall forward, her fingers flat on the Venetian carpet as she stretched out her spine. The caftan molded to her backside.

Standing straight again, she said, "I'm beat. It was a long flight, and I can never sleep on planes. Thank you for a lovely evening."

She came around the table to hug Guy and peck Marnie on the cheek.

Hannigan rose, hugging Marnie and slapping a hand on Guy's back. "We'll see you in the morning. Selena never gets up before eleven when she's not working, so feel free to have the staff make whatever breakfast you'd like."

In their bedroom, as Guy tugged off his clothes, he looked at Marnie. "This is the strangest experience I've ever had."

She shucked out of her dress, hanging it in the ornate armoire. "I still don't get what they want from us."

He slung his slacks over a chair that was probably crafted in the seventeenth century and worth thousands.

"I have no idea. They've got to be playing some game. They can't be this—" He held out his hands, fingers spread. "—ordinary."

"This villa isn't exactly ordinary. And neither was that meal. Or a private tour. It's like they're trying to *appear* ordinary."

Then she was peeling off her bra and panties, and suddenly Guy didn't give a damn about their hosts and what game they were playing.

Right now, all he wanted was to play games with Marnie.

Guy was asleep, snoring softly. His snoring had been a little louder when he was heftier, before his brother died.

Marnie grabbed her phone off the table. Guy hadn't given her time to look at her texts. Almost the moment she'd started taking off her clothes, he'd been on her. God, how she loved it. She never wanted this to stop. And she was racking her brain with ways to make sure it didn't.

She just hadn't come up with anything good. Yet.

She found fancy robes in the bathroom, his and hers, and she wrapped herself in the thick fleece. Padding out to their sitting room, she closed the door softly behind her. Wade would still be at work. She could answer all his texts in one fell swoop, tell him about Selena Rodriguez and Boyd Hannigan and say that she wouldn't be as available over the next few days. End of discussion.

Her phone rang almost immediately after she'd answered the first text.

"Is everything okay, Marnie?"

She tensed at the worry in his voice. She couldn't tell

Wade all the things running around inside her, the guilt, the fear, because it was all about him. "Why do you think something's wrong?" she asked, stalling while she formulated an answer.

"I don't know." She could almost hear him shaking his head. "Something just feels off. Your texts sound stilted. Is this all about Guy's supposed affair?"

She'd confided way too much over the last few months, but the worst was last night, blurting out about Sharon. Besides, hadn't Wade said he didn't want to talk about that? "I was just being stupid. We worked that out and we're fine. The trip to Venice on the train was absolutely amazing. And you'll never believe who we met. Boyd Hannigan and his wife Selena Rodriguez. "

He snorted his disbelief. "You mean *the* Boyd Hannigan and Selena Rodriguez?"

"Yeah, megastars. And they've invited us to stay at their villa. I made Guy pinch me. And it hurt." She didn't tell Wade where Guy had pinched her or about the spark of pleasure that shot through her.

"Wow." Wade wasn't usually a *wow* kind of guy. But if she didn't know better, she'd say he was stunned.

She was still stunned.

"It's been a whirlwind ever since we got on the train. I'm not ignoring you. But you're handling everything, and I'm just rubberstamping what you plan to do."

"I know, but—" He stopped.

In days of old, she would have asked him what the rest of that sentence was, but she was afraid he'd say that he needed contact, needed to hear her voice. In the next moment, she knew Wade would never say that, not even if he thought it. That would be stirring the pot of *something* that brewed between them. Neither of them had ever voiced it, neither had ever made a move.

Wade didn't change that now. "You're right, I've got it handled. It's only a few more days." He laughed softly. "You're indispensable, but I can actually hold down the fort while you're away."

"I know you can. That's why you're my righthand man."

"Go off and enjoy the rest of your holiday with your new friends."

She chuckled, shaking her head. "It's crazy how generous and down to earth they are."

His answering laugh was more of a snort. "Just make sure there's no hidden agendas," and she thought there was a slight edge in his voice.

She shook her head as if he could see. "No hidden agendas at all.

"I'll text to update you. But if you can't answer, just know everything's okay here."

She said goodbye with a sense of relief, as if a huge boulder had been dragged off her bowed back. It was over, it was done. She didn't have to feel guilty anymore. She didn't have to explain anything to Guy.

She felt energized, no longer tired, and something stirred low in her belly. Maybe she should wake Guy...

But there was a text from Linda, wondering how she was doing, if she'd talked to Guy.

She could ease that tension too. It was still midafternoon back home. Linda could take a coffee break.

"Hey there," she said when Linda answered.

"Oh my God. I've been going crazy thinking about how you're doing. I don't know if you've had it out with him."

There was a gleeful note in Linda's voice, as if she was hoping that Guy was truly having an affair. Not that Linda would want Marnie to get a divorce and be miserable, but she did want someone who could understand completely.

"We talked," Marnie said.

"And?" Linda pressed.

"Guy explained it all. And it makes perfect sense. His principal made a pass at him, and he turned her down."

Linda snorted loudly. "And you actually buy that?"

"Yes, I do."

Marnie understood that things could happen. Guy and Sharon were friends, they worked well together, and he probably hadn't recognized her signals. There were parallels with her and Wade. That's why she knew nothing had happened between Sharon and Guy. It would have been written all over him when she confronted him.

"Men can pull the wool over your eyes."

"I know, and I'm really sorry Paul pulled the wool over your eyes and treated you so badly. But that's not Guy. I know him. I would be able to tell if he was lying."

Yet it had taken him two times to get the story right. *No, no, no.* She wouldn't let Linda's suspicious mind influence her. It had taken Guy twice to get the story out because he'd been worried about her reaction, especially after she'd told him she'd seen those texts.

But why had he deleted them? He said it was because he was tired of talking about it. But did that make sense?

"Please, Marnie, don't delude yourself. It'll only hurt worse later."

She couldn't take Linda feeding her doubts anymore, and finally, after months and months, in as gentle a tone as possible, she said, "I'm so sorry for what Paul did to you. It was awful. He was a total scumbag. I know how hard it's been." She paused a beat to catch her breath, then she added as kindly as she could, "But Guy isn't like your ex-husband. I love you for being concerned, but I believe Guy. And I really need you to start believing *me*. Please, Linda, do that for me. I can't have you trying to make me suspect my husband all the time."

It felt like a long time coming, but finally Linda said, almost in a whisper, "I'm sorry. You're my best friend. I just don't want to see you fooled or hurt."

"I'm not. And I know you're always there for me. I love you for that too. I'm always here for you."

"I know I talk too much about him. All my other friends have dropped me because I can't stop talking about him." She still couldn't say Paul's name. "And I'm sorry, I'm really sorry." Then she laughed softly, ending on a sniffle. "You're like my therapist."

Marnie kept her voice low, soothing, but she repeated an idea she'd brought up several times before. "Maybe that's what you need, a real therapist to help you move on."

Linda sniffled again. "Yeah. But a therapist might actually make me think about what I did wrong." It was the most revealing thing Linda had said in a long time.

"You didn't do anything that justified him cheating on you. But maybe a therapist can help you look at other things that might help you move on. We all know that best friends can't tell each other absolutely everything." Just like she'd never told Linda about her mixed feelings over Wade. "There's all those tidbits we have to keep quiet about so we can live with ourselves."

"I tell you absolutely everything," Linda said with a hint of perkiness.

"Yeah, right," Marnie drawled.

Then suddenly Linda laughed, a real laugh. "Yeah, right. We tell each other everything with editing."

They revealed only the things that put themselves in the best light. And telling Linda anything about Wade would not have been Marnie's best light.

"It must be past midnight there. I better let you go."

"Okay, but always remember I love you."

"I love you too."

Marnie was pleased with herself. Two birds with one stone.

GUY COULD HEAR HER VOICE, A LOW, SOFT TONE. SHE'D sneaked out of their bed after he made love to her, picked up her phone, and gone out to the sitting room to call Wade.

He felt his blood boil the same way it had over the past few months.

But she'd said there was nothing. He tried telling himself that sneaking off in the middle of the night was the position he'd put her in. Now she was afraid to talk to her CFO on the phone in front of him.

This was his fault. He'd pushed her into making secret midnight phone calls.

And yet his gut burned.

THERE HADN'T BEEN A SINGLE SOUND FROM SELENA AND Hannigan's suite as Guy and Marnie had glided through the main rooms of the villa. It was a beautiful morning as they walked along the shady side of the canal.

"I wonder if everyone has their own boat to get around in, like we have cars."

"No idea," Guy said, feeling oddly tongue-tied. He'd pretended he was asleep when Marnie came back to bed last night, telling himself that she had been talking about work, and his jealousy was ridiculous.

Unless he chose to believe she'd lied.

Did he?

They strolled along a wide esplanade until they discovered a hole-in-the-wall café. They could have eaten breakfast at the villa, something very Venetian and rich and delicious, but they decided to see some of the city before Selena and Hannigan got up. It was nice to stroll hand in hand, just the two of them.

Guy ordered thick, foamy lattes and a variety of delicacies, from a custard-filled donut called a *krapfen* to a brioche to a slice of Italian strudel and a delectable pastry filled with chocolate cream called a *bignè al cioccolato*. Finding a café table and chairs outside, the sun was now rising over the buildings' rooflines and bathing them in warmth.

Marnie sat back, licking the sugar off her fingers. Then she patted her stomach. "I am so going to have to go on a diet after this trip."

"You look amazing," he said automatically, though it was the truth.

"The problem with being around Selena Rodriguez is that I feel frumpy,"

Almost snorting out the chocolate cream, he said, "Don't be ridiculous. You're the furthest thing from frumpy. You're absolutely gorgeous." But it made him think how different women were, harping on the negative things about their bodies instead of seeing the whole beautiful picture.

He wondered if that was why she'd preened under Hannigan's attention, why she needed affirmation from Wade. She was exquisite, and yet she had to see admiration in a man's eyes before she felt good enough. Maybe what she saw in Guy's eyes wasn't enough anymore. He'd neglected that part of his job, showing her how beautiful and desirable she was. Over the last couple of years, he'd been too focused on his own stuff.

If he asked her, she'd deny needing affirmation. She was attractive and determined and confident, and it would be anathema to her to think she needed a man to tell her she was beautiful. But maybe we deny the thing we need most.

He raised her hand to his lips, her skin scented with citrus lotion. "I love the way you smell."

She laughed. "It's aroma or perfume or scent." She wrinkled her nose. "*Smell* makes me think of bug spray."

His lips still against the back of her hand, he looked up at her through his eyelashes. "Your skin is like the sweetest perfume. Like oranges picked fresh off the tree."

She laughed again. "You're such a schmoozer."

"I mean every word." He leaned close, his arm along the back of her chair, his lips to her ear. "I feel like a caveman. I could drag you back to my lair and make love to you all day on a warm pile of furs."

"You're so romantic." She rolled her eyes, but he saw her pleasure like a flame in her eyes. Then he kissed her, long and deep, with the taste of sugar and cinnamon and sweet milky coffee.

"You're ruining my lipstick," she whispered, but the flame in her eyes became a blaze.

"You better lick it off my mouth," he murmured, nuzzling her cheek before he pulled back.

With her eyes wide, she leaned in, slowly licking his lower lip. The intensity of the moment set a fire alight in his belly.

"It didn't come off." She wiped her finger across his lip. "That's better." Then she tipped her face for him to look at. "What about mine?"

He ran his finger along a slight smudge beneath her lower lip. "You're perfect. You always were, and you are now, more than perfect. And your lipstick belongs on my dipstick."

Her breath quickened, and she stared at him for two seconds, her gaze a little dazed and fixed on his mouth. Then, with delayed reaction, she laughed. "Just like a man, always thinking about your dipstick."

He let his mouth curl into a half smile. "If we weren't in

public and I wasn't afraid of getting arrested in a foreign country, I'd push your hand down there right now."

"Big talker," she muttered, her eyes on his. If they weren't afraid of getting arrested in a foreign country, he knew she would have done it.

Pulling her out of her chair, he wrapped his arm around her waist, hugged her tight against him, and whispered in her ear, "We need to get back to the villa now."

They would have made it, too, if they hadn't taken a wrong turn and gone over the wrong footbridge, then spent an extra laughing, sexy half hour trying to figure out where they were and how to get back.

As they finally bounded up the stairs, Marnie asked, "You think they're still in bed?"

"I sure as hell hope so."

He made her feel deliciously sexy and wicked and desired. Lovemaking wasn't just for the young. A person needed it their whole life long. Why did everyone forget that as they got older?

"Hello there," Boyd called from the dining room. "Were you out enjoying a Venetian breakfast?"

"It was a gorgeous morning, and we wanted to stroll," Guy told him.

Marnie thought about dragging him back to their suite and finishing what they'd started.

Guy had been right, this holiday was exactly what they'd needed to put the pizzazz back in their marriage. Not that he'd said it like that, as if he thought the pizzazz was all gone. It was in the way he'd insisted she couldn't back out, not for any reason, especially not for work.

"We'll be leaving to meet our guide in about five minutes. But you have time for coffee," Selena offered.

Ah well, no time for a quickie. She looked at Guy. He looked at her. And they both smiled, an unspoken promise passing between them. Maybe it would be even better if they had to wait all day.

"I'm glad we made it back in time," she said, still smiling that secret shared smile. "We got a little lost out there."

"It's easy to do," Selena agreed.

Marnie backed toward their suite. "Thanks. I'll skip the coffee and just use the restroom."

When Guy followed her, she was almost sure he'd try to get her lipstick on his dipstick, and the thought delighted her.

He stood behind her after they'd both washed their hands, wrapping his arm around her waist while she fixed her lipstick. He slipped his hand down between her legs, palmed her, his eyes holding hers in the mirror.

"Maybe," he whispered against her ear, sending shivers through her, "we should tell them you're not feeling well, that we're so sorry we have to skip the Doge's Palace and the Basilica but..." He pulled her blouse aside and kissed her neck, giving her more exquisite shivers.

"Why don't we tell them you're the one who's feeling sick?"

He laughed, stepped back. "That wouldn't be manly." Then he shook finger. "You just wait, woman. When I get you alone again, I'm going to make you scream."

She gave him a slow blink and a sexy pout. "Big talker," she murmured.

She'd make sure he followed through.

❧ 23 ❧

arnie slipped her fingers through Guy's as the water taxi motored along the canal, the wind whipping through her hair. It was an exhilarating way to travel. Selena had tied a scarf around her head, but Marnie's hair blew lovely and free, the picture she made so sexy that Guy couldn't help putting his hand on her thigh.

If you thought about sex, you felt sexy. Maybe the key was not letting life intrude. When they got home from work, they needed to turn off everything else, to concentrate on *them*. That's what this holiday was teaching him, to appreciate the beautiful woman who shared his life.

He slipped his arm around Marnie's shoulder, pulled her close, kissed her ear. She sighed, sagging into him.

They weaved through other boats and gondolas with tourists kissing. Most of the buildings were old, some of them freshened up, others closer to crumbling. They passed under ornate footbridges, then turned into a larger canal with much more traffic, and many more people walking along the water's edge. There must have been an organization to the tributaries, but Guy didn't get it.

Hannigan leaned across Selena to say, "This is the Grand Canal."

And it was grand, its waters choppy in the boats' wakes. Their launch pulled up to a dock where they alighted to the view of a striking square structure, its first and second level ringed by intricate arches.

A dark-haired man waited to greet them. "So nice to meet you," their guide said, taking Selena's hand and bowing low, as if he was about to kiss the tender skin. "My name is Marco." He flourished his arm behind him, his look encompassing them all. "The Doge's Palace," he said. "A most magnificent structure."

He was a young man of perhaps twenty-five, his hair thick and so dark that the sun hitting its glossy curls cast it with a hint of blue. Guy supposed he was handsome in the way virile, young Italian men were.

They entered through a special gate, bypassing the crowd in the piazza. The interior was, surprisingly, a large courtyard.

"The Doge's Palace shares a structural wall with the basilica." Marco knew a remarkable amount about the history of the palace, from its origins in the 800s to its destruction by fire in the tenth century to its Gothic incarnation and the many restorations over the years, many of them due to fires. And finally, the eventual linking to the New Prison over the Ponte dei Sospiri, the Bridge of Sighs.

He led them inside to a grand hall with magnificent frescoes painted on the ceiling between gold arches. By some mysterious agreement, they had the hall to themselves for fifteen minutes. Guy wondered how much Hannigan had paid for the privilege. Everyone, including the guards, was deferential, standing back respectfully, no paparazzi allowed. Guy wasn't even sure they'd been recognized, especially with the scarf covering Selena's hair.

"I could stare at the ceiling for hours." Selena whirled

around the marble floor, arms out, head tipped back. "Except I'm getting dizzy, and it makes my neck ache."

Then she simply lay on the floor. No one stopped her.

Marnie gripped Guy's arm. "That's a fabulous idea." She put her hand to the back of her neck. "I'm starting to ache too."

Then they were both lying on the floor, side by side, hands clasped, gazing up at the frescoes. The guide Marco stood over them, glancing at the guards as if to say, *These crazy Americans.*

Guy and Hannigan remained on the sidelines, arms crossed, watching their ladies sprawled on the floor.

"Your wife is crazy woman," Guy said mildly.

Hannigan laughed softly, out of respect for the place. "Yeah. But she's hot," he added as if that said everything.

Maybe it did. "Totally," Guy agreed.

"The sexiest woman on the planet," Hannigan mused.

Guy grinned. "Second sexiest woman on the planet. The sexiest woman is the other crazy lady lying beside her."

"It's all in the eye of the beholder, man." Hannigan tapped the corner of his eye. "Eye of the beholder."

"It most certainly is." And Guy kept his eye on his beautiful wife.

Marnie wore a pretty wrap dress tied at the side of her waist. Guy was glad he'd thought to pack it for her. Unlike Selena, with a scarf covering her dark tresses, Marnie's hair was free. She looked like a teenager, flat on the floor, her ankles crossed as she gazed up.

Yet when he thought about her late-night conversation with Wade in the darkened sitting room, all his doubts assailed him again. He wished to God he'd stepped close enough to hear what she said, but instead, there was just the low intimacy of her voice mocking him.

Hannigan nudged him. "Looks like you two have everything worked out." Then he gave Guy the nudge-nudge-wink-wink from the old *Monty Python* show.

"Yeah," he hedged. "Things are great." If he could just shut down his doubts.

But Hannigan didn't let it go at that. "So you asked her?" The man didn't need to get explicit.

"Yeah, I asked her. She said no. Absolutely not."

Hannigan was silent for a moment. Maybe a telling moment. "You believed her?"

If Hannigan had asked that last night at the dinner table, Guy would have given an unequivocal yes. But now, all his fears were rising up in him again. "Yeah. But it's not like she can just stop talking to the guy. He works for her."

Hannigan eyed the women on the floor as they laughed together, sweet, musical laughter, their hands entwined like old friends or schoolgirls.

"Yeah," Hannigan finally agreed. "It's not like you can return from vacation and tell her she can never talk to him again or you might just have to beat the crap out of him."

Guy got the distinct impression that Boyd Hannigan was no longer talking about Marnie. But he asked, "So what I do now?" The question might not be only for himself.

Hannigan sighed, still watching the delightful display in the middle of the Doge's Palace. "Maybe you need to tell her in no uncertain terms that you're jealous as hell, and make her see that you can't stand hearing her laugh with another man. That it drives you crazy and makes you want to smash something."

Intensity oozed off the man like a fog of testosterone.

"Is that what you'd do?" he asked in the same low tones. "If you were in my shoes?"

Hannigan blinked, gaze still focused on their wives, the muscles in his neck taut. Then he laughed, a little too loudly and a little too late, but his voice remained soft so neither

Marnie nor Selena would hear. "Our situations are completely different. She's got my sanction. But if I were you." He lightly punched Guy's arm, more of a push. "I'd tell her how goddamn jealous I was. Women suck that stuff up if you say it like a man who wants her so bad he can't think straight." He grinned. "Then you get all your manly feelings out." He gave a slight thrust of his hips for punctuation. "And she'll be all over you."

Guy wanted to say that Marnie was all over him anyway. And that he was all over her. That since their night on the train, they couldn't get enough of each other, and he wanted it to go on and on.

If his fears didn't ruin it all first.

THEIR GUIDE, MARCO, WAS A STUDENT OF HISTORY AT THE University of Venice, hence his extensive knowledge.

Marnie had thought, since it was called a palace, that it was actually the doge's home. Which it was, but in addition, trials had been performed here and sentences handed down. It was where men were put away for life or sentenced to a terrible death. Marnie wasn't sure which would have been worse.

She'd never felt the truth of that more than the moment Marco took them up to the Piombi, called the Leads in English, the attic prison cells under the lead roof of the Doge's Palace.

"These cells were used for political prisoners. It was excruciatingly hot in the summer and devastatingly cold in the winter," Marco informed them.

He took them past Casanova's cell, from which he escaped, along with a renegade priest, both of them fleeing over the roof.

"However, if you feel Casanova's circumstances were dire, you will find the Pozzi, the underground prison known as the Wells, to be the more horrific of the two." And Marco led them down.

"The cells are small, with no windows, and no light except that which came through the corridor windows," he explained as they peered into a dank, narrow room illuminated only by a lantern, an example of the only light provided. "And on days of high tide, they could be flooded. Hence the name the Wells. The prisoners had only a table which also served as a bed, a narrow shelf for what meager possessions they were allowed, and a wooden bucket in which to do their business. It was a hell on earth."

"It's terrifying to think they were forced to live this way," Selena said in hushed tones befitting the atmosphere, the fear, the pain, the impending death from loneliness, despair, and slow starvation. She shivered as if she felt the ghosts of the tormented prisoners.

"It's definitely a place of spirits," Marco added, then moved them on. "You will note inscriptions and scrawls on the walls where men scratched their awful tales."

Then he brought them to the cell of Riccardo Perucolo, a fresco painter and a victim of the Inquisition, who had used nails to scratch two masterpieces on his cell walls. "These drawings remained hidden beneath layers of dirt and grime until a restoration was undertaken in the 1980s."

In many spots, the ceilings weren't high enough to stand up in for a man of Guy's size, and barely long enough to walk back and forth for exercise. It would have been a nightmare. When they finally came up out of the dark, Marnie felt like she could breathe again, as if the lingering misery down in the cells had sucked all the air out.

"I know," Marco said, understanding the great gulps of air

she needed. "We cannot go down in the Wells without feeling as if we have entered Dante's Inferno."

It was an apt description. It might be minus the fire and brimstone and all the dead people, but it was Hell.

Marco then took them to the mouth of the famous Bridge of Sighs.

"When the Wells and the Leads could no longer sustain the numbers of prisoners, and the conditions grew too deplorable, to the point where the scent could be detected in the palace's courtyard, it was deemed necessary to build another prison with healthier conditions. And thus you have Le Prigioni Nuove, the new prison." Marco spread his arms wide "After they were tried in the ducal palace, the prisoners were brought across Ponte dei Sospiri, the Bridge of Sighs."

It was the famous arched bridge over the canal that connected the Doge's Palace with the prison next door. It was the strangest thing, perhaps it was the narrow canal between the two buildings, their height, the majesty of the palace, but she could almost hear the sighs of all those people who had walked across the iconic bridge, probably never to be free again.

After roaming the cells, which were admittedly larger and with more light than the Wells, Marnie was thankful to leave the depressing structure when Marco said they would head over to the Basilica di San Marco, on the other side of the Doge's Palace.

Marnie leaned close to Guy to say, "It's amazing that they have Hell on one side and the stairway to Heaven on the other."

He nodded. "Amazing, too, that the Bridge of Sighs is supposed to be the most romantic spot to kiss your lover as you glide beneath it in a gondola. Especially after you know it was really used for conducting prisoners to their fates."

They walked hand in hand toward the magnificent cathedral on Saint Mark's Square, a breath of fresh air after the prisons. They took pictures of the astonishing campanile, the freestanding bell tower in the square, while Marco told them of its spectacular collapse in 1902, after having stood since the tenth century. Of course, the Venetians had to rebuild the beloved landmark.

Standing in the square, Marco gave them the basilica's history, a few tourists stopping nearby to eavesdrop. Entranced by his talk, they didn't seem to recognize the two celebrities in their midst. Perhaps it was Boyd's dark sunglasses and Selena's scarf.

"This is actually the third church on the site," Marco told them. "The rebuilding started somewhere around 1063. Many of the columns and sculptures were brought back from Constantinople during the Fourth Crusade." He waved an arm toward the entrance. "The four bronze horses you see over the entryway were some of the artefacts transported here." He gave a very Italian shrug. "These are replicas. The originals have been removed to the museum to protect them from pollution."

After a discussion of the architecture and when the gorgeous exterior reliefs were added, Marco led them inside. The walls and vaulted ceilings were spectacular. "The pictures are all gold leaf mosaic," Marco informed them.

The interior literally gleamed. Marnie wanted to lay down again as they had in the Doge's Palace, but there were far too many people. And she probably would have been arrested.

Selena looped her arm through Marnie's, and they strolled ahead of Guy and Boyd, arm in arm. As they observed the mosaics, the statues, the ornate balustrades of the choir box, Marco grew silent, letting them absorb the splendor.

Until finally Selena declared, "I'm famished. Let's find a little restaurant." Outside the basilica, Marco bowed slightly, hands together. "Thank you for the opportunity to show you these beautiful icons of my city."

"Please join us," Selena said, touching his arm. Marco had in no way acted starstruck, yet deferential to all of them, Marnie and Guy included.

But he backed away. "Thank you, but I'm unable to. I do hope you enjoyed the tour."

"It was spectacular," Boyd said, drawing him aside where, Marnie was sure, he tipped the man generously.

They found an open-air café a couple of streets away from the piazza. And once again, no one stared or snapped pictures, as if they had no idea who was in their midst.

Under big umbrellas shading them from the sun's glare, they dined on lobster gnocchi, pasta with scampi and asparagus, risotto with seasonal vegetables, sea bass baked with olives, tomatoes, capers and potatoes, all four of them sharing everything. It was delicious, and not one of them had room for dessert.

When Boyd brought out his wallet, Guy stayed his hand. "Please, let me get it. It's the least we can do for giving us such a great day."

When Boyd's face clouded a moment, Selena touched his arm, saying, "Thank you. We're so glad you wanted to come out with us." Then she clapped her hands. "Now, I know it looks like a terribly long walk back to the villa since we came along the canal." She pointed behind her, though Marnie had no bearings. "But it's not that far, just over the Rialto Bridge. And we can see so much more of the city if we walk it."

Marnie glanced down at Selena's sandals.

The woman chuckled. "They look fashionable, but they're quite comfortable. There's a wonderful shop by the Spanish Steps in Rome, with a marvelous shoe clerk, Giancarlo. You must ask for him when you go there." She angled her feet. "They're dainty, but they have a back so they don't slip, and no thong between the toes. And the soles have a decent arch. Not only that, I've added moleskin even though I've already broken them in. Just in case."

Marnie marveled again how down to earth Selena was. All right, not everyone could buy their shoes at a fancy shop by Rome's Spanish Steps, but really, what celebrity would care about owning good walking shoes?

They strolled, Selena a little slower, letting the men get ahead of them.

"They make an imposing pair."

"They do," Marnie agreed.

The streets were narrow, many of them in pavers of different patterns and sizes. One could find an old stone façade on one side, columns on the other, then a modern glass and chrome storefront. Cafés abounded, people laughing, eating, enjoying the day. They meandered along narrow waterways, many with steps so boats could let off their passengers. Marnie snapped pictures of the tourists in their gondolas. They passed couples arm in arm, women with shopping bags, teenagers engrossed in their phones, tourists taking pictures.

"I'm surprised no one has recognized you or Boyd."

Selena laughed softly, tapping her scarf, then her oversized sunglasses. "I look like any other fashionable tourist with these on." She jutted her chin at Boyd. "No one will recognize him with his sunglasses and that silly Panama hat." She giggled. "And all the scruff shaved off his face." She leaned into Marnie, lowering her voice. "I much prefer him that way, without all that horrible stubble they always make the men wear these days. It's so unattractive, and when we're together, I make him shave it all off so I can feel all that smooth skin." She laughed, looking at Marnie, lowering her sunglasses and waggling her eyebrows lasciviously. "It's so much nicer for certain lovely activities, don't you think?"

Like sex. That's what Selena meant.

"But let's talk about your hotheaded Guy."

"Why do you say that?" Guy was the least hotheaded man she knew. If anything, he was more on the passive-aggressive spectrum. But not in a bad way. When he was angry, he simply didn't talk. He'd had to work himself up to that confrontation in their stateroom.

Selena squeezed her arm. "He gets hot under the collar whenever Boyd looks at you."

Marnie's skin prickled with apprehension. Did Selena know about Boyd's proposition? Was she angry? Was she about to punish Marnie in unimaginable ways?

"Your husband doesn't look at me," she denied.

Selena laughed loud enough to make both Guy and Boyd to turn around. She slapped a hand over her mouth, then called out, "We're fine. Go on. We're following." Then she whispered to Marnie. "We don't want to attract attention."

There was no mistaking Selena Rodriguez's laugh, but other than Guy and Boyd, no one seemed to take much notice.

Selena hugged Marnie's arm close again. "You probably don't know that he and I sometimes..." She let the sentence hang a moment. "Step out," she added smoothly, but they both knew what she meant.

"Yes, I gathered that."

"But I'm very glad you didn't take him up on any offers he might have made." She looked ahead at their men. "He prefers married women, especially if their husbands agree. Then there's no entanglement later on."

Guy had minded. "Is that why you're glad he didn't make an offer, so there were no entanglements?"

Selena laughed again. "No, my darling woman. It's because then we couldn't be friends, and we wouldn't be able to have this lovely holiday."

Marnie wasn't completely getting it. "So does that mean you *are* jealous?"

Selena let out a long breath. "I wouldn't say *jealous*." She smiled with those ruby red lips. "I'm more what you'd call territorial."

Now Marnie really wasn't getting it. "But then why do you both have..." She let the sentence hang just the way Selena had. "You know?"

"Other lovers?" Selena supplied softly. She tucked away a tendril of hair that had slipped from beneath her scarf. "Because we're apart so much. And a woman really can't go without sex for that long."

"What about a man? Can he go without it for that long?"

Selena's chuckle was sweet and musical. "Some men, absolutely." She looked at Guy specifically. "But other men?" She shook her head. "I wouldn't want to put it to the test. This way I know exactly what he's doing. And I know he's not doing it while we're together. If he did, I'd shoot his balls off."

The thought came to Marnie and she decided to say it. Because why not? Of course, Selena could kick them out of the villa, but other than that, what could she do? And she'd already revealed so much. "You have the strangest union I've ever heard of."

Selena giggled like a schoolgirl. "The craziest. But it works for us." She patted Marnie's arm as they strolled. "In a marriage, you need total honesty, about everything. About your needs. About his needs. About which of your needs aren't being met."

Marnie felt guilt wiggling through her like a worm, eating her insides. She hadn't given Guy total honesty. He'd asked, and she'd denied everything, even her own feelings. But if she'd told him the truth, what would he have done? Her marriage wasn't like Selena and Boyd's. She and Guy hadn't granted each other carte blanche to go off with somebody when they weren't together. If he'd known she had feelings about Wade, even though she'd tamped them down and never done anything, she didn't know what he'd do.

"Honesty about everything?" she asked. "What about little white lies that save your spouse's feelings?"

"Did you watch that show *Big Little Lies*?" Selena lowered her sunglasses to look over the rims at Marnie.

"I saw the show and read the book."

"Well, little white lies often turn into big little lies. And your life can fall apart."

"I'm not talking about *those* lies."

Selena laughed again. "Well, I certainly wouldn't tell Boyd his penis is too small."

Marnie gasped, and Selena leaned in, bumping shoulders, her laughter about to turn hysterical. "I'm joking. Honestly."

"Thank God. I certainly wouldn't want to walk around with that knowledge in my head."

Selena squeezed her arm. "Oh Marnie, I do so like you."

But Marnie still felt that worm of guilt for denying that she'd ever had feelings for Wade. Was it a little white lie? Or a big little lie?

And would it come back to bite her in the ass?

24

They explored Venice for what seemed like hours to Guy, but it was probably only five miles. Selena Rodriguez knew every nook and cranny of the floating city, and she wanted to see everything, all while ostensibly on their way back to the villa. It was good to be with someone who knew all the hidden gems, as Selena called them. They meandered through cobblestoned streets, past open-air markets and restaurants, bars and stores. She took them to an ancient bookshop where the books were stacked like bolts of fabric or stored in old row boats and gondolas, stairs were made of old hardbacks, and friendly cats wanted a scratch behind the ears.

They crossed the Grand Canal over the Rialto Bridge, which was crowded with tourists browsing the shops and taking pictures. They walked small bridges and larger bridges. Venice was the land of bridges, with waterways snaking everywhere.

After wending their way through the crowds, they often turned to less populated streets. They crossed the Grand Canal once again at the Ponte degli Scalzi, which was quite close to the train station where they'd arrived. They wandered through another magnificent church, Chiesa di Santa Maria di Nazareth, filled with marble statues and gold relief and unbelievable frescoes, the sun streaming through the windows as if the angels were looking down.

And still Selena wasn't done with her walk back to the villa. They strolled through a maze of hotels, discovered an Irish pub where they all ordered a beer. There were beautiful churches and colorful three- or four-story buildings fronting the canals, all with their own boat docks. They crossed over the Cannaregio Canal by way of the Ponte delle Guglie, with gargoyles decorating its arches.

"Do you actually know how to get back to the villa?" Hannigan finally asked.

Selena's laughter tinkled through the streets. "Eventually," she said, grabbing his hand and running with him to a narrow bridge that didn't have a single guard rail. It was breathtaking to stand above the water as a small boat arrowed under the bridge, its occupant waving at them.

When they finally got back to the villa, Selena said, "Let's stay in for dinner since we've been out all day." She always seemed so excited about everything. He'd have thought a megastar like her would be jaded. But then they'd spent the prior evening playing gin rummy.

"That sounds wonderful," Marnie agreed.

"But first let's do drinks on the balcony." Selena rang a bell and when their butler appeared, she politely asked. "What is a specialty drink of Venice?"

He grinned broadly. "You must have a Venetian Spritz." Turning on his heel, he left, while Hannigan opened the big French doors to the balcony.

For the next hour they enjoyed refreshing Venetian Spritzes made with Aperol, an Italian liqueur, Prosecco, and soda water. They watched the traffic on the canal and

Hannigan regaled them with funny stories from his many location shoots.

"I'm going to make a list of all these movies," Marnie said, "so when we watch them, we'll have some behind-the-scenes laughter."

After their second spritz, Selena clapped her hands. "I'm going to dress up for dinner again. How does that to sound everyone?"

Guy felt like groaning, especially when Marnie said with a hint of breathlessness, "Oh, what fun."

Knowing he was stuck, he and Hannigan exchanged a look of mutual disgust.

"You want to take a shower first?" he asked Marnie as they closed their suite door.

"No," she said, shaking her head. "You go ahead."

She already had her hand on her phone.

"I thought we could take a shower together," he said lasciviously, just short of pervy.

"I would have loved that." She blushed even as she waggled her phone at him. "But I've got all these texts stacking up. Let me just get rid of these before dinner."

He felt the burner on his blood turn to simmer, and he thought about what Hannigan had said, that women liked a little jealousy. But Marnie had never enjoyed all that he-man stuff. She thought it was demeaning, as if he didn't trust her.

But then there was Wade. And Wade seemed like an entirely different issue.

He allowed himself a snarl, because that's how he felt, like a lion curling his lip. "Talking to Wade again?"

Her head snapped up, and while normally a remark like that would have pissed her off, this time there was a flicker of something else. Was it fear? Why would she be afraid?

Unless she had something to hide.

And the burner on his blood turned up a couple of notches.

"I just have to take care of any issues," she said, not meeting his eye. "You know that." But it was as if she was somehow unsure of her answer. Or was she unsure of him? Maybe the discussion they'd had the other night was having its effect, making her feel she had to watch herself because he thought she was having an affair. At least she wasn't sneaking out of bed in the middle of the night.

They should have been over that. She'd told him there was nothing between her and Wade, and he needed to believe it. Yet he voiced his thoughts anyway. "I don't like the idea of that man stealing my shower time with you."

She clutched her phone. "Just let me finish this and then I'll join you."

She was still choosing work over him. Choosing Wade. But instead of snapping at him and reminding him that she'd told him all along she'd have to work during this vacation, she looked almost guilty. As if she'd begun to understand how Wade and her workaholism affected their marriage.

When she left him for the privacy of the sitting room—and her texting with Wade—he took his shower alone.

She didn't join him.

THE DINNER WAS ONCE AGAIN FABULOUS.

"Your chef is the best," Marnie said. She knew the food was good. Quail on a bed of gorgonzola and lettuce, delicately fried fish nuggets with guacamole and lime mayonnaise, artichokes, lobster-stuffed ravioli, the main courses followed by Venetian fried cream and a chocolate cake filled with a warm chocolate center, vanilla ice cream on the side.

But somehow everything tasted like straw in her mouth.

Despite Wade having said just last night that everything was fine, there were issues, the call taking longer than she'd anticipated. By the time she was done, Guy was already out of the shower. After the good day they'd had, she felt his brooding as if it were a cloud descending.

Maybe his gloominess wasn't justified, because she truly did have work to do, but she could have done the work later, after a shower. She wasn't even sure why she hadn't just put the phone down and followed him. She hadn't been giddy reading Wade's texts. But she did feel guilty that she'd felt that giddiness previously. Had she been looking forward to hearing his voice more than she wanted to climb in the shower with her husband?

No, she didn't think so. There was just that push-pull between what work needed and what Guy wanted.

And it was tearing her apart.

After an evening of drinks and cards, as they got ready for bed, Marnie's phone beeped again, and she saw the lines tightening on Guy's face.

She had only one choice, and she shut off her phone, plugging it into the charger. But amid her guilt was a growing resentment. Now she wasn't even allowed to do her job.

The moment her phone was silent, Guy grabbed her up and dropped her on the bed.

The resentment vanished at his touch, and her heart thrilled.

He crawled over her, thrusting his hands in her hair and kissing her with a delicious ferocity that made her skin tingle.

"You're mine," he murmured against her lips.

Her blood thrummed with the possessive words. She grabbed his ears, pulling him down until she had to look at him cross-eyed. "And you're mine."

Their lovemaking that night was feral, animalistic, and the best she'd ever known.

Their last couple of days and nights continued like that, laughing and handholding during the day's tours, mouthwatering Venetian delicacies, hours of drinks and games on the balcony with the backdrop of the Venice canal, and lovemaking that grew more delicious every night. Guy was insatiable. And she matched him.

Then, once he was softly snoring, Marnie would sneak out to the sitting room with her phone and answer Wade's texts.

"I GET THE IMPRESSION THEY'RE AT WAR." SELENA STROLLED hand-in-hand with Boyd, the Slades several paces ahead of them.

She stopped to read a gravestone, her fascination with the old graveyard evident, especially as it was a Venetian site she hadn't visited before. Boyd loved how everything was interesting to her. They'd taken a waterbus to *Isola di San Michele*, a former prison island, which had been turned into Venice's cemetery during Napoleon's time. The island's old church was run by Franciscan monks, and the gardens for the dead were separated by Cypress trees and filled with markers and monuments and a profusion of flowers decorating the graves.

"I told you he's having issues about her CFO and his principal," Boyd reminded her.

She looked up at him. "I thought you said they talked about it and cleared the air."

"They did." He and Guy had discussed it the day they'd visited the Doge's Palace, as they'd walked the streets, alleyways, and bridges of Venice. "But things like that don't blow over with just one talk. He hasn't come to terms with the fact that she has to speak with her CFO on a daily basis."

She shook her head, her gorgeous tresses tumbling around her shoulders. On the cemetery island, relatively free of tourists, she'd pulled off the scarf. And still no one had recognized them.

"I told Marnie that all they needed was complete honesty." She stood once more, squeezing Boyd's hand. "Like we have. No secrets. Everything out in the open. It's the only way for a marriage to survive. They just need to talk."

Boyd smiled, as if agreeing with her. Yet he appreciated the irony that they didn't have honesty at all. He'd made love to her like there was no tomorrow, like there was no director waiting for her at the shoot and dying to crawl back into her bed. He hadn't told her how his belly boiled at the thought. He hadn't told her that their relationship was no more honest than the Slades' marriage. And it never would be. Unless he found the courage to tell her his true feelings.

He could battle directors and screenwriters and executive producers and production company bigwigs. He could battle his agent and the paparazzi and the fans who sometimes threatened to overwhelm him. But he was exactly like Guy, afraid to be completely honest and open with his beautiful, seductive, sensual wife.

Until he did, they would never have a real marriage.

ON THEIR LAST FULL DAY IN VENICE, SELENA SHOWED them sites that were all new to her as well, a cemetery island, then a seventeenth-century pharmacy with beautiful old fixtures and intricately carved cabinetry filled with exotic perfumes. They visited the Palazzo Mocenigo, a museum for textiles, costumes, and perfumes, which, to his amazement, Guy found fascinating. They ended with dinner at the rooftop garden restaurant of an old hotel, the view of the canal stunning and the food delectable. And though they'd tried to excuse themselves early to pack for the flight home the next day, Hannigan and Selena were having none of that.

"Your flight isn't at the crack of dawn. You can pack in the morning," Selena said with a pout. So Guy and Marnie stayed for drinks and delightful conversation on the balcony.

Once alone, like every night they'd spent in the luxurious villa, Marnie turned off her phone. Then they had their wicked way with each other after a day of tormenting touches and kisses and dirty little vignettes about what they were going to do to each other that night. They made love like wildcats, until he forced a scream out of Marnie even though she was worried the celebrities would hear. He loved her moans and groans, her cries and shouts of pleasure, the way her head thrashed on the pillow as she came.

Finally, they fell asleep in each other's arms.

Or so it seemed.

Then Marnie, thinking he was in dreamland, crawled out of his bed, grabbed her phone off the bedside table and her robe off the floor or the chair or wherever they'd thrown it in their passion.

On those other nights, he'd wait ten minutes after he heard the snick of the door. Then he'd climb out of bed while she was busy with her texting—which he feared was sexting—and open the door slightly to see her.

There was always a phone call as well. It was maddening, making his blood boil until the whites of his eyes turned red like a devil. After long minutes of soft talk, her voice would rise and she would say her goodbyes, while Guy softly closed the door and crawled back into bed.

It was demeaning and unmanly to lay there controlling his breathing and adding a soft snore, especially when she'd lay awake for fifteen minutes before finally falling asleep.

What did she think about during those tormenting

minutes? All the work she had to return to? Or Wade? Did she fall asleep to fantasies of him?

Guy was sure those nights would push him over the edge into violence. Not that he would ever be violent with Marnie. But he imagined punching bags with Wade's face on them. He imagined walls with Wade's picture that he could pound his fists into.

If he didn't do something, his marriage would crack under the strain. *He* would crack.

And this night, their last night in Venice, he couldn't take it anymore. He thought of sitting on a plane with Marnie for ten hours. He'd never make it through without doing damage to someone.

So tonight, he didn't open the door and listen. He didn't watch the seductive moves of her body as she talked to Wade. He didn't listen to the intimacy of her low, husky voice, even if he'd never been able to make out her words.

Instead, he lay awake in the bed, eyes open, staring at the beautiful molding around the ceilings and the intricate plaster designs stretching out like a sunburst from the chandelier. The moon reflected off the canal and streamed through the open curtains, creating a light show across the ceiling.

When Marnie finally returned, he didn't turn over and modulate his breathing. He stacked his hands behind his head.

The moment she realized he was awake, her steps faltered before she regained her composure by the side of the bed. "Sorry if I woke you. I thought I'd just take care of a few emails and texts since you were sleeping."

She said it as if she had nothing to feel guilty about. Maybe in her mind she didn't. Because Guy believed her when she said she'd never had sex with Wade. At least not in the physical world. But he didn't believe that was true in her fantasy world, at night or when she was driving to work or eating her lunch or working out or on the drive home to her husband. They were all times for daydreams about Wade.

Guy felt himself rising to the boil, his blood bubbling. "I'm sick and tired of you crawling out of our bed to talk to him."

She reeled back as the bitter animosity slipped through his grinding teeth. Then she obviously decided to lie. "What you talking about? You and I make love every night, I turn off my phone, I sleep in your arms."

"What about tonight?"

"There were so many texts. I had answer to them."

"Is the first night you've left my bed to answer Wade's summons?"

She had to know she was caught, but instead of the admitting the truth, she turned it around on him. "What do you expect me to do? I have to talk to him. There are work things that need to be discussed. Unless you want me to quit my job." She snapped out the words with a click so hard it might have chipped her teeth.

He didn't expect her to quit her job. It was her lifeblood. She loved being CEO. She loved the power. She did an excellent job against people who would have crushed her if they could, the board, underlings who thought they should have her job, women who thought she'd slept her way to the top. Marnie had battled them all and won. He was damn proud of her.

He needed only one thing. "I want you to stop talking to him late at night in that intimate voice you use only with him."

She climbed on the bed on hands and knees, towering over him in the dark. "Have you been spying on me?"

What had he been doing? Was it spying? Was it wrong? Was it the only thing a man could do if he wasn't to go insane?

"If you want to call it spying, yeah. I heard you get out of bed, grab your phone, close the door, and then sit on that chair talking in that seductive voice of yours with a man who isn't your husband."

She swallowed as she recognized how bad it looked, but she didn't give him a single concession. "Half the time I'm talking to Linda."

He threw his anger back at her. "Why do have to talk to Linda so late at night?"

She leaned close, a sneer on her face. "Because you made me terrified to even glance at my phone during the day. All those ugly looks and then your silences, they drive me crazy. So the only time I can answer my texts and talk to Wade or Linda is at night when you're not hovering over me."

It was true. He'd put her in an untenable position. If she took her phone into the bathroom to answer texts while he wasn't "hovering," he glowered at her. If she brought her phone along on their day trips, he glared at her. If she dared to set it on the dinner table, he raked her with a gaze that would have flayed flash.

In his gut, he knew he was to blame. But if she hadn't gone overboard in the first place, he wouldn't have resorted to such childish behavior. But now he attacked on a completely different level. "Tell me exactly what you were talking so intimately to Linda about in the middle of the night? Me? My supposed affair with Sharon?"

Linda's tirades against him had been another bone of contention. If it weren't for Linda, Marnie might never have started questioning his relationship with his principal.

Yet a little voice said that if he'd told Marnie about the incident in Sharon's office and hadn't deleted that text string, she never would have been suspicious. It was the omissions that got you. The spouse always figured it out.

"You've bought into everything she says, haven't you?" But

the new roiling in his gut had to less to do with Marnie's transgressions than his own.

Instead of railing at him, she sat back on her haunches, hands on her thighs, the robe gaping over her cleavage and doing something to his insides that had no place in the middle of this argument.

"No, I don't believe her." She paused a beat long enough to set his nerves jangling and leaned back to snap on the bedside light, illuminating him. "But then I don't truly believe everything you say either."

Try as he might, he couldn't stop his guilt from rising up and spilling onto his face. The sensations in that moment, the things he'd thought...

Marnie saw it all. "Oh my God." Shock and anger registered on her features, as if she'd only been testing him, and he'd fallen right into the trap. "You actually kissed her back."

25

He stared at her, the light behind her glistening through her hair, her skin above the robe so creamy and beckoning.

From somewhere came the echo of Boyd Hannigan's voice. *Just tell her the truth.*

He thought of his anger over Marnie's seemingly intimate conversations with her CFO. Even if it was only once, he'd committed the same transgression. He'd thought of another woman.

It was time to give his wife exactly what she'd asked for. His confession. "I didn't sleep with her. I would never sleep with her. You're the only woman I want." He swallowed, almost choking himself. "But there was a moment when I wondered what it would be like." His pulse thrummed across his eardrums, but he didn't stop. "A moment when she was kissing me and I didn't push her away. And I wondered how she'd taste."

He closed his eyes because he couldn't stand to look at Marnie, the horror and pain etching her face into ragged lines. "But then I remembered how you taste, so sweet, so exquisite, and I knew no one could ever be as good for me as you are. That no one could make love to me the way you do. That no one could make my heart beat so hard." He paused, just a second, hearing only her breathing. "I pushed her away and told her that nothing like that could ever happen again or I'd have to quit."

He could barely breathe but the truth was out there. And he felt a sense of relief right along with the fear that she would leave.

When he opened his eyes, her face was scored with pain. Somehow it was worse than anger. It was worse than having her scream at him. It was as if he'd broken something inside her.

He wanted to go on, explain that it was only a moment, not even a second, certainly nothing as long as five seconds. She didn't rage or shout or throw things. And that was even harder. He knew how to handle a manic Marnie. But he didn't know how to handle the quiet pain creasing her face.

And finally, she said, "Why did you do it?"

He knew what she meant. Why had he needed to think before he pushed Sharon away? He swallowed again, hard, but this time he looked at her, really saw her, the anguish but also the guilt in her eyes. It seemed they'd stopped talking so long ago, stopped sharing their deepest thoughts. But if they were going to have any chance, they needed to have it out. Now.

And he gave her the truth. "Because I hate the way you talk to Wade. Sometimes I'll come down for a glass of juice or to look for a book I left in the family room, and I hear you. I recognize that voice. It's the one you use to whisper the sexy, dirty, beautiful, mind-boggling things you want me to do to you. And it scares me that you talk to him that way. It doesn't matter what you say to him. It's that sexy, seductive voice of yours. It makes me question everything. I thought if I got you away from him for this trip, I could show you that you don't need him."

She blinked, and a teardrop pooled on her eyelashes, finally trickling down her cheek. "It was work," she said very softly

She closed her eyes, telling him that wasn't the whole the truth. His insides shriveled.

Her eyes remained closed even as another tear slid down. And she said what he already knew. "But that's only half the truth. I never had sex with him. I never kissed him. I never even daydreamed about it." Finally, she looked at him. "But it wasn't always business."

His breath stalled in his throat, but he managed to say, "You talked about me. About our marriage."

She closed her eyes again and nodded. But this time her lids only remained closed for a second. "I was so angry that you didn't want to be principal. And Wade listened to me when I needed to talk. All Linda talked about was Paul and the divorce. I never should have mentioned to her that the new principal was an attractive woman because then she wouldn't let up. And if I told her anything about us, she would have gone on and on about how you were ignoring me because you were having an affair. So my dinner chats with her were pretty one-sided." She sighed out a long breath.

"I'm sorry. I always thought you had Linda to talk to." And he'd resented that Linda warned Marnie about husbands who had affairs, as if he was one of them.

She looked down, almost in shame, as she said, "I did tell her about that text from Sharon. It was like I thought it would be. She wouldn't leave it alone, wanting me to confront you." She swiped at a tear. "I didn't even tell her I was having trouble getting away for this trip because I knew I'd never hear the end of it. I don't know why I thought it would help to talk about the text. It's as if she thinks my marriage is her marriage, and that if she gets me to accept that all men cheat, I can put a stop to the downward spiral in a way she never could." She blinked, focused on him. "But you've been spiraling downward since your brother died."

Her words were a direct hit to his solar plexus and stole his breath. He missed Chris so damn much. "I just didn't want the same thing to happen to me. I didn't tell you about the job, because I didn't want it. I felt like I hadn't accomplished enough for my scholarship kids, and that if I became principal, I'd lose my chance to be involved. I want to feel like I've done something really good for them."

Only then did she reach out to him, cupping his cheek. "But you've done so much. Look at all the kids that have gone on to attend great colleges and start amazing careers. Lawyers, doctors, engineers, computer experts, businesspeople."

She'd never acted as if she was aware of it. "But you haven't wanted to be a part of it."

She pulled back, quickly, almost guiltily. "I'm just so busy. I know you've asked me to help in the fundraising, but it takes so much time I don't have. I want to help, but I can't. And since you won't let me talk about work, I can't explain all that to you." She let out a breath and dropped her voice to a whisper. "That's why I talk to Wade. Because you won't listen to me anymore. You won't talk to me anymore. Remember that Chinese dinner I brought home before we left on the trip, when I told you that I might not be able to go?" He remembered. He'd been so damned pissed at her. "And you were telling me about Randall the bully as if I knew all the details about him. But I didn't know a thing. You shut me out. It wasn't just about the job opening. It was before that." She shook her head, looking deep. "I think it was even before your brother died. It was like you just stopped talking to me. And when I had a work problem, you'd say, 'We have an agreement.'" She hiccupped as if her tears weren't over. "But I don't remember any agreement that we should stop talking to each other." She lifted her shoulders, let them drop in defeat. "So I started talking to Wade more and more." She held out her hand. "There was nothing sexual about it. He just listened to me. He had good advice. He was the one who told me that I could make this trip, that I could do everything by text or on conference calls or emails. He made that possible."

He felt like a corkscrew was drilling straight to his gut. "I was the one who told you that."

Finally, after a long five seconds, she nodded. "You're right. But when you said it, I felt like I was being pulled in two. I needed to work it out with my people." She'd needed Wade to tell her it was okay. And he felt his heart break into little pieces. Unable to express herself with her own husband, she'd turned to someone who would listen.

Then she twisted the corkscrew deeper. "When did you stop talking to me? When did you stop listening to me? I know part of it's my fault, because I work too much, because I can't ever seem to shut it off." She bit her lip, and he was sure she was holding in a sob. "I know that I left you to do most of the stuff with the kids. But you were so good at it. I felt like I was at loggerheads with them all the time. But you could talk to them. They listened to you."

He nodded. Since they were telling the truth, he gave it to her. "They talked to me because you were never there. You left it all up to me. I know we both agreed in the beginning that I'd take that job at the school so that we could send the boys there and it wouldn't cost an arm and a leg. But then it seemed as if you just abandoned all your responsibilities. I was doing it, so you didn't need to."

"But I was trying to bring home the money to save for college, to pay for the mortgage and the cars. I paid for our lifestyle."

"But we didn't need all that. If you weren't making so much money, we could have gotten them scholarships to college."

She stared at him, blinking, a sheen of tears over her eyes. "You never wanted any of that?"

He couldn't bear it another moment, and rising to her level, he wrapped his hand around her nape, pulled her into his arms, hugging her tight. "I love our house. I appreciate that the boys are getting the best educations. I love that you're making that possible. I just wanted you to see that I was doing my part. It wasn't always about money or that we were having to scrimp because my job didn't pay as much. We never had to scrimp, but you seemed to make it your justification for working so hard and leaving us alone all the time."

Then she did cry, huge sobs against his chest. "I was just so stressed," she said between gulps of air. "I was always stressed. Sometimes I had to rush to the ladies' room and just sit on the toilet lid and breathe deeply. But if I told you about that, you would have said I was working too hard, that I should come home by six every night and I shouldn't be going in on the weekends or spend so much time thinking about work. But the board was always hammering on me. And Wade was someone who would listen, because he felt the same pressures."

His heart pounded with what he'd put her through. Because he wouldn't listen. Because he thought she didn't believe he was pulling his weight. Because they'd lost the ability to talk about all of it.

Hands on her shoulders, he held her away and reached out to stroke a tear from her cheek. "It was never that I didn't want to listen. It was just that I've always felt so inadequate. As if I should be doing more. As if driving the boys around and going to their games and doing the laundry and all the house things wasn't good enough. That all you cared about was that I got a better job and made more money. And your talk about work just made me feel less and less important in the scheme of things, as if home didn't matter to you anymore. But I'm so sorry you couldn't come to me when you were stressed."

She laughed softly at that, then wiped away her tears. "And I'm sorry. I never meant to make you feel underrated. I valued everything you did. I didn't have to worry about the house or what the boys were doing. I could concentrate on the job. But I'm sorry I never told you how much I appreciated everything you did to back me up. All I did was nag you as if it wasn't enough, as if you couldn't do anything right. I'm so sorry. I was just so mired in my own crap."

"And I was mired in mine."

"I think I understand now why you wanted me to stop talking about work. But why did you stop talking to me? It wasn't just Chris. It started before we lost him."

He bowed his head. "After the boys went to college, when Jay was finally at Columbia, and our sex life was so damn amazing at first, I thought everything was going to change. That we could start traveling together, that we'd spend the weekends hiking or taking drives, just being together. But that never happened. It was as if now that you didn't have the boys to come home to you were free to work until all hours of the night. Sometimes it was nine or ten before you got home. And even then, you'd talk on the phone with Wade. It felt like I didn't get any facetime at all, especially the times you went into work on the weekends as well."

She whispered, "But there's college to pay for. And the board just seems to be riding me harder and harder the older I get, as if they think menopause has suddenly fried my brain." She snorted softly. "Now *that* I can talk to Linda about."

He stroked her hair, pushed it behind her ear. "I didn't

understand. And that's all on me. Because I wouldn't let you talk. I'm so sorry."

He cupped her cheeks, kissed the tears from her eyelashes. Then he told her another truth. "And that makes me even more terrified about Wade, the times you call him at night, all those hours you spend with him, so many more than you get to spend with me. And especially the business trips."

FOR THE FIRST TIME, MARNIE TRULY FELT THE PAIN GUY had bottled up for so long. She'd always blown off his feelings as being over the top, distrusting, even ridiculous. Because she'd never considered that she'd done anything wrong.

But then she thought of all those late-night calls, the hours she'd spent in the office talking things through with Wade, the business trips where they hung out in the hotel bar talking until the wee hours. And she told him things about her marriage. She told him personal feelings. He'd been a very good listener, yes, but she should never have given him that window into her relationship with Guy. She should never have felt the things she did, the closeness, the camaraderie, the ease with him that she'd somehow stopped feeling with Guy.

Since that fight on the train, she'd known her culpability. She'd had to admit to herself that she'd had some feelings. Even if they weren't sexual, they were dangerous feelings because unchecked, they could lead to all the things Guy feared.

He had told her his shameful secret about sharing that kiss with Sharon, about thinking of letting it go on. His words had been like swords through her heart and that had been only one time. She'd confided to Wade over and over again.

But Guy deserved the truth, not a little white lie to save

his feelings, as well as protect hers. If they didn't get this out in the open... No, if *she* didn't get this out, she would never be able to text or call Wade again. Those unacknowledged feelings would always hang over her. And she would always be afraid that Guy was angry.

It was the hardest thing she'd ever done, and there was no easy way.

"I told Wade things about our relationship," she admitted. "That I was afraid you were having an affair." She rolled her lips between her teeth and clamped down to keep the tears at bay.

Guy backed off, the distance growing between them as stared at her with fathomless eyes, her reflection in them obscuring any expression.

She had to go on. "I told him how upset I was that you didn't take Sharon's job when it was offered to you, that I worried about the boys' tuition, and about how bad it felt that the board was always ragging on me. I told him how angry I was because you didn't call a plumber or fix a leaky toilet or listen to me when I had a problem." She closed her eyes, breathing in and out, but she had to look at him again. Because looking at him kept her honest. "I told him so many things I shouldn't have. He became my confidant when I thought you weren't there for me anymore. And maybe..." She swallowed hard, because this was the most difficult part of all. "Maybe I felt things I shouldn't have." She held her hand, entreating him, as if he might leave her right then.

But he just looked at her, still on the bed, still within arm's reach, but so very far away.

"I never thought about having sex with him. But I was way too dependent on him. And it had the potential to become more if I had a weak moment." She had to breathe again before she told him the next truth. "He never said anything, but I think his relationship with me was why he got divorced. I think his wife didn't like all the time we spent together, that he wasn't home with his family but always working. She was suspicious."

She could barely stand the stony cast of his face, and she rushed her words to get them over with. "But there was never ever anything like that. It was just talking. And now that I really think about it, it was always me telling him, which is maybe the worst thing of all." She raised her shoulders, let them slump. "I'm so, so sorry. I never showed you how important all the things you did were to me, to the boys. Without you, they would have felt neglected. I always made it sound like what I contributed was more important than your part. But that was so wrong. And I never thought about how my dependency on Wade would make you feel. I never even really thought that I was doing anything wrong. But after I saw that text with Sharon, even as I was denying it, I was starting to see how my relationship with Wade might look to you. I'm sorry."

She simply couldn't go on anymore. Confession was supposed to be good for the soul, but it just made her ache deep inside. Especially when Guy hadn't said a word.

He was silent for long, agonizing moments.

Then finally he closed all the distance that had grown between them, their knees touching, his hands on his thighs.

"Do you know why I really didn't talk to you when they wanted me to be principal?"

She was sure the truth was going to hurt. "Because you knew I'd try to force you into taking it."

He shook his head slowly. "Because I knew you'd have made me see all the good, logical reasons why I should take it. You'd have made me admit to myself how much it would ease your burden, so you wouldn't have to think about the next tuition payment, that it would help you be less afraid of the future and where our retirement was going to come from."

She closed her eyes, unable look at her reflection in his. All her good, logical reasons would have been about alleviating *her* fear, not about what *he* wanted or the kids he loved working with.

"You would have made me face how selfish I was by turning down that job," he whispered.

She heard him move then, felt his hand on her knee. She couldn't look at him, she could only look at his hand on her, big and strong. "It wasn't selfishness," she said. "It was that you knew I wouldn't be able to understand what you needed."

He stroked her thigh. "I should have told you everything I was feeling about Chris's death."

"But you did. I knew how you felt. I just didn't realize how scared you were. I understood that it made you think about your own mortality, but I never thought that you might feel like you were heading down his path to destruction. You used to tell me about all the kids' petty squabbles, and I thought that here was a way you could leave all that behind. That you could deal with only the upper-level stuff. I just didn't realize you actually loved the petty squabbles, loved figuring out how to help them."

He took her hand, kissed her knuckles. "That's our problem. We didn't know how the other felt, all because we stopped talking. Maybe it was Chris's death. Maybe it was Linda's divorce. Maybe it was my jealousy of Wade. Maybe it's the pressure the board has put on you. Maybe it was being empty nesters. Maybe it's all those things. We stopped talking and everything fell apart." He smiled, a gentle smile that touched her deep inside. "Do you know who made me realize that?"

She shook her head as if he was actually waiting for an answer.

"Boyd Hannigan."

"Boyd?" she said with just the right amount of disbelief.

"Yeah, Hannigan. He told me that the way he and his wife made it through their separations while they were off making movies was simply not to talk about what they were actually doing out there. And he made me realize that while not talking worked for his marriage, it wasn't working for us." He laughed humorlessly, shook his head. "He even made me see that I needed to tell you about what happened with Sharon. But what I told you at first, about the kid and the meetings with his parents, that didn't really explain her text. And I knew you'd just keep on thinking something happened until I told you the whole truth."

She felt another wave of emotion that actually made her dizzy. "But why did you delete everything?"

He tipped his head back, closed his eyes, let out a low laugh. "Because I was so sick of dealing with it. I didn't want to have to see all that every time I went into my phone." He looked at her. "And because I felt guilty, because I took too long to push her away."

They both had their guilt.

"My knees are aching." He tugged her down onto the bed, stuffing their pillows beneath their heads. "I'm getting old."

"You're not old."

"I am." He pulled her close, his hand at the small of her back. "Too old to fill up our marriage with guilt trips. We need to talk and listen, to be there for each other. I know how hard it is with our busy lives." He rubbed his nose against hers. "But we have to make the effort."

She wanted to. More than anything. "I'll start coming home earlier, as much as I can. And when I'm home, I'm going to make it all about us, as much as I can." She knew there would be times that work would call with an emergency. "Maybe we can make that cassoulet and the lentil relish from Chef Badeaux on the train. And I can start my fabulous Cluny masterpiece."

"I'll help you pick out the colors." He slid his hand beneath her hair, his eyes going milk chocolate. "I'm glad you like it even though I forced it on you."

She leaned into his touch. "I'm glad we got it. I would have gone home and told myself how stupid I was for not buying it. I just couldn't think past all the work issues." Maybe the needlepoint was a symbol of how far she'd let work take over, to the point where something she'd loved all her life became just another stressor. "But I'm going to make time for more than just my job. It's important but I won't have it for the rest of my life."

"But you'll have me," he pledged. "And I don't want you to be afraid to tell me about work anymore. I want to hear everything. I want to talk through the issues, whatever they are. I'm not going to shut you out because I feel inadequate."

She kissed him softly. "You are not inadequate, so far from it. You're the best teacher there ever was. I love how much you love your students. I want to hear all about them and to help more on the scholarship program, with your fundraisers. I want to make it a priority."

The warmth of his body filled her up as he hitched her closer. "I know you're still going to be busy. I don't want to overload you. Let's just make talking to each other our priority. The other stuff will work itself out."

She sighed. "When this product release is done," she started.

He put his finger to her lips. "There's always going to be something. You're CEO. You're top dog. You'll always be needed. And I don't want to add extra pressure." His brows raised naturally as he said, "I just want to make sure we talk. And that we do our best to make time for each other."

She smiled from deep down inside. "I want to make sure we talk in the bedroom."

He leaned in for a sweet, swift kiss. "Oh, we've been

talking pretty damn good in the bedroom for the last few nights."

"Hmm," she murmured. "Then why don't you tell me more about how seductive and sexy my voice is when I'm talking on the phone?" She waggled her eyebrows. "Maybe I should call you every day on my way home from work and talk sexy to you."

He pulled her tight, let her feel how hard he suddenly was. "Maybe you should start right now."

Then he kissed her, put his hands all over her, and she whispered, in her sexiest, most seductive voice, telling him everything she wanted him to do to her.

26

Selena kissed him, a lazy, gentle, oh-so-sweet kiss. "That was amazing, lover."

Boyd didn't like it when she called him *lover*. It made it sound as if he was just another in her string of men.

She stretched languidly, humming her pleasure. Her gorgeous olive skin beckoned him to lick his way from her collarbone to that luscious tuft of hair between her legs.

But Selena rolled out of bed, coming to standard gracefully on her feet, then bending at the waist, her sweet heart-shaped bottom beckoning him. She frog-marched to the window, stretching her legs, then threw open the curtains to gaze out over the balustrade.

"You better watch out, dear, the paparazzi might be spying."

She waved a hand at him, still gazing at the stars, her beautiful naked body aglow in the moonlight. "No one even knows where we are."

"The press and your fans know you're in Venice, and you can be darn sure they're scouring the hotels and rentals looking for you."

She turned, stalked back to him, her smile wide, the brightest thing being her white teeth. "Darling," she drawled. "They've all seen me in the buff. The whole world has seen me in the buff. Nobody cares about naked pictures of Selena Rodriguez."

"Oh, you'd be surprised what they're interested in."

He propped himself on his elbow as she climbed onto the bed again, sitting cross-legged, her beautiful breasts tempting him. "*This* is something far more interesting." He thought about how much more interesting he could make things, but Selena said, "The Slades. I think they were trying to get away from us tonight." She leaned in as if she was telling a salacious secret. "I think they were dying to have sex."

"They needed to pack." But Boyd agreed. There was something in the looks that had passed between Marnie and Guy.

She snorted. If her fans or the paparazzi heard that snort, they'd be appalled. But in private, Selena was her true self, laughing uproariously in a very undignified manner, snorting when she felt like it.

"What is it you really like about these people?" He knew what he liked, but he hadn't figured out why Selena had taken them under her wing.

She raised her arms, her breasts rising temptingly as she fluffed her hair. "Just that they're so freaking normal." She looked down at him. "I love their quarrels, the little silences that are so telling. You know everything about them, when they're fighting, when they've just made love, when they're giddy. They don't have to hide anything. Not like us, who have to hide everything."

He knew exactly what she meant. Being a celebrity, they always had to be on their guard for that hidden camera, the sly photographer trailing them in public, waiting to capture them at their worst. Selena never ventured outside, not even to get the mail, without having her face and hair on. The paparazzi stuck their cameras on long sticks for a view over their high walls or helicopters flew overhead with a zoom lens. Selena decided what everyone saw, not the paparazzi. And she didn't mind if someone had taken a picture of her through the villa window because *she* chose it. She was gorgeous and confident in her nudity. And she had displayed her beautiful assets up on the big screen often enough.

She had, however, closed the curtains so the paparazzi couldn't photograph their lovemaking.

"So tell me what interests you about the Slades." She smiled wickedly, as if she suspected he was attracted to Marnie Slade. He was. Any man would be. But he'd never pursued another woman once he met Selena. Besides, with his ability to read people, which might have been because of his training as an actor, he knew neither of the Slades would take him up on his offer, not even for a million dollars. In fact, that might have made it even less likely. They valued their marriage, even when it seemed they were at odds.

"Just like you, I enjoy how normal they are. And I like that they're unseduceable." He enjoyed making up the word.

"No one is unseduceable." Selena winked.

And that wink poked all his open wounds, his gut suddenly roiling with exactly who she'd seduced and how many times. And how many different men.

"So you asked them?" she pressed.

He wasn't sure if it was a statement or a question, but he admitted the truth. "I asked. They turned me down." Then he went for broke. "That's another thing about them that attracts me, their monogamy."

She laughed that beautiful, seductive, tinkling laugh. "But, darling, we're monogamous."

He let one second elapse before he said, "Except when we're not."

She didn't hear the pause. Or she chose to ignore it. "We're monogamous when we're together and that's what counts."

"Except that we're apart far more than we're together."

He saw an infinitesimal flicker in her eyes, despite the darkness of the room, despite the moon behind her. She said very softly, "That's what keeps our marriage alive, the fact that we're not in each other's pockets all the time and that we're free but discreet when we're part." She hummed a little note as if she was mulling. "We could never be like the Slades. When I'm not around, could you really stop looking at other women or taking them to bed?"

This was his opening. He could say it now or forever hold his peace. "I'll never stop looking at other women. I appreciate beauty. I even appreciate a good-looking man. But I don't sleep with them."

"I know you don't sleep with the men." Had she deliberately misinterpreted?

He waited four long beats. He could almost hear her heart in the quiet. He could certainly feel his own. "I haven't slept with any other women, not since the first day I met you."

She blinked too many times, and he could see that she understood. But she didn't want to. "Of course you don't sleep with them. You have your wicked way, and then you send them home."

He slowly shook his head, waited for her to say something. She didn't. And finally, he added. "No. I haven't. I've been monogamous since the day I met you and fell instantly in love and wanted you for my wife."

He was taken by a sudden terror that she would leap off the bed and run screaming, calling over her shoulder that she wanted a divorce.

But apparently she was too stunned to run, so he said the rest of it. "I want to be monogamous with you."

Even when he saw the light dying in her eyes, he went on. "And I want you to be monogamous with me. Whenever I think about you with your directors or your leading men, I want to smash things. I can't take it anymore. I want you to be all mine without the specter of other men in your bed. Even when we're not together."

Her answer came out in a whisper, as if she couldn't believe what he was saying. "But what about when we're apart. All those months. What are we supposed to do? How will we get relief?"

"We'll find a way to work it out."

She was staring at him, her mouth agape, like a fish out of water because Selena never gaped. "It just can't work."

"It will if we want it to." And he let that hang a beat too.

She didn't answer, as if she couldn't form words or even a coherent thought on that precise subject. Instead, she asked, "You really haven't touched or kissed or had sex with another woman since you met me?"

He shook his head, but he could read nothing in her expression. Maybe it was the light, not enough of it. Maybe it was just her incredulity.

"So you've been lying to me this whole time?" she asked.

He should have known she would pick on that. "I didn't lie. We just never talk about the other people we sleep with."

"That's mincing words," she shot back. "We were supposed to have total honesty. I told Marnie that marriage only works when you have total and complete honesty. And you made me into a liar." Her voice deepened with each word until it was a growl. "We had an agreement and you broke it."

"But we have a perfect marriage," he argued, his belly turning into fire. "Still together after fifteen years, more than most Hollywood couples, and we still love each other."

But she wouldn't let it go. "How can we have a good marriage if you've been lying to me for fifteen years?"

She slid off the bed, stood, the moon outlining her perfection. "I can't think about this anymore. I can't talk about it. Our relationship was based on honesty and now I find out how dishonest you really are."

She stomped around the bed, flung open the armoire doors in the moonlight, dragged out clothing, and slipped into her one of her favorite caftans, no panties, no bra.

Then she turned and stared at him. "I can't be with you now. I can't stand to look at you."

She grabbed her phone off the table, then she was gone, throwing the bedroom door open, not even closing it behind her.

And leaving him all alone in the dark.

BOYD HAD PACED THE ROOM SO MANY TIMES HE COULD SEE his footprints wearing down the terrazzo tile. Where the hell was she? It was the middle of the night, for God's sake. Venice wasn't a crime-infested island, but this was Selena Rodriguez. If anyone recognized her, God only knew what could happen. Kidnapping?

All the terrible scenarios ran through his mind. He realized that now he shouldn't have told her the truth. At the very least, he should have followed her. Why the hell hadn't he?

There were no answers. There was just his own folly. He should have told her in the very beginning that he didn't want to share. Day one, fifteen years ago, when he fell so hard he'd made himself dizzy. That's what Selena did to him. She turned him upside down, inside out, shaking him up, then knocking him out cold. There would never be anyone for him but her. He'd been in love before, he'd been married. He'd thought he was happy until things didn't work out. But he'd never felt for anyone what he did for Selena. If he lost her, his life would have no meaning. He wouldn't be able to work, he would be able to eat, he wouldn't be able to breathe.

He was about to call the police and say Selena Rodriguez was missing when the front door opened.

His knees were suddenly so weak he thought he might collapse to the floor.

She was flushed when she appeared in the doorway. It could have been the night air, it could have been anger.

And he began to grovel. "I'm sorry. I should have told you the truth all along. It's totally my fault."

She held up her hands. "Don't talk to me." Then she stomped to the armoire, pulled out her suitcase, and threw it open on the bed.

For a trip that was only a few days, she'd brought an incredible amount of paraphernalia. But Selena never packed for herself, and now she simply threw things in. Dresses, caftans, shorts, leggings, tank tops, shoes, purses.

He asked the stupidly obvious question. "What are you doing?"

She gave him the painfully obvious answer. "I'm leaving."

His chest started to spasm like he was having a heart attack. "Don't leave. Please. Let's talk about this."

She marched into the bathroom, tossed all her makeup and various sundries into a huge bag, then stomped back out to him. "I have to get back to work. We have nothing to talk about."

"Can't you at least let me explain?"

She never stopped moving. "There's nothing to explain, Boyd. You lied. My whole thing has been about total honesty. An open book. Especially with each other. That's what I staked my reputation on. That's what my fans expect, the press, everyone who's ever watched my movies."

He didn't dare tell her she was being too dramatic.

She went on. "Honesty. That's all I asked from you. Complete honesty. You could sleep with whatever woman you wanted and I would never question it. But when you're with me, you're with me. And now I find out you've been lying to me." She was utterly gorgeous in her fury, her hands jammed on her hips, her hair flying everywhere, her lips the juiciest cherry red.

"Don't you even get the irony in that? You're angry with me because I *didn't* sleep with another woman. Because I never slept with any other woman after I met you. And certainly never since we've been married. Don't you see how odd that is?"

Emotion streaked across her face. It wasn't anger, it was more like pain. Then she turned away from him, slamming the suitcase shut, kneeling on the top so she could zip it.

Then she turned on him again. "Don't *you* get it? You're making me play the part of the cheating wife. Now I'm the one who's done something terrible."

She hefted the case off the bed and almost dropped it. He rushed to help her, and she wrenched it away from him. "Leave me alone," she snarled.

And he suddenly understood. They'd had an agreement. She was only doing the same thing she thought he was, taking their separate pleasures when they were away from each other. They'd been on an even playing field. Until he'd changed that. And now she was the only one taking other lovers. It wasn't just the lack of honesty. It was the fact that he'd written himself into the script as the good guy and written her off as the villain.

"I didn't mean it that way. I don't think any less of you."

But Selena was beyond listening, and she kept right on rolling the case out the door. "I'm going. Don't try to stop me."

He had to ask, pathetically, "Are you leaving me?"

She turned in the doorway. "I'm leaving you for now. I don't know about later. I have to think about it. And you need to think about what you've done."

He followed her out just as a boatman was rushing up the stairs to help her with the case. He was losing her.

Maybe he'd lost her the moment he'd decided not to live by her rules.

He stood on the edge of the canal as the boatman helped her into the launch. "Where you going?" he asked.

"To finish my job. I should never have come here. My charter is waiting for me at the airport."

She'd been making all her arrangements since the moment she'd rushed out of their bedroom. And now she sat with her back to him as the boatman pulled out onto the canal and whisked her away into the early morning darkness.

Whisked her away from him, maybe forever.

Hannigan was seated at the dining table when they rolled their suitcases out of their suite the next morning.

He waved them over. "Have some coffee and breakfast. I've called for a motor launch. It'll be coming in about half an hour, and I've already ordered the limousine to the airport."

"Thank you. That's really kind of you," Marnie said.

Though Hannigan smiled, it was somehow weak, entirely different than his movie star smile. "I'm flying home with you. They had an open first-class seat."

Or they bumped someone else so they could give it to Hannigan. Guy snorted his disbelief. "Why on earth would you go to San Francisco? Don't you live done in L.A. somewhere?"

Hannigan wagged his head, not really a nod. "We've got a flat in San Francisco. I thought I'd spend the night there, get over the jet lag."

That was weird. It would have been faster to fly straight to LAX. "What about Selena? Don't you two usually charter?"

The look Hannigan gave him was more a grimace than a grin. "She's gone."

Before Guy could ask, Marnie tipped her head. "Gone where?"

"She flew back to Colorado. Did I tell you she was making a Western?" he added conversationally. "Female revenge plot."

Marnie couldn't seem to stop asking for more. "Was there an emergency? I didn't think she was leaving for another few days."

They sat, and Hannigan poured them coffee. Marnie took a pastry for the two of them to split.

"No, it wasn't planned," he said. "She's left me."

His words stunned Guy. What the hell? They seemed so happy, so in love. They couldn't stop touching each other. "You mean *left you* as in separation or divorce?"

Hannigan nodded

"But why?"

Marnie said at almost the same moment, "It wasn't because of us, was it?"

Hannigan held up both hands. "It had nothing to do with you guys. I just told her something she didn't want to hear."

Guy couldn't help himself. "And she left just like that? Because she didn't like what you said? That doesn't make sense."

Hannigan rolled his lips together, breathed in a deep belly breath, let it out slowly as if he was meditating. Then he said, "Selena doesn't like dishonesty."

"What were you dishonest about?" Marnie wanted to know.

He swirled his coffee in the cup. "I told her that I hadn't slept with another woman since she and I met."

Guy was speechless. But Marnie wasn't. "She left you because you *didn't* sleep with another woman?" Her voice rose on a note of hysterical laughter that she tamped down before it got out.

Hannigan sighed again, heavily. "As you both know, she and I have an agreement. We're allowed to play with other people when we're separated by our work."

Guy hurried him along. "You're stalling. Get to the point."

Hannigan's smile, though it wasn't his usual high wattage, was at least real. "All right, all right. I never wanted anyone but Selena, and when she told me what our marriage was going to be like, I agreed because I knew there was no other way I could have her."

"Wow," was all Marnie said.

Hannigan shrugged. "Call me pussy-whipped. But I agreed. I never asked her what she did. And she never told me. We just never talk about it."

"Wow," Marnie said again, as if she honestly couldn't believe what she was hearing. "So, like," she said very slowly, "what would have happened if I took you up on your offer on the train?"

Hannigan gave her a sheepish grin. "I'm good at reading people. I knew you wouldn't. And Guy would never agree either. So you were a safe bet."

"Wow," she said a third time. And Guy had to agree. "I don't even get why you asked me? Just to see if you guessed right?"

He puffed out an odd laugh. "It's a game. I ask, the answer no, then I can say I tried, which means I'm sort of following Selena's rules."

"And yet not," Marnie said. "Boy, you are pussy-whipped. I never would have guessed it after watching your movies. You're always Mr. Tough Alpha Male."

This time he truly laughed. "I'm really just a pussycat."

Because it was a lady's prerogative to keep asking questions when a man would have shut up long ago, Marnie asked,

"So what prompted the argument? Did Selena think you'd slept with me and get upset?"

Hannigan shook his head slowly, his chin jutted. "No." He gave another of those heavy sighs. "I finally decided I didn't want her to be with other men anymore. I want to be normal. I want to have a marriage like yours."

Guy had to look at Marnie to see the expression on her face. And he found her looking back at him in silent communication.

With the tiniest nod, she gave him permission. "Our marriage isn't perfect," he said. "We have just as many problems, though they're different from yours." That was the understatement of the year. "You already know things were rocky when we were on that train."

Hannigan looked from him to Marnie. "Yeah. But it's just the two of you. And you're always together."

Marnie added quickly, "We have full-time jobs and I travel. So it's not *always*."

Hannigan shook his head. "You're not apart for months at a time." He paused a moment. "And you don't sleep with other men while you're away."

Marnie curled her fingers around Guy's. "No, I don't sleep with other men. Guy is all I want."

Hannigan closed his eyes. It was a strange thing, but Guy actually felt his pain. That was how he'd felt when he feared Marnie was having an affair with Wade.

And finally, Hannigan said, "I don't want perfection. I just want her. And now she's gone."

That wasn't enough for Marnie. "But what did she say when you told her? That she wouldn't stop?"

He hung his head. "We never actually got that far. She was angry because I lied. Because I hadn't slept with anyone and she had. And that turned her into the plot's villain and me into the good guy."

Marnie leaned an elbow on the table and put her forehead in her hand. "Absolutely. Now she has to take all the blame."

"But I told her there's no one to blame," Hannigan said. "We both agreed to it."

"Sure you both agreed," Guy said. "But then you didn't do it and she did."

Hannigan exhaled once more from deep in his belly, the sound agonized. "I get it. I really do. And maybe if it hadn't gone on so long, things wouldn't have been so bad either."

"You've been married for fifteen years," Marnie said. "That's a long time to hide something like that."

He nodded. "Yeah. It's a long, long time to live a lie."

"But you're not living a lie anymore. Now she knows."

He snorted. It was either disgust or terror. "But how do I fix it?"

MARNIE HAD BEEN RUMINATING ON BOYD'S PROBLEM SINCE they'd left the villa. And she still had no idea how he was supposed to fix it. He and Selena had a fundamental difference. It was like a couple who got married when one of them wanted children and the other didn't. How do you resolve that?

The trip to the airport was twenty minutes, and with Boyd, it was first class all the way. They'd taken their last ride along the canal, where they'd been dropped off for their limo drive across the bridge to the mainland. And though Boyd had booked his ticket last minute, he had the agent shuffling everything around so that he was seated by Marnie and Guy for the long leg of the trip. After a brief layover in Paris, they'd boarded the flight for San Francisco. They each had their pod, but up front was a bar and small seating area, with complementary drinks. Unless Boyd had paid without them seeing.

"You need to grovel," Guy said. It was a very guy thing to say, not just in terms of him, but in terms of being male.

Boyd grumbled, "I already groveled. She left anyway."

"You need to make this all about her," Marnie mused, getting more excited as plans came to her. "Tell her what you want, and make her believe it's what she wants as well."

Guy looked at her, his eyebrows high. "That never worked on you."

She smiled sweetly. "Maybe you never really tried it."

But she had tried it on him. She'd wanted that kitchen remodel, even if she was stressed out about where the college tuition money would come from. But she'd figured they needed to spend a little on themselves, and she'd gotten Guy to see that too. They both loved the kitchen. Now she was determined to use it more, cooking together, spending time together.

Suddenly seeming to get where she was heading, Guy winked. "You said that Selena was a sensual woman who couldn't do without lovemaking for that long a period of time."

Boyd shot Marnie a look, as if he wasn't quite sure he wanted her to hear this discussion. Then he shrugged. "Yeah?"

"You need to figure out how you can give that to her."

He raised a brow. "But sometimes we're so far apart, different countries even, that it's hard to do."

Marnie picked up where Guy left off. "You're a smart man. Use your brains."

Boyd laughed like he hadn't laughed since he'd told them Selena had left him. "Don't you remember I told you my coach said I could make it on my looks but not my smarts?"

She winked at him. "You're not as dumb as you'd like us to believe. Put on your thinking cap." She tapped her temple.

He held his head in both hands, pursed his lips, jutted his chin, making hilarious faces. The man was a comic genius, but thank goodness there was no one else in the bar area to see or hear. And finally, he said, "We can act as if going on location is like being in prison."

"Huh?" Guy grunted.

Boyd smiled his true smile, the one that bowled women over, even from the movie screen. "Like conjugal visits in prison. We'll have it put into our contracts that we get time off for a conjugal visit every—" He wriggled his lips like a movie villain. "—three weeks or a month, whatever Selena needs."

Marnie put her hand over her mouth, laughing. "You see, I said you were a genius. If it truly is about just needing physical connection, and not about needing variety, that should solve all your problems."

Boyd punched his fist in the air. "Woo-hoo!" He waved his hand, called the flight attendant over. "Get this woman another champagne cocktail." And then, because he was ever so polite, he added, "Please."

THE FLIGHT HAD BEEN DELIGHTFUL, AND AFTER DINNER and their brainstorming session over Boyd's sorrowful plight, Marnie stretched out in her pod and went to sleep. It wasn't the middle of the night, but traveling tired her out, though first class was far better than economy.

"I never want to fly any other way," she whispered to Guy before she drifted off. And she dreamed about more holidays they would take together.

When they touched down in San Francisco, they were

first off the plane, and magically, only celebrities knew how, their luggage rolled off first as well.

Once they were out in the arrivals hall, Boyd gave her a big hug, practically hauling her off her feet. The two men did a back-slap man hug.

No one had paid much attention to them on the flight, probably because they saw celebrities in first class all the time. But here in the international terminal arrivals hall at SFO, they were the center of attention. They'd even been the objects of a few pointing fingers.

But Boyd didn't seem to care, if he actually noticed. He pulled out his phone and handed it to Marnie. "Put your address in here as well as your email. And I've already got your phone numbers since you sent those photos from my phone."

She typed in the info. Then she asked, shyly, because he was a huge celebrity, "May we have your address?" She was old school and wanted to send a thank you card for all Boyd and Selena had done. A text or email didn't cut it. "Thank you for letting us stay at your wonderful villa. And for all your hospitality."

"Don't thank me. Meeting the two of you was what made me see I had to change things with Selena." He laughed and slapped Guy on the back again. "I'm totally jealous of you guys." He leaned in close as if he was revealing major secrets. "That's really why I flew back to SFO with you both instead of going to LAX. I wanted to pick your brains some more on all my marital issues."

Marnie hoped there were no paparazzi lurking with special microphones that picked up conversations yards or even miles away.

When he said, "Give me your phone, and I'll type in our address," Marnie opened her contacts and handed him her cell.

When he was done typing, he pointed to a limousine that had pulled up outside the door. "That's probably me. Can I give you a lift?"

Guy waved his hand. "You've done enough. And we're heading south while you're going into the city." Then Guy boldly said, "You're welcome to stay at our house if you don't want to be alone tonight."

Boyd shook his head. "Thanks. But I have a lot of thinking to do." He rubbed his temple. "Lots of stuff going on in here. You guys have given me food for thought. And you've made me confident that I can work this out with Selena."

Marnie put her hand on his arm. "I know you'll figure it out. I've got faith in you. And in Selena. You two are so in love."

A shadow passed through his eyes again, but finally he smiled. "Thanks."

Then he pulled up the handle of his bag and rolled it through the doors, people watching him avidly the whole way, then turning their eyes on Guy and Marnie as if they knew the secrets of the universe.

When they'd gathered the bags and headed out to catch their ride, Boyd's limousine had disappeared as if the celebrity was a genie sucked back into his bottle.

Or maybe he'd never existed at all.

IT WAS LONG PAST DINNERTIME WHEN THEY ARRIVED HOME. Guy felt like he'd been gone forever, as if so much had changed. Indeed, he felt like a new man.

"Should we run out to the store to get milk and stuff?" Marnie asked.

He cupped the side of her neck. "I'll take care of it tomorrow. I'm not going into school." He nuzzled her cheek. "And there's something else I'm hungry for tonight."

She leaned into his touch. "I just want a champagne cocktail and a bowl of popcorn."

He had to laugh. "Maybe we should watch a Boyd Hannigan movie."

Waving her phone at him, she said, "I can't believe I have Boyd Hannigan's address in my contacts list."

"It's pretty freaking amazing. The guy actually wanted to hang out with us because he was jealous and wanted to be normal like us."

She socked his arm lightly. "There's a lot to be jealous of."

He reeled her in for a long, delicious kiss. "Oh yeah, there's a lot to be jealous of." Then he added, "Are you tired?"

She rubbed her nose against his. "I slept on the plane, remember?"

He waggled his eyebrows lecherously. "I can think of a lot better things to do than watching Boyd Hannigan movies."

A cloud suddenly fell over her gaze, and she held up her phone again. "Now don't get mad, but I really need to take care of the texts that came in while we were on the flight."

He felt a tickle of irritation, yet he was able to stop himself. "You have a job. I have a job. We both have to deal with crap all the time. I'm not going to be such an asshole about it anymore."

"And I'm not going to call Wade after work unless it's an emergency. But I really feel like we've been on the flight so long that I should check in." She clamped her lips together, looked at him a moment, and added, "I'm also going to tell him I'm not coming in tomorrow."

That stopped him. "You're kidding."

She shook her head. "No joking. We've been on the go for almost twenty hours. I'd like a day to relax. Wade and the rest of my team are perfectly capable of handling any issues." She squeezed his hand. "You can listen to the conversation if you want. I don't mind. There's nothing you can't hear."

His heart swelled. They'd turned a corner, and she was making an effort. They'd still have issues, because they were a normal couple, just like Hannigan said. But they'd made it through this truly rough patch, and they'd make it through anything else that got in their way.

Raising her hand to his lips, he kissed her knuckles. "I don't need to listen. I'll make that champagne cocktail and run you a bath."

She smiled. "Don't forget the popcorn."

She would always make him laugh. And she would make his blood boil again in good ways as well as bad. But he would always love her with everything in him.

❧ 28 ☙

Marnie had worn leggings on the plane, and now she was curled comfortably in her office reading chair. She'd gone through the texts, but there wasn't much. Everything was on track with a new plan they'd come up with on how to handle the earlier issues.

But she called Wade anyway. He answered on the second ring. "Hey there, back from the land of Oz?"

"We got back about an hour ago," she said.

"You didn't have to call right away."

"I know, but I wanted to tell I'm taking an extra day. It was a long flight."

"Sure. There's nothing pressing. Rest up."

"Have you got any immediate issues we need to talk about?"

"No." She could almost hear him shaking his head.

And she moved on to the real reason for her call. "I want to apologize. Over the last few months—" She chuckled because it was a lot longer than that. "—I unloaded a lot of my personal stuff on you. That was wrong, and I'm sorry. I won't do that anymore. We work great together, but that doesn't mean you need to listen to all of my *stuff*." She gave the word extra emphasis.

"You don't need to apologize. You've got a tough job."

He was good at making excuses for her. "I appreciate how much you took care of while I was gone. I couldn't have taken this trip without your support. You guys didn't even need me."

He laughed softly. "We need you, Marnie. But you don't need to give the company your all twenty-four-seven."

She'd learned the truth of those words. "And you don't need to either. I apologize for all the times I texted you so late at night, as if you were supposed to deal with things during your family time. I'm sure your wife found it irritating. And I hope that didn't cause problems in your marriage."

Like the problems it had caused in her marriage.

"My issues were my own, nothing to do with you or work. No need to apologize. I was the one who picked up the phone and called you when I could have left it till the morning."

"Well, I'm turning over a new leaf. This trip made me realize I need more balance in my life."

"I totally support that. We all need balance. But if you have a weak moment and send me a work text, I promise to ignore it until the next day." He ended with a chuckle.

She felt as if he was relieved to hear it. There'd be no more late-night talks in the office about her personal stuff. She'd gone too far, leaning on Wade because she hadn't believed she couldn't lean on Guy. Guy had done the same thing, turning away from her, because he didn't think he had her support. All that was going to change.

"I also want to say that I realize I've been a bit of a micro-manager." She noticed he didn't jump in to deny it. "But I've got a great team, especially you, and I need to remember that."

"You've got a great team because you built it. And that means you can relax. We've got your back."

"Thank you. That means a lot." She sighed out her relief. "I'll see you on Thursday."

"Sounds great, Marnie."

They said their goodbyes, and when she hung up the phone, she felt lighter.

She needed balance. She needed to work on her Cluny masterpiece. She needed to watch Boyd Hannigan movies with Guy. She needed day hikes, weekend getaways, home-made cassoulets and lentil relish, and visits with the boys back East.

She wanted to do all that with Guy.

She smelled the popcorn as she stepped out of her office, but Guy wasn't in the kitchen, and she followed the lingering scent up the stairs to their master suite

In the bathroom, he'd lit candles around their big soaker tub. Shutting off the taps, he pointed to the water. "Your bath, madame, along with your champagne and popcorn."

"You are so sweet," she murmured, wanting to drag him into the tub with her.

But he picked up a piece of paper from the bathroom counter. "I found this in my briefcase."

It wasn't until he stood beside her that she realized it was a photo. "It's from the carousel," she said, putting her fingers to her lips, remembering the happiness.

"Yeah. But if you want to know the truth, I didn't like it."

His words twisted inside her. "Why? It was a wonderful night. The carousel was fun."

"I remember looking at that photo and thinking we weren't that happy, fun-loving couple." He cupped her face. "But now it's makes me realize that's who we need to be. And what a bear I've been, always growling at you, when really it's been about all my crap in here." He held the photo against his heart. "I'm making a solemn vow to you right now that we're going to be the couple in that photo. And the next picture we take on a carousel, I'll be kissing you." His smile broke through, his beautiful, manly smile.

She rose up to kiss him. "Let's go to Santa Cruz Beach Boardwalk next weekend and take another photo."

He looked taken aback, his mouth an *O* of surprise. "But don't you have lots of catching up to do?"

She palmed his cheek. "Yes. I have lots of catching up to do with you."

He chuckled, a deliciously sexy sound. "Then maybe I need to help you undress."

The tingles started from deep in her body, spreading out.

He unbuttoned her blouse, his knuckles brushing her nipples, then he slid it off her shoulders and down her arms, his touch warm along her skin. She wore the sexy camisole underneath.

And he whispered, "Are you trying to make me crazy, woman?"

Maybe that's exactly why she'd worn it. "You're the one who said you wanted to undress me."

Bending, he sucked a peak into his mouth, right through the lacy material. She hissed in a breath at the electrifying sensation.

He pulled the camisole over her head and tossed it on the vanity chair along with her blouse. He went to work on the matching bra, undoing the front clasp, stroking his fingers lightly over her breasts as he slid aside the cups. It was sensual and erotic, her body liquifying.

Hooking his thumbs in the waist of her leggings, he stood so close she could see her reflection in his dark, sizzling eyes. Then he helped her step out of the leggings and guided her into the bath where she sank down into the luscious heat and neck-high bubbles.

And all she wanted was him. He was all she'd ever wanted.

Guy wanted her so much his heart felt like it would burst. Sitting on the edge of the tub, he made love to her with his fingers until she cried out her pleasure. Then he climbed in, and took her to even greater heights with his mouth as she leaned against the lip of the tub.

Afterward, he dried her slowly and rubbed her lotion in until her skin was silky smooth, then made love to her in their big bed long into the night. He never wanted this to end. If they worked at it, it didn't have to end.

Like they'd said to Boyd, they weren't perfect, and they would have their rough patches again. But they would work through them. All they had to do was talk to each other.

That was what he'd learned from Boyd Hannigan and Selena Rodriguez, that a marriage needed open and honest communication, even if the movie stars hadn't achieved it.

So the next morning, he said to Marnie, "I have the day off, but I need to go in to talk to Sharon."

There was an infinitesimal flinch on her face. Then it was gone. "I understand. You want to settle things between you and her."

"I need a good working relationship with her. I absolutely don't want this to stand in the way of the kids."

She held his face between her warm hands. "Do whatever you have to do."

He felt the trust in her touch, saw the reflection of his own in her eyes. Leaning his forehead against hers, he whispered, "I love you. I always have. I always will."

She rubbed her lips against his. "I never stopped loving you, not from the moment I saw you."

Finally, after thirty years, he knew their love was forever.

EPILOGUE

They'd been home for close to two weeks. The first Saturday, they'd gone to the Santa Cruz Beach Boardwalk and taken another carousel photo. Guy felt the joy without question. The couple in that photo was exactly who he wanted them to be.

Last Saturday they'd driven to the wine country for an overnighter. They'd felt like honeymooners, walking hand in hand, sneaking kisses and touches, and talking, *really* talking.

But they didn't need an outing every weekend to experience togetherness. Next weekend they'd planned a day to work in the garden. He'd helped Marnie order the floss for the Cluny tapestry. She was home by six or seven every night. He opened himself up to her, listening to the details of her day. The board members were still a bunch of assholes, and Wade still needed handholding—Guy's take on it, not Marnie's.

Being able to tell him and get it all out seemed to calm her, just as telling her about his day with the kids calmed him too. He'd told her about his conversation with Sharon word for word. The principal had agreed the kiss was an aberration. She'd been elated at their success and lost control. It wouldn't happen again.

Guy would make sure it never did.

They were doing the dishes after dinner on a Wednesday when their phones pinged simultaneously. It had to be one of the boys. With his hands in soapy dishwater, he said, "Can you get it?"

Marnie thwacked his butt with the dish towel and grabbed her phone. Only to gasp moments later. "Oh my God."

His heart pumped triple time. "What's wrong?"

She waved off his worry with, "The kids are fine." Then she added, "But you have got to see this. Better yet, we need to watch it on the big screen."

Heading into the family room, she turned on the smart TV. He followed to find she'd already queued up a video, it's caption reading "Are America's sweethearts totally sweet on each other?" Marnie made the video full screen.

Selena Rodriquez came to life on their eighty-inch TV, a Selena they barely recognized. In a dingy sod cabin with only one window, she wore a raggedy gingham dress that might have once been blue and white. Her hair hung in tangles around her face, and she was weathered beyond her years, dirt crusted in lines on her face.

And her gaze was murderous.

"You git, Jake McAllister. Or I'll blow your head off." The rifle in her hands didn't tremble one bit.

Before she could take her shot, a door burst open, banging the wall of the cabin and showering her with dirt clods from the roof. The rifle's direction shifted, and Selena screeched, "What are you doing here?"

The camera swung then, and it didn't find the hapless Jake

McAllister. Instead, it focused on Boyd Hannigan, backlit by the sun but recognizable nonetheless. He wasn't decked out in Old West garb, but wore cargo shorts with a button-down shirt and boat shoes.

No one yelled "Cut," though he obviously wasn't part of the picture.

He marched resolutely to Selena, the lens following his every step. "What am I doing here?" He took the rifle, which had been pointed at his chest, and handed it to someone off camera. "I'm here to grovel. To beg you to forgive me. To take me back." He went down on one knee. "Please, Selena, you're all I've ever wanted. All I'll ever want."

"Get up," she snapped. "You look ridiculous." She pointed. "And turn off that camera."

It kept rolling, the angle moving to capture both their faces.

She tugged on Hannigan's hand, forcing him to his feet. "I'm working," she hissed. "We can talk about this later."

"We can't talk about this later. Later will be too late. You'll have made up your mind, and I won't be able to help you change it."

"I've already made up my mind." Her nostrils flared, and that murderous look she had for Jake McAllister was now trained like a rifle sight on Hannigan.

"I made a mistake, but I love you, Selena. It can be just about us and no one else. We can fix it."

"I don't think this is the way to fix it," Guy said, afraid the poor man had made a huge tactical error. This wasn't what they'd discussed on the plane.

Marnie replied, "Oh yes, it is. She loves the public display. Can't you tell?"

He couldn't. But Marnie saw with a woman's eye.

"You lied, Boyd," Selena cried dramatically. "There's no way to take that back."

"I lied because I love you."

"Good Lord," Marnie breathed out. "He's not going to say he doesn't want her to have sex with other men, is he?"

But Hannigan was a bit smarter than that. "Help me figure out how to fix it. Whatever you need. I can stay here, right in Colorado, be your lapdog, at your beck and call. I don't need to be in L.A. And we can figure out a plan for when we're apart." He circled her wrist with his fingers and pulled her in, whispering something the camera didn't pick up.

"He's telling her about the conjugal visits," Marnie whispered as if they'd be overheard.

On the screen, Selena hissed, "You're crazy. It'll never work."

Keeping her close—with the camera zooming in—Hannigan said, "I love you so much, I'll make it work. We can do this. Don't leave me, Selena. I'm begging you."

The camera was close enough to illuminate the flicker of indecision on her face.

"He's going too far," Guy said. "His male fans will think he's turned weak."

"He's perfect. Their fans will go crazy."

"They'll think he cheated."

Marnie elbowed him lightly. "There's nothing better than a reformed and groveling rake."

Obviously, Selena thought so too. After making her fans wait at least half a minute for her next words as her soulful coffee-colored eyes roamed his face, she grabbed Hannigan by the ears and hauled him in for the most spectacular on-screen kiss ever, rivaling Rhett and Scarlett.

"All right," she said, her lips now a bee-stung red. "I'll give you one more chance. Don't screw it up." She kissed him again, sweetly, and lowered her voice. "I love you. I always have."

Hannigan whooped and picked her up in his arms, whirling her around. The camera caught every moment. Then he carried her from the dingy cabin and disappeared into the bright sunshine outside.

"Oh my God," Marnie breathed out. "That was so romantic. Just like Richard Gere carrying Debra Winger out of the paper factory in *An Officer and a Gentleman*."

The video had gone viral, with a million likes. Guy laughed, mostly because he was stunned. "I wonder if they planned the whole thing."

"Maybe," she said. "But who cares? He won her back."

The doorbell rang as if on cue. "Who the hell could that be?"

Guy answered to find a delivery man on the doorstep. "You gotta sign for this." He held out a device and a legal-size envelope.

"It's not a summons, is it?" Marnie asked when Guy had taken possession of the envelope and closed the door.

"I sure as hell hope not." He tore open the package, pulling out two envelopes, one cream-colored with their names in fancy cursive lettering. Opening that, too, he read aloud. "Selena Rodriguez and Boyd Hannigan request your presence as they pledge their love anew on June fifteenth."

Marnie gasped. "How on earth did they get this together so fast?"

"I think that video's a week old. And Hannigan's a fast worker."

"What's that say?" She pointed to an almost indecipherable scribble at the bottom.

Guy held it closer, making out the words. "You two are our first invite. Without you, none of this would have been possible. If you don't show up, we'll be sending out the goon squad to drag you here."

"What's in the other envelope?"

Guy tore it open and two first-class tickets fluttered out, along with a reservation for the InterContinental Hotel in Los Angeles. "This is a joke, right?"

Marnie shook her head. "I don't think so, sweetheart. I think Boyd and Selena are very serious."

He looked at her. She looked at him.

And finally, he said, "Then let's go do some stargazing."

She kissed his cheek. "I'll go stargazing with you anywhere, anyhow, anytime."

Once Again, a later-in-life series that will whisk you away to fabulous foreign locales where love always gets a second chance.

Look for **Memories of Santorini** coming your way soon!

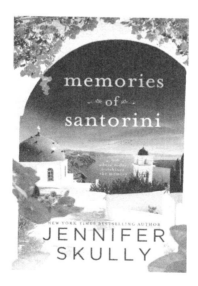

The *Once Again* series, where love is in the stars.

JENNIFER SKULLY

Dreaming of Provence | Wishing in Rome
Dancing in Ireland | Under the Northern Lights
Stargazing on the Orient Express

And coming soon...
Memories of Santorini

ABOUT THE AUTHOR

NY Times and *USA Today* bestselling author Jennifer Skully is a lover of contemporary romance, bringing you poignant tales peopled with characters that will make you laugh and make you cry. Look for *The Maverick Billionaires* written with Bella Andre, starting with *Breathless in Love*, along with Jennifer's new later-in-life holiday romance series, *Once Again*, where readers can travel to fabulous faraway locales. Up first is a trip to Provence in *Dreaming of Provence*. Writing as Jasmine Haynes, Jennifer authors classy, sensual romance tales about real issues such as growing older, facing divorce, starting over. Her books have passion and heart and humor and happy endings, even if they aren't always traditional. She also writes gritty, paranormal mysteries in the Max Starr series. Having penned stories since the moment she learned to write, Jennifer now lives in the Redwoods of Northern California with her husband and their adorable nuisance of a cat who totally runs the household.

Learn more about Jennifer/Jasmine and join her newsletter for free books, exclusive contests and excerpts, plus updates on sales and new releases at **http://bit.ly/SkullyNews**

ALSO BY JENNIFER SKULLY/JASMINE HAYNES

Somebody's Wife

The Jackson Brothers: 3-Book Bundle

Castle Inc

The Fortune Hunter | Show and Tell

Fair Game

Open Invitation

Invitation to Seduction | Invitation to Pleasure

Invitation to Passion

Open Invitation: 3-Book Bundle

Wives & Neighbors

Wives & Neighbors: The Complete Story

Prescott Twins

Double the Pleasure | Skin Deep

Prescott Twins Complete Set

Lessons After Hours

Past Midnight | What Happens After Dark

The Principal's Office | The Naughty Corner

The Lesson Plan

Stand-alone

Take Your Pleasure | Take Your Pick

Take Your Pleasure Take Your Pick Duo

Anthology: Beauty or the Bitch & Free Fall

Printed in Great Britain
by Amazon